THE RELUCTANT DETECTIVE GOES SOUTH

A Martin Hayden Mystery

by

Adrian Spalding

CONTENTS

Chapter One 1
Chapter Two..15
Chapter Three 30
Chapter Four 40
Chapter Five 58
Chapter Six 77
Chapter Seven 109
Chapter Eight..132
Chapter Nine 161
Chapter Ten 187
Chapter Eleven..205
Chapter Twelve...213
Chapter Thirteen...222
Chapter Fourteen 232
Chapter Fifteen...241
Chapter Sixteen...245
Chapter Seventeen 260
Chapter Eighteen..271
Chapter Nineteen 278
Chapter Twenty 282

CHAPTER ONE

Martin Hayden loved hangovers; it proved he'd had an excellent evening. Last night there had been a lot of champagne plus a significant number of oysters consumed. Not that he especially liked oysters, it was just oysters had been the key to solving the very first case that Hayden Investigations undertook. Consequently, it was considered by everyone present a fitting food to consume. Martin had not planned to spend the whole night eating shellfish and quaffing champagne; in much the same way he had never planned to have any clients or staff for his detective agency. It had been, from the very start just an easy way of duping his mother into believing that her son was doing real work, hence he could claim a rather large monthly allowance from the family fortune.

The problem Martin had with his mother was her ability to interfere and shape his life. He had no problems with such involvement when he was a child. When he became a teenager it was more irritating. Now he was a lot older, he had hoped to be free of her arched, disapproving eyes but no such luck. A month after he had opened the doors of Hayden Investigations, she insisted that he should take on a secretary to help the business expand.

Giving in yet again, he employed Susan. Sweet, young Susan, who was so pleased to get a job, especially as it involved no actual work. It was Susan's misguided (so Martin thought) passion for helping people that had led to him having to carry out detective work, something he was not anxious to do. He looked across the office to where she was fast asleep on the black leather sofa, if Martin's head ached, then she was going to have the mother of all hangovers when she eventually opened her pretty eyes.

Susan had two drinking problems. The first was she could not hold her liquor. The second, she had a total inability to calculate how much she was consuming. This combination resulted in being asked to leave the up-market champagne and oyster bar they were celebrating in, when she had decided to dance along the glass bar counter singing: 'Hey Big Spender'.

Susan had insisted through her slurred words that she wanted to return to the office where she recalled, through her alcohol-fuelled haze, there was the champagne they had not finished earlier. Unfortunately, Martin had sufficient alcohol at the time to think it was a good idea. So, together they staggered back to the office of Hayden Investigations, where they consumed a further two bottles before either falling asleep or passing out, Martin could not be sure exactly which.

Quietly Martin stood up, walked across the office past a snoring Susan, into the small kitchenette to make himself a strong black coffee. The noise of the electric kettle did nothing to help his headache, so he turned it off. A lukewarm coffee was preferable to the cacophony caused by the kettle.

There was a timid knock at the office door before it opened. Ernie was the elderly receptionist employed by the owners of the shared office space. He was also the security guard, caretaker, general handyman and anything else he might be needed for. He poked his head around the door.

"Sorry to trouble you, Mister Hayden, there are just two things I need to tell you."

"Go for it, Ernie, what's up?"

"Your friend Colin, the one who dresses like a lady, I found him asleep in the cleaner's cupboard. I left him like that; I do hope that's OK with you. Or do you want me to wake him up?"

Martin, in the haze of his hangover, had forgotten that Colin was with them last night. He did recall Colin threatening to leave the champagne bar unless Susan sang: 'Girls Just Want to Have Fun'. Sadly or fortunately, depending on your musical taste, Susan was thrown out before she had the chance, at which point Martin had lost track of Colin, confident that as a man in his sixties, even dressed in a skirt and blouse, he could handle himself well enough.

"If he's not in the way, Ernie, then leave him. I'm sure the longer he sleeps the better he will feel when he finally wakes."

"Some celebration last night, Mister Hayden."

"It was a little excessive, I'll admit. What was the second thing?"

"Oh, yes, there's a lady to see you here. She came along with your mother yesterday, but you were all out. I think you might have a new client. Business is on the up, Mister Hayden, that's good news."

Martin was not so sure. There were several words in Ernie's sentence that worried him: business, new client, Mother; none of which he would describe as good news.

"Could you ask her to...." before Martin could finish his sentence, the door flew open, and an elderly lady pushed herself past Ernie. She swept into the room like a tornado, stopped just short of Martin and announced in a rather loud, authoritative voice, resembling a sergeant major that Martin had once met at Sandhurst:

"I am Lavinia Barrington-Smythe. Your mother has told me that you are some sort of private detective, whom I thought one could only find in America. We live in strange times, often described as the modern era. Not that I need a private detective, it is your relationship with my son that we need to talk about."

"Your son?" Martin was not sure he was happy with the word relationship and her son in the same sentence, the implications were a little strange. He was glad that Susan was asleep and Ernie had returned to his desk.

"Paul," Lavinia stated, "you went to boarding school with him. Not that I ever wanted him to go, it was his father's idea. Idiotic, if you ask me, but that was my husband for you, full of stupid ideas."

There was a flash of recall on Martin's face. "How is Paul? I haven't seen him in ages."

"Maybe that is because you and your fellow pupils decided that it would be funny to call him Piggy Paul. Although I would be the first to admit that he was a little on the obese side given his height. Again, it was his father, letting him have all that rich food, never agreed with it. Learn to eat modest amounts, that is my motto, and nothing fried."

"I think it was more to do with the fact that he could make a hell of a noise with a conch shell rather than his weight. Plus, he was always the rational one in our group."

"My son has now lost weight, since his father died."

"I am sorry to hear that. What did he die of?"

"He died while lion hunting, serves him right. I have never agreed with any form of hunting animals unless you are going to eat what you kill. For someone who only ate chicken and salmon, lion hunting was a damned stupid thing to do."

"My God! Did the lion kill him?" Martin had the vision of a lion first mauling, then tearing off body parts before consuming Paul's father, and leaving the family with just a few bones to bury.

"No, it was a Rhinoceros that crept up on him and gored him to death. Serves him right."

Martin tried to sound shocked, but he could not remove from his mind the question of just how a Rhino creeps up on anyone. In the end, all he managed was a very limp sounding, "Oh."

At this point Martin should have remained silent, allowing Mrs Barrington-Smythe to continue with the reason she had come to his office. He would later that day blame the residual alcohol in his body for asking the stupid question, "Is it fair to say that you did not agree much with your husband?"

"Absolutely. Hated the man."

"But you married him?" Again, it was the residual alcohol asking, not Martin's rational side.

"Never wanted to, but the Smythe family, my family, were up against the wall, financially you understand. Consequently, they pimped me out to the wealthier Barrington family, so it was my duty, which, of course, I carried out. Now, back to Paul, I need your help."

Martin offered the seat at his desk to her, while he pulled Susan's chair a little away, hoping to lessen the impact her loud voice was having on his hangover. As she sat down, her eyes drifted toward the sleeping, no longer snoring, Susan, "Is she dead?"

Now at this stage the residual alcohol was eager to say, 'yes, all good private detectives have a dead body in their office to practice on.' It was fortunate that the black coffee was now starting to dilute last night's champagne out of Martin's brain.

"Hungover, I'm afraid," was the answer, he thankfully managed.

"So that is Susan. Yes, your mother did warn me about her habits."

Lavinia took off her leather gloves, laid them gently on the top of her leather handbag, which she had already carefully placed on her lap.

"I am worried about Paul. He has been frequenting a very disagreeable place for the last four weeks. Let me explain further. Two days a week he spends the whole day at some sort of place for homeless people. I always thought homeless people stayed on the streets begging, but now, I understand, they have some sort of centre where they can congregate. Which begs the question, just how homeless are they really?"

Apart from buying the Big Issue on occasions, Martin had never been renowned for his sympathy toward charities and the less fortunate. However he felt like Mother Teresa compared to the viewpoint being shared with him by Paul's mother.

Lavinia glanced briefly at Susan, gave a disapproving look, then continued,

"Paul tells me that it is good to be charitable. I never brought him up like that; I would imagine it was his father putting socialist ideas into his head when he was an impressionable teenager. If people drink their way onto the street and end up homeless, then that is totally their fault. Good people like my Paul should not be expected to make things better for them. They should help themselves, be independent." She leaned forward, and lowered her voice, "I think you will find a lot of these homeless men are just plain lazy."

"A lot of people would think that Paul was doing a good thing by helping out at such a centre," Martin whispered back.

She returned to her upright position and her commanding voice, "Maybe socialists and communists think that way, and they have a lot to answer for. Nevertheless Mr Hayden, I would like you to speak to Paul, to find out just why he has suddenly taken it into his head to act like a Marxist. I am sure there must be more to it than him just wanting to be charitable. Your mother has agreed that you would not charge for this service as it is more helping a friend than an investigation."

Martin resisted pointing out that she was asking, albeit in a roundabout way, for charity. Paul was, after all, a friend that he had not seen for a few years, so it would be fun to catch up with him. It could also be interesting to learn just why he was spending time at a homeless centre, presumably making tea and serving sandwiches. That sounded nothing like the Piggy Paul he remembered from school.

"I'll arrange a lunch with him and see what I can find out."

"Thank you, Mr Hayden, I will..." Lavinia was interrupted by the still sleeping Susan, who turned over, farted loudly and pulled the coat, which Martin had earlier laid over her, closer to her shoulders. Lavinia huffed a sigh of disapproval, stood up, put on her gloves, then formally shook Martin's hand. "I will look forward to your report. Good day."

***

Martin could not decide if he should wake Susan or leave her to sleep. In the end he made another coffee and waited. Most of the time he spent watching her sleeping, which he felt was probably the calm before the storm.

Just under an hour later she turned once more, farted, coughed and then sat up, letting his coat fall to the floor as she wiped the dribble from her lips.

She looked around her, stared at Martin, swung her legs around so that she was sitting, even if in a most unladylike fashion, and scratched her head with a look of being lost.

"Did I get to sing, 'Girls just wanna have fun'?"

"Sadly, no."

"Did Colin sing it?"

"No, but he made it back to the cleaner's cupboard without incident."

"It's the bubbles in the champagne that gets you pissed; you know."

Martin walked over, sat down beside her and put his arm around her shoulder.

"Again, I have to say no. Bubbles are full of nothing either harmful or intoxicating. I think, with hindsight, it was the volume of champagne that you drank that resulted in your now rather dishevelled appearance."

Susan looked at him, confusion showed on her face. Then she asked, "Was there a posh-sounding lady at the bar, with a loud voice?"

"There might have been, or would you be referring to a lady who has recently visited our humble office, whose voice, no doubt, could easily wake the dead or a sozzled Susan."

"Next time I suggest continuing the party after we have been thrown out of a drinking establishment, could you do the right thing as my boss and say no, even if I get violent?" Not waiting for an answer, she continued, "So, who was the woman in the office?"

Susan listened carefully as Martin explained the reason behind the arrival of Lavinia Barrington-Smythe and her request for him to speak to her well-meaning son, Paul.

"I'm going to arrange a social lunch with an old school friend."

"You have never mentioned him before, was he a good friend?" Susan asked.

"Not really, he was a strange boy; had a weird habit which meant everyone tried to avoid him, although invariably as he was in the same dormitory as me, I had to be at least civil to him."

"What disgusting habit did he have?"

"Paul? Well, it was an odd habit; he has no doubt grown out of it now."

"What was this habit?" Susan was pushing the question, as it was clear to her that Martin was avoiding answering it.

"Really nothing that a young lady like yourself need to worry about."

"I want to know now."

"Well I'm not going to tell you now or anytime soon. In order to avoid any form of confrontation with you, I'm off for a well-deserved shower and change of clothes; something you might consider doing as well. I'll see you tomorrow morning when we should both be fresh and breezy. Oh, by the way, Colin is still in the cleaning cupboard, but I'll knock on the door to make sure he's OK before I go."

***

To avoid slumping back onto the sofa and spending another few hours asleep; which she often did after a night on the town, Susan decided that it would be better to keep moving around the office for a while before finding her way onto a tube and home. It would not normally be her first thought, but to tidy up the office seemed a good idea in her still slightly inebriated mind, especially given the state of it after yesterday's celebrations. She began by clearing the empty champagne bottles, plastic beakers, empty packets of smoky bacon crisps as well as vacuuming the ones that had been trodden into the carpet. Considering there had only been three of them celebrating, they had made one hell of a mess, she thought.

Before long Susan was carried away with making the whole office neat and tidy. Exactly why she felt that particular need, she had no clue; especially as her own flat was anything but immaculate. Maybe it was just that she felt so good about working with Martin. He had, after all, employed her even though her C.V. contained very few facts. Her working life had been a constant flow between jobs that either she hated, or they hated her. Either way, here at Hayden Investigations, she felt Martin liked having her around, plus it was so cool doing things that a P.I. does, just like her hero TV detective Jim Rockford.

Martin's desk was next in line for a tidy up. She began to think how comfortable she felt in his company, which was not surprising given his star sign. His birthday was March 2nd, a Pisces: gentle, wise and musical; almost a perfect match for her star sign of Leo.

She liked Martin's cute boyish ways. She looked at a parking ticket on his desk with the words, 'punishment paid' written on it, that was his sense of humour. Then, amongst other papers, she found another parking ticket, 'punishment paid', then yet another. In all there were seven parking tickets, all paid promptly, all for Martin's car. Weirdly, she thought, all for the same road in Lewisham. Susan laid the tickets out on the desk. They were all, not only for the same road, but all were between eight and nine in the morning, and all of them were on the same day of the week: Wednesday.

Susan looked at the dates. The second penalty notice she knew for a fact that Martin had been in the office at that time as he was interviewing her for her current dream job. Apart from that occasion, she had never known Martin admit to getting out of bed before eight in the morning, let alone be in south London at that time of the day. She considered if he might have lent his car to someone, but soon dismissed that idea, knowing how protective he was of his car. Why would the car be in the same place at the same time every Wednesday? It could not, she was sure, be Martin's car. It had to be a car, using a false number plate.

"Christ, Suzie Baby, what exactly are you doing? Hangover cures tend to be either large, greasy breakfasts or simply more alcohol. Never in my glitzy life, have I been told that spring cleaning clears a hangover."

Colin stood in the doorway, his mascara smudged, lipstick long gone and hair, not as well-groomed as it had been at the start of last night. His skirt was creased and tired looking, as were his eyes. He also sported a very unfeminine five o'clock shadow.

"I find it very cathartic; I'll have you know," Susan retorted.

Colin walked over to the desk where Susan was standing and plonked himself on the seat. "You have no idea, darling, what that means, but I get your gist. Anyway, since when have you been laying out Martin's paperwork in such a regimented fashion?"

"They're parking tickets."

"Well I can see that. My ex-wife, she made it her mission in life to collect as many as possible, I think she was trying to get into the Guinness Book of Records. Either that or she just enjoyed seeing me pay out, less money for my wardrobe."

"Do you still see much of her?"

"Since the divorce, not a lot really, unless she has a tap that needs fixing; I'm cheaper than a plumber. I see more of my two boys. They think it really cool having a transvestite as a dad. It means they can come to me for advice on what clothes they can buy their wives. Every cloud has a silver lining, Suzie Baby." Colin looked at the parking tickets on the desk. "Tell me, why exactly have you lined these all up?"

Susan leaned in close to him. "They are for the same road in south London, the same day each week and all between eight and nine in the morning."

"Well, at that time of the morning they're not Martin's, that's for sure."

"That's what I thought."

"Looks like someone has cloned his number plate, common enough these days, so what's the plan?"

"I'll speak to him about it in the morning."

"A lot of good that will do. You know he will not be bothered about following them up or appealing against them, too much hassle. Not that you would ever listen to me or anyone else for that matter."

"I can but try."

"By the way, thank you for not pointing out the obvious when I surfaced from my deep, champagne induced, sleep."

Susan hugged him, "What? How I was pleased to see you come out of the closet? But it was a cupboard, so I'm not sure how that works."

Colin laughed, kissed Susan on the forehead, "Well if you need me, just call. I'm off to freshen up. Bye."

CHAPTER TWO

The next morning Martin sat holding his freshly poured coffee, half listening to Susan read out his horoscope for the day. There had been a time when he had insisted that she need not bother for the simple reason he did not believe in 'the stars'. Sadly, that had only encouraged her to persist. In the end he found it was easier to sit back and take in the predicted highlights of his forthcoming day as worked out by 'Stars R Us' or whatever internet site Susan pulled the absurd nonsense from.

'Today for Pisces, the moon leaves your fifth house of romance.' He had recently learnt he was a Piscean. The other bits, moon rising, sun in your house of money and all the other terms Susan used to explain the authority of the stars, were way too complex for him. He guessed leaving and romance in the same sentence was not going to be good. 'Long term associations will be tested, and love will be lost.' Martin thought he was getting good at predicting what they were going to say, which only served to reinforce his opinion of what tosh they were. He then had to endure Susan telling him what her day had in store for her, which he was even less interested in, although previous experience had led him to nod occasionally and make interested sounds as she read. Now that 'the stars' had been recited, this ensured he would be able to open the newspaper and read in peace for the remainder of the morning. Today, however, he was not going to be allowed to.

"How come you have all those parking tickets?" Susan asked. A question that Martin would have described as a supplementary question, further delaying his morning read.

"Well, I guess I parked on some sort of yellow line, that is what generally happens. They are all paid for within the seven days."

"But they can't be yours; they are far too early in the morning and all for the same place in Lewisham, south London, Turner Road. So why pay them, you can contest them, you know."

Martin closed his broadsheet newspaper. He sensed this would not be easy to explain to Susan, who liked to question everything and stand-up for the oppressed.

"I pay them for the simple fact that it is a lot easier. I did, a while ago, have a jolly good ruck with a traffic warden who had placed a ticket on my windscreen. I tore up the ticket and threw it in his face. I still got a copy in the post and I still had to pay. The flip side is that if I do decide to, as you say, 'contest them' they might look at my file and notice that I don't actually possess a driving licence with which I can legally drive the car I have received a fixed penalty for. Thus, I'd rather play safe and just pay up."

"But it's not right. If this person, who must have cloned your number plate sticks to a routine, then he'll be back in Lewisham tomorrow morning getting another parking ticket which in time you'll pay for him. I think we should both go down there in the morning and get this sorted, once and for all."

"Susan, it is far too early in the morning for me to be on the streets of south London. If you want to pop down, please feel free, just be careful, don't do a Jim Rockford. It is most likely a traffic warden with dyscalculia getting his numbers mixed up."

"You mean dyslexia."

"No, that is to do with words, I'm talking numbers."

"Well, there are letters on the number plate as well, so it could be either."

"Whichever way, I plan just to pay up and not rattle the cage of the DVLA and expose my non-existent driving licence."

Martin looked at his watch, folded his newspaper and stood up, having decided that it might make for a quieter morning if he left early for his lunch with Paul. Once Susan had a bee in her bonnet, that's where it stayed.

Last night he had called Paul, who seemed somewhat less than enthusiastic about meeting up with his old school friend. Martin guessed it might be a simple case of Paul recalling how badly he had been treated by his classmates.

"I'm off to have lunch with Paul. It would seem his social diary is a little on the thin side. I doubt if I'll be back today, you know what us old boys are like once we start drinking and chatting."

"This disgusting habit he has, will it hinder your lunch?"

"I sincerely hope not."

"Come on, Martin, what was, or is, his disgusting habit?"

"I told you before, it is not for the ears of a lady. I'll see you in the morning."

"In that case, I'm off to do a bit of bargain hunting this afternoon, and I'll be coming in late in the morning. I'm sorting out your parking tickets for you."

"Good luck with that one."

***

Examining the wine list, Martin searched for some sort of acceptable wine. When it came to wine, Martin was a traditionalist, it had to be red, from France and preferably with a real, natural cork. The wine needed lots of body and had to have that flavour that comes with an oak-aged wine. After careful consideration, he reluctantly decided upon the Pinot Noir from some place in Italy that he had never heard of, regretting asking Paul to choose the restaurant.

At school Paul had shown little good taste. Now looking at the wines on offer at this mediocre, over-decorated, Italian restaurant, Martin concluded that his classmate had not changed one iota, except for the loss of weight.

Paul leaned forward placing his lunchtime specials menu on the table, "It is very kind of you to buy me lunch. It must be, what, six years since we were last in contact?"

"Seven," Martin replied without hesitation or looking away from the wine list. "It was Stephen's wedding, to that really ugly girl he found, with the Homeric laugh."

Paul leaned back into his chair, "I'm just glad he didn't let out one of his loud burps during the service. I recall he took every opportunity to do so during classes."

"That was a strange habit," Martin thoughtfully agreed, "but we all grow up in the end."

"He was not the only one with strange habits," Paul ventured.

"We all had odd habits, that is what becomes of cramming boys into a boarding school dormitory."

"I was thinking of Alan. The one who collected pencils and had them arranged in a drawer under his bed in colour order. Yes, although he was mostly harmless, that is unless you had a pencil that he wanted for his collection, then he could get really rough. I wonder what he is doing now?"

Martin smiled then added, "Don't forget Nigel, who played that hideous pop song: 'Macarena', non-stop in the dorm."

"God, and that dance that went with it. All madness at the time, but looking back, fun times. I see you still have your chipped tooth, I thought you would have had it fixed by now."

"It sounds good, when I recall it was when I was playing rugby that I was injured, makes me sound tough."

"I guess you never mention the exact circumstances. The slipping in the shower after the game."

"No, I keep that part quiet," Martin smiled.

Paul emptied his glass of wine. "I hadn't seen Stephen since his wedding, until I bumped into him in Lewisham High Street a couple of months ago. We ended up going to lunch at some pasta place in Eltham that he loved. Weird place called: 'Pasta Postcard'. As the name suggests it has walls full of tacky postcards. Anyway, apart from him either divorcing his wife, or she left him, he was less than clear, he's now an estate agent and likes to be called Steve; how times change" Paul refilled his glass, ignoring Martin's and continued, "I also saw you, not that long ago, having an minor disagreement with a traffic warden who had given you a ticket. When I saw you shrug your shoulders and throw the ticket into the car, I thought, 'Martin has not changed much since his schooldays.' Forever one for the easy life."

"Well you cannot fight the system and win. I just pay them now without question, they always manage put the guilt back on you, even if I honestly did not see the times of the red route or whatever rules they make up"

Together they started recalling their school days as Martin fought his way through sticky pasta coated with far too much crème fraiche. Paul seemed not to notice the food, he seemed relaxed and pleased to be spending time with a school mate that everyone had looked up to. Not that Martin was any sort of special student, it was his family and the wealth they had accumulated selling simple screws around the world that made him stand out in the class.

As they finished the meal with a coffee and fresh fruit, Paul asked how the detective agency was doing.

"Is my business a success, you ask?" Martin repeated Paul's question. "Well, I always planned to have no staff, no work, no clients and no cases to solve. By that test, my business is a total failure. My interfering mother has a lot to do with that, which brings me to the reason I wanted to meet you for lunch."

Paul listened carefully, as Martin painted a verbal picture of Paul's mother, bursting into the office, taking total command of the space and issuing instructions to those around her, which in this case was just Martin, as Susan was fast asleep. She wanted to know what Paul might be doing at the homeless centre. Martin himself, did not especially care, he made that clear. But had he refused Paul's mother, then that would have filtered back to his own mother, which in turn, might have caused him even more problems trying to avoid work. Paul sat back in his chair, silent for a moment, before leaning forward towards Martin.

"If I tell you, it's our secret?"

Martin nodded, "Of course, school dorm' rules apply, as always."

"I'm doing community service."

"What, like a volunteer?" Martin asked.

"No, as in restitution for a crime."

Now, Martin could easily imagine Paul volunteering for the good of mankind, but being a criminal was harder to picture. "A crime, like breaking the law type of crime?"

"Yes, for common assault. I have to do one hundred and twenty hours of community service. I have chosen to do it as far away from where I live as possible. Hopefully, no one finds out, especially Mother."

"Piggy Paul a villain, well I've heard it all now, so what happened?"

Paul spoke quietly, "Well, let me first explain. My girlfriend, Vicky, lives in a run-down flat above a fish and chip shop. She does not have the sort of background my mother would approve of; hence Mother knows nothing about her."

Martin tapped the side of his nose, "Mum's the word, do carry on."

"The landlord does nothing but take rent. So, I was there one day fixing the toilet cistern, a job I am not well suited to, as it was overflowing and making everywhere wet. She had told me she called the landlord earlier, who had said he would try and come around and have a look, but no promises. I'm halfway through stopping the overflow, trousers and shirt soaking wet, not too pleased I can tell you, when the doorbell rang. Vicky looked surprised. 'Might actually be the landlord', Vicky said. 'Is it now,' I say. There is one long flight of stairs going down to the street door, I stomp down the stairs, winding myself up to give this man a piece of my mind.

"I opened the door, the red mist flowing over me, so without bothering to say a word, I land a punch squarely on the face of the man standing in front of me. I then follow it up with another heavy punch to the person's stomach, then I plant a firm right hook into his face."

Martin had never considered Paul to be the aggressive type. At school he would not say boo to a goose. How people change after puberty.

Paul continued, "As the third punch connected, I noticed the brown uniform plus the 'London Delivery Company' logo on the man's shirt, which by now was collecting blood from the poor man's nose as he staggered backwards.

"Of course, I was apologetic, and helped stem the flow of blood with a wet flannel. Even so, the police were called. Apparently, it is company policy to call the police for this sort of thing. Which I understand, I am a dispatch manager myself, so I could see their side.

"I was charged with common assault, so in front of the magistrate, of course I pleaded guilty, I had little choice. Hence, I ended up with the community service. So now you see why I would rather my mother know nothing about this episode."

Martin leaned back in his chair and laughed loudly, that story more than made up for the insipid restaurant that he'd had to endure.

When he had composed himself, Martin asked, "That is some predicament you are in. How many more hours do you need to do at this homeless centre?"

"The thing is, it does not matter I plan to continue at the centre, it's a way of still getting to see Vicky and concealing her from Mother. A clever idea, you must agree."

***

Martin slumped into his leather office chair; the pasta was laying heavily in his stomach. He dug out some indigestion tablets from his untidy desk drawer and chewed the white chalky tablets before finally washing them down with water.

He had not planned to come back to the now empty office. Susan had already left to go shopping. After the lunch, which had given him chronic indigestion, he had no choice. He knew it was pointless going home as his mother did not believe in new-fangled, manufactured medicines like aspirin, paracetamol or what he craved: two Rennie tablets.

Mother's medicine cabinet looked more like an herbal tea emporium, putting any Chinese medication shop to shame. She had tea for just about any illness that Martin might contract, as well as some he had never heard of. As a child, he was regularly tortured with foul tasting hot fluids, which not so much stopped the symptoms, as persuaded him not to complain about them. Two chewable Rennie tablets were a far easier solution than a ginger and fennel tea.

On one level, the lunch had been disappointing; the food and the wine were mediocre to say the least. On another level, learning that the Piggy Paul from school was now a villain was, to Martin's mind, a revelation.

Martin would have liked to tell Paul's mother face to face so he could see the look on it when she discovered that her sweet, innocent son was doing community service. But a school dorm promise is a solemn promise that cannot be broken. Martin was just going to have to explain to the old lady that her son was giving something back to that section of the community that is at a disadvantage. No doubt she would denounce him as a paid-up member of the Communist Party, but in her eyes, Martin guessed, that was marginally better than being told your son is a criminal. He might even go further, break it to her that Paul planned to continue volunteering for the foreseeable future, maybe even offering a home to some of the homeless men that he encountered. Although, Martin thought, that last part was probably going a bit too far.

There was a knock at the door and in walked Ian Shillingford.

In Martin's life, Ian Shillingford represented two distinct and very different roles. He was first and foremost the landlord of the tall, prestigious Victorian building just off Regent Street where Martin rented one of twelve office spaces. In fact, Ian owned a significant number of properties across London, some residential, some commercial, some left empty as an investment. Martin was just one of many tenants that Ian had, so a visit was very rare indeed. During his last visit, Ian had realised that Martin did not actually pay any rent for the property. His business had been designated as a charity, which was not a total lie, Martin liked to think, as he never actually had any plans to work or make any money, so it was a sort of charity. Ian's second role was the reason that Martin was able to have the office space rent-free, thanks to Jenny Shillingford. Apart from being Ian's wife, Jenny was having an affair with a younger man and that younger man was Martin. Helpfully she had arranged through subterfuge, as a favour to her lover, for him to have the office rent-free.

"Mind if I sit down," Ian didn't wait for a reply, just took the seat opposite Martin. "How are things doing in the charity world, Martin? You know I think it is a wonderful job you guys do, helping women who are subjugated, modern slavery as they call it. There was a piece in The Times the other week about the problem and the way the government are just not providing the funding to support such great charities as yours."

Martin nodded as he recalled the last time Ian had sat in the office and Susan had made up the elaborate story about modern slavery. Although, as she later pointed out, it was not a total lie as their first case had been connected to that problem. Martin just hoped and prayed that Ian had not uncovered a victim of slavery and was going to ask him to help.

"Your attractive assistant is out doing good work, I guess."

Martin just nodded again. His indigestion was getting worse as he tried to imagine just why Ian was in the office without his own personal assistant who, Martin knew thanks to Jenny, always travelled along with him. Martin had a bad feeling, and it was not just the burning pain in his stomach.

"I'm glad she's not here, to be honest Martin, as the conversation I need to have with you is a little personal and best talked about just between us men."

Now, hearing his lover's husband say that, Martin was more than tempted to stand up, meander nonchalantly towards the door, then run. Ian was a lot bigger than him and looked as if he could easily take down his wife's lover. He decided to stay put for the moment, as fleeing would be an instant admission of guilt.

"I have come in today to ask for your help. Now, I know you're not a 'real detective', that it is just a cover for your charity, but I heard from Ernie on the front desk, that you did do some detecting recently to help a friend and you were very successful."

At this point Martin was going to butt in and explain that it was a total fluke, but Ian held his hand up to stop the interruption.

"Then I realised that in your charity work there is, perhaps, a lot of detective work required, to safeguard your clients. That is perfect for what I want. I need someone to carry out some discreet enquiries for me, nothing official. That is why I am not going to a conventional detective agency, yours is perfect. You see, Martin, I hate to admit it, but I think my wife is having an affair."

Martin would have got up and run away then and there, had it not been for the simple fact that his now frightened blood rushed to his head to hide, making him feel faint and unable for the moment to use his legs in order to escape. He was trapped, so instead he spoke,

"An affair?" he repeated, trying to sound surprised.

"I'm afraid so, Martin. There have been worrying signs recently and I just want to see if my suspicions are founded, or if I'm just being silly. She is an attractive woman, Martin, I think you might have met her when you first moved in here, so you know."

"I think I was too focused on the contract to really notice your wife, Jenny, you say," Martin tried to sound relaxed, he was not sure how successful he was. "What sort of things are making you suspicious?"

Ian explained that Jenny had nights away, staying with friends or family. She often went to dancing classes, or so she said. She was also very vague about who she was going to lunch with, just one of the girls was her favourite quote as she walked out of the door. Of course, Ian admitted that he spent many hours working, which meant he could not give her the attention he would like to.

"If you could just spend some time following her, see where she goes, who she meets, that would be so helpful. I am hoping it will be just her girlfriends and family, but if there is another man, I would want to know just who he is."

"Look Ian, I know you help my charity with free accommodation, so I would absolutely love to help you, but I am not sure I am the best person for this matter. I am sure a real detective would do a far better job."

Martin tried to rationalise what he was saying, which was in effect, get a good investigator and you will have more chance of finding out if she is having an affair. At first this almost seemed suicidal to Martin, until he realised that knowing there was going to be a detective following her, he could simply warn Jenny. Tell her that they should not see each other for a few weeks, while she was being investigated. The conclusion would be that she was not having an affair and then they could go back to their old ways. The fly in the ointment was that Ian was a man who expected people to do exactly as he wanted.

"Martin, it has to be you. I do not want someone I do not know and trust poking around in mine and my wife's life. I feel you are a very honest man, come from a good family and whatever you found out would only be between the two of us. I would hate it if she thought I suspected that she was having an affair, when in fact she was not. The last person I want to know of my suspicions is Jenny."

Martin thought to himself, as he came to the realisation that he was not going to be able to wriggle out of this request, Jenny would, in fact, be the first person to know.

"I will certainly pay you for your time and trouble, shall we say a donation to the charity? That way there is nothing in my accounts which says: 'paying private investigator to follow wife', which would be an embarrassment when the auditor comes around. I'll look forward to hearing from you in a couple of days."

Ian stood up, firmly shook hands with Martin, then left the office. Martin sat down and ferreted around in his desk draw searching for more indigestion tablets. The lunch with Paul was, no longer, the principal cause of his heartburn.

CHAPTER THREE

Being part of the early morning rush hour was something that Susan did not enjoy one little bit. It reminded her of when she had a real job and had to get up in the dark in order to catch a bus and be at her desk by nine o' clock. Work was so different for her now; it was well after nine when she caught the tube from her home to Oxford Circus. She could now stroll into the office whenever she wanted to; she felt so relaxed working for Martin.

Today Susan parked her well-worn Ford Fiesta and peered through the dirty windscreen. Turner Road was lined with post-war council blocks of flats, grand, brick-built constructions that had aged well. They were nothing like the tower blocks of the late seventies; these blocks were just four stories high and had a character to them. As Susan looked along the road as it curved left and carried on, she realised that her plan had a small, yet significant, flaw in it. Turner Road was a long road, so just where the Honda Civic with Martin's number plates on might park, she had no idea. She decided she would leave her car and start walking up and down the road, until she either saw the car parked or saw it driving past her.

It took her seven minutes to walk along the damp, chewing gum-stained pavement to the opposite end of

Turner Road, where she stopped for a moment and looked across at the small parade of six shops. The smell emanating from the working man's cafe was tempting her to walk back up the other side of Turner Road with a bacon roll. It was then she noticed a traffic warden, casually leaning against some iron railings, quietly enjoying a cigarette. Susan had a Jim Rockford inspired idea, although really it was just common sense. She crossed the road towards the traffic warden.

"Are you waiting for a Honda?"

He stood up straight, crushed his half-smoked cigarette under his boot, acting as if he had been caught doing something wrong, which in fact he had been. It was just he had no idea who exactly was addressing him. Part of him hoped she was not some under-cover supervisor who was about to reprimand him for smoking on duty. The other part hoped that she was not connected in any way to the owner of the Honda that regularly parked close by, which in fact she was, but not in the way the startled traffic warden thought.

"Why do you ask?" He wanted to know exactly who, or what, she might be.

"Because someone has been giving parking tickets to a Honda that has false number plates."

"Ah, that'd be me. Now I thought it strange that he turned up every Wednesday about this time and got a ticket. Works well for me, chance to grab a sausage sandwich from the cafe, have a fag, and issue a ticket, sweet life. So, do you know this dude?"

"No, but I know the dude with the legitimate number plates."

"Well, he can appeal you know, prove he was elsewhere. I can't do a thing about it now; it's up to them back at the office."

"You never thought it odd, that a driver turns up once a week and gets a ticket without moaning about it, or perhaps, once in a while, just parking legally?"

"I'm paid to stick fixed penalty notices on windscreens, not to think. People do all sorts of funny stuff; I see lots walking around these parts especially."

"That's it then, as long as you traffic wardens give out tickets, you're happy and satisfied. No need to actually think," Susan retorted mockingly.

"Actually, I am a Civil Enforcement Officer."

"Well, aren't you the lucky one."

"Look out, here we go."

The civil enforcement officer pointed towards the corner of Turner Road. They both watched as a blue Honda Civic, looking exactly like Martin's Susan thought, parked up on the double yellow lines close to the corner. The door opened and a tall man got out. He was dressed in casual trousers, black brogue shoes, a bulky overcoat with the collar turned up and a baseball cap with the bill pulled down shielding his eyes.

"Watch him!" The civil enforcement officer then commentated, "He'll go to the back of his car, get out a plastic bag and take a brief look around, before going into that block of flats over there. He looks a big bastard, so I wait till he goes in and then I stick him on. No point having a confrontation."

As predicted, the man took out a bulky plastic bag from the rear of the hatchback and walked into the block of flats. He re-appeared on the first-floor open walkway and knocked on a faded red door. Before Susan could ask any more questions, the traffic warden, or however he liked to be described, scampered across the road, stood in front of the Honda and produced a ticket, which he swiftly attached to the windscreen before walking briskly up Turner Road away from the Honda and Susan.

Having decided that she wanted to know what was going on, Susan continued to watch as the man entered through the red painted door. It was getting cold and she had not dressed for a stake out, but she need not have worried, it was maybe only five or six minutes later when the man reappeared at the doorway and emerged from the flat. He took a cautious look around him before walking back to his car. Susan had been unable to see who might be living in the flat.

Now was her chance to confront the man beside his car, but as she stepped off the pavement, she heard a cry from beside her. A woman, maybe in her seventies, stared down at the shopping bag that had split leaving a sorry pile of groceries on the damp pavement, as well as a large navel orange which was rolling out into the road.

Susan hesitated, the old lady or the shady looking Honda driver? Any bookmaker would have put the old lady as favourite, and they would have been right. As Susan knelt to help the aged lady recover her shopping, she saw, out of the corner of her eye, the Honda drive away.

Once the shopping and navel orange had been recovered, Susan looked up at the flat the driver had visited and made her way towards it. She crossed the road, took the concrete stairs to the first-floor walkway and knocked confidently on the door, with its faded peeling paint. The door half opened on a bleached-blonde woman, at least in her fifties, wearing bright red lipstick plus a serious amount of blue eye make-up. She took one look at Susan and without any hesitation beckoned her in.

"Hello luv, what's yer poison?"

Susan stood in the cluttered hallway uncomfortably close to the plump woman, who Susan now realised had strong smoker's breath.

"I was wondering if you..." Susan was distracted as a small naked boy, who could only have been a few months old, crawled along the stained, frayed carpet towards the woman. The small child settled at her feet and smiled up at Susan.

"Don't mind him, he's me mate's little boy, as soon as yer put him in clothes, off they'd come. Haven't seen you around here before, new on the estate?"

"You could say that. I was wondering..."

"Got Oxy today, just arrived, not often in me cupboard, if you fancy some of that?"

"Oxy?" Susan asked.

"Or benzo pills if that's yer fing?"

"You are selling pills?"

Susan's question sparked a look of unease in the woman's tired brown eyes. "Maybe, who's asking? You from 'round 'ere?"

Susan did not want to get into a long conversation with the woman, who now looked to be getting agitated, as Susan clearly was not decided between oxys and benzos. Susan went for it, "The bloke in the blue Honda who was just here, who is he?"

"None of your fucking business. You'd better go now, young lady, or else you'll regret it."

Susan did not want to give up just yet, "He's using my boss's number plates on his car, and I want to know who he is so I can get this all sorted out."

It was then Susan noticed the hammer the woman was holding in her hand. It looked as if the young toddler had handed it to her, maybe he did, as Susan was absolutely sure that it was not in her hand a moment ago. The blonde raised the hammer in front of her large bosom making certain that Susan would see the weapon.

"I think you had better sod off right now and forget ever being in this flat, and it would be a lot better for yous to not worry about any men in blue cars."

The plump woman with the bright lipstick, bleached hair and the hammer, opened the door again. The naked boy was the first to make a break for the outside world, only to be thwarted when the woman trapped him between her ankles. Susan took her lead from the baby and stepped outside with a defiant, "I'll be back." The door slammed shut behind her.

Susan stood outside the cafe, allowing the warmth to wash over her. 'That went well,' she thought sarcastically to herself. 'I couldn't have made a worse job of that if I tried. Jim Rockford would have solved things on that one visit,' she admitted to herself.

To console herself, Susan stepped into the cafe and ordered a double bacon roll. She would ask Martin to come back later with her, have it out with the bleached blonde. She knew full well that he would try and get out of such confrontation, a more certain bet was to ask Colin. Yes, that would be a far better plan. What could go wrong having a sixty-year-old transvestite threaten a middle-aged drug dealer?

***

"You have got to be joking! He asked you, you of all people, to find out if his wife is having an affair?" Susan sounded stunned after hearing what had gone on in the office yesterday. She now stood, unbuttoning her coat, having just arrived back from Turner Road and looked at a perplexed Martin. Then she burst out laughing before adding, "That is just like asking the fox to guard the henhouse."

"I know. Sounds so daft," Martin shrugged his shoulders.

"Well I'd say it's his own fault, choosing you over a real detective to save money, I bet that's the real reason behind him asking you. All that money and he is, no doubt, as tight as a duck's arse. So, what are you going to tell him?"

"Well, I'm meeting with Jenny later today. I have heard about a really discreet restaurant tucked away in south London, no chance of bumping into anyone we might know. I'll tell her then."

"Bad plan. You just do not understand women, do you Martin? You go telling her that her husband is having her tailed 'cause he thinks she is having an affair, and then, most likely, she will go ballistic and have a blazing row with him. Best not to say a word."

"Well, she thinks something is up already as we're going to south London. Apparently, she has never been to Eltham before. She did sound a little concerned that I am taking her into the outer regions of London to eat, so I'll have to say something."

"No, don't say a word, just go out with her as normal. Tell her you wanted to show her the rough side of London for a change. Then give it a couple of days and tell her old man that she is being a good girl. Job done; everyone is happy."

Martin looked at his watch, stood up and picked up his coat getting ready to leave the office.

"I can't do that; I have to tell her. Think of this, Susan: what if her old man suspects that I am the guilty party? He might have already employed a real detective to follow me. Then he would be able to prove I'm lying and throw me out of here."

"Don't be silly, why would he bother telling you, or at least asking you, then employing a real detective to follow you; that's plain stupid. If he suspected you, he would have confronted you, I'm sure. Best not tell Jenny."

"Susan, you're just reading too much into this, he is asking me for a favour, so I'm telling her and that's final. She'll understand."

"Trust me, Martin, women do not understand men, and in the same way, men do not understand women. Are you coming back to the office later?"

Martin knew that sort of question needed a neutral answer. A definitive response, without knowing the full consequences, was not something he did. Susan had a habit of asking an innocuous question, only to trap him into some sort of outrageous scheme. "Why?"

"Well, you know these parking tickets that you are always getting, I've found out why. Your car has been cloned and I need a strong man beside me in order to confront someone who is connected with the said cloned car."

"Susan, you have lost me totally with that sentence. I have always paid my parking tickets. I have no idea whatsoever what a cloned car is; mine is a Honda. As for requiring a strong man beside you, I do not think I am that man."

With Martin standing at the door, coat on and itching to get away from the office, patiently he listened to Susan talk about the parking tickets that were not his. Not that he fully comprehended just how a car was cloned, but Susan seemed to have a handle on that one. He impatiently checked his watch as she wittered on about a blue Honda, a shady-looking man, an old blonde woman with a naked baby and a hammer. None of these endeared Martin to agree to her request for him to be the strong man to help her confront the old blonde.

"I admire your concern for my finances, Susan, I really do. But I think I would rather pay a few parking tickets than confront a rough old blonde with a hammer; that is not going to end well. Just forget it, Susan, the tickets will stop in due course, or I'll sell the car, I am thinking about it; Jenny says the Honda is too boring."

"But it's not right that some low-life is using your number plates to avoid who knows what, for now it's parking tickets, tomorrow it could be speeding tickets, bank robberies, anything, and it will be your door the police will come knocking on. We've got to sort this out now, Martin. We'll go along there later, tell her to speak to the Honda driver and then I'm sure it will sort itself out."

"Susan, I need to leave now, get home, change, or I'm going to be late, and I am not sure that Jenny will be happy waiting for me in a restaurant in an area which she considers to be an uncharted wilderness. If you are so set on dealing with this matter, then ask Colin to go along. If this blonde is as despicable as you say, I am sure a couple of Colin's harsh comments on her fashion choices should have her begging for mercy."

"I'll call Colin now, just as I knew I would have to," she shouted after Martin as he walked out of the door.

CHAPTER FOUR

The moment Susan had asked Colin to help, he was eagerly putting on his coat telling her, 'Let's get over there now and get this thing sorted.'

Colin strode towards Susan, his high-heeled black boots tapped out a rhythm on the pavement. He wore clean, blue, straight-cut jeans tucked into the boots, in what he considered to be a fashionable way; Susan was not so sure. It was not the jeans that caught her eye, or the heavy foundation, rouge lipstick and blue mascara that he wore, even the pearl drop earrings did not bother her, it was the polyester faux fur, zebra skin jacket he was wearing, which drew several disapproving looks from a number of passers-by. Obviously, transvestites were not a common sight around this council estate. He kissed her on both cheeks.

"Right, so where is this drug dealer we need to sort out?" He asked.

"Why are you wearing such a hideous jacket?"

Colin looked down at the jacket, brushed the faux fur downwards then looked at Susan, the look in his eyes could be interpreted as either serious or just hurt.

"I thought I'd try and blend in with the common locals, think I might have failed, still, it is warm. Let's get to work, shall we, and not worry too much about my dress sense today; we all have bad days."

Susan shrugged her shoulders, tutted and said, "Follow me."

Susan outlined what she had witnessed the driver of the car with the cloned number plates do. How he had made a brief visit to a flat and her own subsequent visit to it. How, whilst there, she had felt threatened with a hammer and wanted a man with her to help ask more questions of the bleached blonde occupant.

To the less knowledgeable, Colin might not look exactly tough; however, Susan knew from experience that Colin was more than able to handle himself. The years that he had spent in the police force had given him a worldly experience. Susan's plan was for Colin to knock on the door and then when it opened both of them to slip inside.

Colin banged on the door. A moment later the bleached blonde peered around it, took one look at Colin and then took a second look, before opening the door wider and letting him in. Susan moved into sight and followed him; the bleached blonde did not look happy.

"You again, young lady. Told you before I don't want you here so piss off and take yer poofy friend with you, I don't want yer business here." She held the door wide open and pointed the way out for them just in case there was any misunderstanding.

"Flossie Roberts, that's not the way to greet an old friend." Colin smiled at her.

She peered closely at his face, an inquisitive frown across her own, "How come you know me; I don't know any trannies."

He took advantage of the distraction to close the door behind him. "Let's not tell the whole neighbourhood who you are." The door clicked shut, leaving the three of them a little too close together in the crammed hallway, with its dim single bare light bulb. The naked baby with a hammer was nowhere in sight.

"DS Higgins?" Flossie sounded unsure. If he was not the policeman she was thinking of, there was a striking resemblance.

"There you go Flossie, that wasn't hard, was it?"

"What yer doing here? All dressed up, are you doing undercover stuff?"

At this point a slightly confused Susan asked just how the two of them knew each other.

Colin explained at length, as he liked to do, that while he had been a Detective Sergeant based at the Elephant and Castle Police station, he had encountered many of the local villains and characters. Flossie Roberts was one of those local personalities that he got to know well during his time as a police officer.

Flossie Roberts lived, at the time she knew Colin, on the Heygate Estate. A sprawling grey estate of concrete council boxes stacked on top of each other. Her third husband had just left her and the resulting shock, or so she said, had left her with a form of agoraphobia, which meant that she could not work. Somehow, through sheer determination, she was able to wander down to the local shops and the White Horse pub for a tipple whenever it suited her but otherwise, she remained firmly in her flat. To supplement her measly benefit payments, she took up some home working. She opened a lending library of very adult VHS tapes. Men used to pop in to buy a tape or two from her, then, if they liked, they could return the tape a week or two later and get some money off their next purchase. A business model Blockbuster would have been proud of.

She also offered an additional service that not many high street video libraries were able to provide. Nothing too sordid, she made that clear, just a hand job for the bloke which, of course, was at an extra cost. She told friends no way was she going to lay on her back for her customers, but the occasional hand job, well, it helped pay the rent and finance her nights in the White Horse pub.

All was going well; Flossie had a regular clientele and a steady income. She was even able to put money away in a biscuit tin hidden away in the airing cupboard. Then the world moved onto DVDs and the internet took off. Pornography was now available directly into homes and Flossie saw fewer and fewer customers knocking on her door; things started to decline. It was during this downturn that one of her regular customers who was not computer literate in the least, at eighty-three years old suffered towards the end of his regular hand job, a massive fatal heart attack. DS Colin Higgins attended and thought the whole thing hilarious. He also thought Flossie should have been more careful who she gave her services to, telling her she would do well to do a risk assessment on her customers in the future. Flossie got a caution and her dead client was deemed to have died of natural causes whilst visiting a friend.

After that episode still fewer men turned up at her door and having said she would never go any further, Flossie now offered a new service: the full works, laying on her back for her customers. This new service soon attracted several fresh faces to her flat. It also attracted the wrath of local housewives who heard what she was up to. One Tuesday, Flossie returned from shopping to see her flat ablaze. She lost everything, including her biscuit tin hidden in the airing cupboard. It was again DS Higgins who investigated the allegation of arson, which it was, and he had no doubt it was a confederation of local women that had had enough of Flossie and her services. It was also DS Higgins that helped her move out of the area into the care of the neighbouring borough of Lewisham. After that he heard nothing more from her.

"So, how come you're no longer a copper?"

"Seriously Flossie, look at the way I prefer to dress now; I ain't going to make commissioner, am I?"

"You could have been a Woman Police Officer."

"Doesn't work that way, Flossie. But that's enough about me; it seems you're selling pills now."

"I just sells them to the local lassies around here, helps them to relax at the end of the day. Them poor girls with kiddies, it can be such hard work, they need a little something, help 'em rest before the little blighters get up. No harm done."

"Benzo's and Oxi's, I guess. Any weed?"

"Honest, Mr Higgins, nothing naughty, just pills you get from the doctor. There's nothing wrong about that; I wouldn't do drug dealing, that's so bad."

"And who's this?" Colin pointed at the arriving naked baby, crawling towards Flossie and then attaching himself to her leg.

"This is little Reggie; say hello to the nice man." Even at his tender age, little Reggie gave Colin a look of disbelief. "He's not mine, I look after him for a neighbour when she's at work, do it as a favour."

"You're such a martyr," Colin commented sarcastically. "Anyway, Flossie, I'm sure you have guessed why we are here. Your man, who I guess supply's your stock, has chosen the very same number plates as Susan's boss. She and her boss, as well as myself, would like you to either ask him to change them, or if it suits you, we can talk to him direct. Choice is yours, Flossie."

Flossie shuffled around, she looked uncomfortable with the choice: side with the law or side with the man who supplies her stuff and would not take kindly to being told what to do by her. His reaction could be either a good slap around the head to remind her to behave, or he'd find someone else to sell his wares to. In the hard life-experienced head of Flossie, there was only one choice.

"Mr Higgins, you know I can't go telling someone who I do this sort of business with to change his plates; he wouldn't take kindly, I know."

"Flossie, all he needs do is go on Auto Trader or some such magazine, look up blue Hondas and find a picture of one with the registration plates clearly showing, get a plate made up with that number, job done and Susan's boss here stops getting tickets; it really is that easy."

"I'll ask him Mr Higgins, honest I will, but he can be a mean bastard, so I can't promise." She agreed knowing it would never happen but hoping it would get these two out of her flat for the time being.

"I'm sure you'll do your best."

***

Susan and Colin sat in a café, the atmosphere as humid as a tropical rain forest. The windows were steamed up with rivers of condensation rolling downwards. Susan stirred her tea in a mug, which celebrated one of the Queen's many Jubilees, with a little chip on the rim.

"I thought you'd be a lot tougher on her not just politely ask her. You of all people should have noticed that she is breaking the law in there, selling prescription drugs and looking after kids in that squalor. Maybe we should report it all to the police."

Colin bit into the fried egg sandwich that had been constructed with two very thick slices of white bread. The result was a trickle of yellow egg yolk running down from his lips, which he quickly wiped with a paper napkin, avoiding smearing his lipstick.

"She's a victim, Suzie Baby, trust me that is exactly what she is. There is no point treating her like a criminal."

"How can she be a victim? She's selling drugs, that's illegal whichever way you look at it."

"Ok, I agree, by the letter of the law, yes, she is selling drugs and that's unlawful. She is childminding, for which I would guess she has no qualifications, even if the flat reached the required standard, which it would not. So yes, she could be charged, and no doubt found guilty. Yet, my sweet Suzie, she is just one of hundreds, maybe thousands, of women across the United Kingdom who are struggling, living in a poverty trap. People, who can only find jobs which pay the minimum or less, then they would need to get child-care, which totally strips them of any money that they might earn in the first place. Consequently, they stay at home, live on benefits, which might keep you from starving, but does not help you live in a modern world.

"All those things we take for granted: a warm home, a clean home, have you seen the price of cleaning materials? Reasonable clothes for you and your children. We're not living in the Victorian era now, your kid turns up at school in frayed and patched clothes, he or she will be the butt of jokes and ridicule. Plus, it's not just single parents, lots of people have trouble coping with everyday life. Those who have mental issues, those who cannot get a job, they rely on the generosity of the state; a generosity which can change on a political whim."

Colin held up his hand to stop Susan interrupting. He lubricated his throat with his tea and wiped the final crumbs from his mouth before continuing,

"Then let's not forget, we do live in a very material world, TVs, mobile phones, faux fashion names, all bear the same importance as food on the table. People like Flossie make themselves available to those in the shady world of the criminal underworld, just to make a few pounds here and there. George Orwell once wrote: 'poverty frees them from ordinary standards of behaviour, just as money frees people from work'. Flossie and those like her sell a few pills, nick the odd bottle of spirits from the supermarket, screw over mail order companies, do all sorts of things that no one in middle England would ever dream of doing. They make a few pounds here and there, it's those doing the supplying who are making the real profits."

"Who's George Orwell?"

"Suzie Baby, you are such a philistine. George Orwell, famous author who wrote 'Animal Farm'."

"Wasn't that a children's book?"

"No. Have you ever read it?"

"OK, so it's not a children's book. I thought it was about some farm animals and things."

"Well it is, to a point, but it's not a children's story."

Susan stood up having finished her tea and buttoned up her coat.

"I'd best be going. Do you think Flossie will tell him?"

"Oh, she'll tell him something, but what she says will depend on how she is feeling at the time. Don't expect the flow of parking tickets to stop just yet."

***

Just off Eltham High Street is a road that resembles a narrow alleyway. Apart from the two boarded-up and long closed shops, there is a small Italian restaurant. When you open the door to 'Pasta Postcard', you must negotiate a trifling step down into a small vestibule before turning right through a glass door into the main part of the long narrow restaurant. The walls are almost entirely covered in frames of various sizes, each filled with numerous postcards. Some display the picture on the front, some the writing on the back; it gives a dull look to the restaurant. It is an awkward entrance, no one would question that, but in winter the double door system keeps all the diners free of icy blasts when the street door opens.

Martin was sitting below a large frame of postcards depicting Scottish Lochs, located halfway down the restaurant on the right waiting for Jenny to arrive. But for the staff, he was the only person there, which concerned him. He always believed the best restaurants were busy, so there had to be a reason why he was the only person here. He hoped the reason was not connected to any hygiene issues in the kitchen.

Jenny fought her way through the complex double door system, hindered by the three large shopping bags she carried. She did not look at all happy as she sat down opposite Martin.

"This had better be worth it, Martin. You cannot imagine the difficulties I have had to endure to get to this..." She stopped, looked around the décor with a very disapproving eye before giving her verdict: "Drab-looking restaurant with tacky crass postcards, hideous things, in a location which would endear itself to any secret society looking for a hideaway. I hailed a cab outside of Peter Jones, I had some things I simply had to buy, gave him the address and he said: 'No', can you believe it? 'I isn't taking you, lady; too bloody far'," her attempt at impersonating a south London cabbie failed totally. Although Martin wanted to, he declined to point that fact out to her.

"I tried four other cabs, and you know what, today I have learnt that they can refuse if the destination is more than twelve miles away or takes longer than an hour. I ask you, is a train the only way to get to this place called Eltham, which I had never heard of until you mentioned it? No way will I go on a train crammed against all those common people."

Once more Martin declined to point out she could have caught a bus, as that would have been a waste of his breath.

"Lucky for me, taxi driver number five was happy to do it as he was just going off duty. Mind you, he demanded I pay him in cash; I suspect the journey was not recorded. So, this rendezvous had better be worth the fifty pounds I have had to spend to get here."

Martin smiled. "Well, I'm pleased you are here. Shall we order?" He knew it was best to ignore the rant and just get on with eating and enjoying a glass of wine, hopefully then Jenny would forget her hazardous expedition into the wilderness that she considered south London to be.

By the time they had both finished their desserts of tiramisu, (which the menu described as homemade but looked suspiciously as if it had come out of a carton), not only had other diners arrived at the restaurant, but Jenny had calmed down enough, Martin hoped, to allow him to broach the subject of her husband's suspicions.

"Your husband thinks that you are having an affair!" Martin blurted it out against Ian's request and more importantly, against the advice Susan had given him. He was greeted by a brief silence from Jenny as she took in the statement.

"Don't be so bloody stupid, Martin; all Ian ever thinks about is making money. As long I turn up at his charity events or join him meeting clients when he wants me to, he cares little about what I do."

"That is not the impression I got when he popped into the office."

Martin then gave a potted version of Ian's visit to the bemused Jenny. He related the conversation he'd had with her husband. Jenny was less than impressed, she knew her husband a lot better than most people.

"Well if I were you, I'd take him for a real ride, charge him a bloody fortune, and string out the investigation for as long as you can. That will teach the old sod thinking I'm having an affair indeed."

"Well, you are."

"That's not the point, Martin, we are just having fun, something that Ian does not understand. His idea of fun is assessing the growth of his property portfolio. At times it is like he is playing bloody Monopoly." Jenny stopped, emptied her glass, slammed it down on the table, then stated, "The bastard! You know why he's asked you to investigate to see if I am having an affair, he's fishing."

Martin was now confused. "Fishing?" he repeated.

"Yes, he wants to know if I'm having an affair, if I am and he has proof, he can then divorce me and cut down any settlement I might get. He could portray me as some sort of unfaithful wife."

Martin was going to point out the obvious to her but decided once again against making the point. Martin was beginning to think he should have listened to Susan after all.

Jenny continued, "Now I can see his plan, he's having an affair and wants to expose mine first. God, he's a bastard at times. Martin, do me a favour, investigate Ian and see if he's having an affair, trail him around, see what he's up to. Get some hard evidence for me."

Martin slumped back into his chair, refilled his glass and started to pull at his ear lobe; his nerves were becoming frayed. He was, for a moment, tempted to walk out of the restaurant and leave Jenny to her own imagination. The danger was that he might never see her again. He doubted that she would ever make it out of Eltham alive without his help. Being the gentleman he was, he stayed.

Jenny explained to Martin about the young attractive women at the office and all the empty flats Ian had, which were perfect for him to have an affair. Martin didn't listen to her instead he thought to himself: 'how come everyone wants me to investigate?' Susan wanted his help with her blonde drug dealer, then the enquiry about Jenny for Ian and now Jenny wanted him to follow Ian. This was not the sort of life he had envisaged when he first started the detective agency.

"Stop right there!"

Martin sat up straight, put his empty glass on the table and held his palm up to stop Jenny as she decided that the regular trips to Newcastle her husband made could well be a cover for an affair.

"As I don't have to follow you to see if you are having an affair, I already know the answer to that, which means I will have time to follow Ian and see what he is up to. I'll let you know what I find."

Martin had no intention of following Ian, why should he? He planned to do nothing, wait a while and then tell Jenny that her husband was as pure as the driven snow. Everyone ends up happy and life goes on as before.

"Can I possibly help you at all Sir?"

A tall man dressed in a well-tailored blue suit stood over them. His Italian accent seemed diluted, but Martin could see that he had the olive dusty skin tone that Italians often have. He was also good looking, judging by the admiring look Jenny was giving him. Martin then realised that his hand was still in the air as if he wanted to attract the attention of a passing waiter, although this man in the blue suit did not look like a waiter.

"Sorry, I was just gesticulating to my companion," Martin admitted, laying his hand back on the table. "Plainly, you're not a waiter, but do you work here?" Martin asked not having been to Eltham in his entire life, in case the man in the blue suit standing over them had nothing to do with the restaurant. For all Martin knew he could be a random stranger that travelled Eltham restaurants seeing if he could help people.

"Not exactly, Sir, I own the restaurant and I always want my guests to be well looked after."

He looked at Jenny as at the same time his right and left hand pulled up the belt of his trousers, as if he thought they were falling down, which they did not appear to be. This action resulted in his right and left shoulders coming up level with his ears. It briefly appeared that his head had been swallowed by his body and reminded Martin of a tortoise shrinking back into its shell, an odd look. Martin still harboured a misgiving that the man standing next to them could be a local loony.

"I know your face, such a beautiful face," the alleged owner claimed while studying Jenny's appearance. "Of course," a look of recognition appeared in his eyes, "we shared a lunch table at a conference in Liverpool, about a year ago. You are the wife of Ian Shillingford."

"Well, yes," Jenny admitted cautiously.

"The conference: 'Liver Bird Bedsits', promoting houses around Liverpool and the many opportunities to buy cheap and rent high. I own several properties as well as this restaurant," he seemed to crow the fact. "Jenny, that's your name. I am not that good with names but I eventually get there in the end. I'm Derek, Derek Primm. I was just another man hanging around your very successful husband hoping some of his magic profit dust would land on my shoulder."

Oddly, once again Derek pulled his trouser belt upwards with his hands and once again his shoulders appeared to attempt to swallow his head. Martin thought, that if any magic profit dust had landed on Derek's shoulder, it would soon be shaken off.

"Pleased to meet you, again," Jenny added offering her hand expecting it to be shaken, but instead Derek leaned forward, cradled her hand and kissed it. Jenny was clearly relishing the attention.

"Love the décor of your establishment and all these charming postcards, such a wonderful idea. Did you have an interior designer suggest the theme?"

Martin wondered if the affectionate attention had any influence on her revised opinion of the restaurant. He suspected it did.

"It is my little hobby since I was a teenager. I began collecting postcards from around the world. I thought it was better to display my, dare I say myself, impressive collection, instead of just having them sit in boxes in the corner of my room. Collecting them gives some 'me time' away from the pressure of running a property empire as well as this indulgence," he gestured around the restaurant. "I'm a bit of a foodie," he smirked.

"And there I was thinking that you must have been some sort of male model," Jenny admired.

"You are just too kind."

'And you are a creepy dick', Martin thought to himself.

As if he heard those thoughts, Derek looked towards Martin. Somehow, without the need for any spoken words, he seemed to be asking just who this male was with Jenny. He clearly knew that it was not her husband with the magic profit dust. Jenny quickly ventured an explanation, sadly a rash one.

"Let me introduce you to Mikhail, my bodyguard. Ian insists that I should always have a man around. You just can't be too careful these days with kidnaps, ransom notes and streets full of odd people."

"Pleased to meet you, Mikhail, you seem to have lost your Russian accent?"

Martin found himself lost for words, both English and Russian. This was mainly due to the simple fact that he was unsure which of the recent statements that had been made about him he should rectify. In the end, it was Jenny who answered,

"Mikhail's family came here when he was a small child, so he has never actually spoken Russian, have you, Mikhail?"

"Correct, Madam. She always insists that I call her madam, avoids anyone thinking that we are anything but employer and employee."

"I understand," Derek's tone was sarcastic. "You look too mild and meek to be a conventional bodyguard, so I guess your talents are elsewhere and well hidden. Such misunderstandings must be common." Derek turned his attention back to Jenny. "Please give my regards to your husband. I do hope that one day you will return with him to allow me the pleasure of offering you a complementary meal and wine."

Derek left the table and returned to his place beside the small bar that doubled as the payment point. With his back to Jenny and Martin, they did not see the wry smile on his face. He was overall a very observant man; it was his nature and it worked well for his business. Derek was sure that real bodyguards do not arrive twenty minutes before the person they are meant to be protecting. He was certain such knowledge could be put to good use in the future.

CHAPTER FIVE

Susan planned to explain to Martin what had happened yesterday with Colin. She also planned to make a small confession. Last night she had made a short call which part of her this morning was beginning to regret. Before any of this could happen, Martin's mobile phone rang.

Mornings in the office were normally relaxed. Susan would arrive first and make coffee for them both. Martin would appear about ten o'clock carrying a brown paper bag with a Danish pastry for her and a wrapped bacon bap for himself, both from the local bakers.

Today coffee was interrupted as Martin answered his ringing mobile phone. When he heard the female voice on the other end of the telephone line, the atmosphere of their morning coffee session changed.

"Mother, this is not a good time," Martin reacted as he always did to his mother, avoiding any conversation unless absolutely necessary. The downside of this strategy was that his mother fully expected this response and simply continued talking. Looking back, Martin understood that there were very few decisions that he had ever made that had not included some sort of input from Mother. She believed, in the same way a religious fanatic believes their specific Heaven is an indisputable fact, that it was her right to dictate and direct her son, hiding behind the quote: 'it is for his own good'. Martin knew she just enjoyed people doing exactly as she told them without any sort of questioning.

Susan sat back in her chair smiling, she liked to watch Martin squirm.

"Alright, what is it, Mother? I am expecting a client at any moment," he lied.

"Martin, I have been speaking to Lavinia, and we have both agreed..."

'Wait for it', Martin thought.

"... we want you to see exactly what this homeless centre where Paul is offering his services looks like."

"Why?" Martin asked; he should have known better.

"What a silly question to ask, Martin. Lavinia, his mother, is terribly worried about him, just as any mother would be. If you ever have children, and frankly I doubt you ever will provide grandchildren for me, then you will realise that parents worry about their children."

Martin thought the worry she had shown him was more about interference and control. But now was not the time to get any sort of definition out of his mother; that much he had learnt.

"You are aware I know that Paul has, for some inexplicable reason, decided that it would be good to do charitable work. Not that I am against doing charity work; I, for one, have attended some very worthwhile charity events at the Savoy and I am sure raised lots of money for them. But to actually go into the provinces and be amongst these people, well, it is just plain stupidity. That is what charity workers are for, not the children of established and well-respected families like the Barrington's."

"Mother, he is not in the provinces, he is in London, the same as you and I."

"No Martin, I must correct you. The true London is central London and a little to the west. Anything beyond Drayton Gardens, I simply do not regard as true London. Sweet, timid Paul working in south London is frankly dangerous."

"Come on, Mother, he's working in a place called Deptford, it's on the Docklands Light Railway, linking it directly to Canary Wharf, the banking capital of the world. Lots of young people are moving into the area. I've heard they even have a Waitrose there."

"Sometimes, Martin, I despair at the youth of today and their carefree attitude. Do you not read the papers or listen to the news? There are crimes being committed in places like south London, hideous crimes. Paul is working in a homeless centre in south London. Imagine, Martin, just for one single moment, the sort of people who frequent a homeless centre in Deptford: drug addicts, alcoholics, drunks, no doubt women who wear dungarees. There will, I am sure, be tattooed men who smoke funny cigarettes and who are without a good upbringing. Single women, who let their many children run wild while they watch daytime television. Tramps who have not washed for weeks, plus, I would guess, reprobates. I suppose they all would be drawn to such a centre. Dare I add homosexuals and Trotskyists? Lavinia and I feel that Paul could be in real danger. She is terrified that he will be kidnapped, and a ransom demanded; I, on the other hand, have a more balanced approach."

'Really?' Martin thought.

"I think he might be beaten up and robbed. Therefore, Martin I want you to go down there and see for yourself the sort of people that he is mixing with. Then, we would like you to convince Paul to give up this ridiculous notion of doing charity work in south London."

"Mother, Paul is a grown man, he knows what he is doing, and I am sure he is more than able to cope with anyone he might meet in or out of a homeless centre."

"At times, Martin, you are so exasperating. You went to school with the irksome, little boy, or should I say obese, irksome boy; thus, you know exactly what a wimp he is. Happy to be bullied; always full of odd ideas, none of which have ever, up until now, included charity work. The boy is, and always will be, a dreamer. I want you to be a good boy and pop along to this charity centre today and convince him to give the whole thing up, for the sake of his poor mother.

"I must go now. I look forward to hearing from you later, darling. Goodbye." She put her phone down, leaving Martin listening to silence.

"Instructions from on high?" Susan sarcastically asked.

In between eating mouthfuls of his now cold bacon bap, Martin summed up his mother's request, leaving out the bigotry which he knew Susan would not approve of.

"She wants me to go and see Paul at the homeless centre and convince him to give up volunteering. Of course, doing so would mean ending his community service early and thus entailing the wrath of the courts. Hence I can't see me being able to convince him."

"You could have mentioned that small fact to your mother, I'm sure she would be sympathetic."

Martin laughed at Susan's glib comment and finished his coffee.

"Right, when are we going?" Susan asked.

"Going? I told you there is no point; I'll just tell Mother that he didn't want to give up the good work."

"Then when Paul's mother asks: 'Did Martin visit you today?' He'll say what, exactly?"

She watched the thoughtful look wash across Martin's face; she had a good point.

"I'll call Paul, tell him the situation and he'll cover for me, that's what old boys do."

"This is the same Paul who, I think you recently mentioned, has trouble lying. Didn't you tell me that at school when three of you boys were called up before the headteacher for having magazines full of naked women, that you had already collaborated on a story of total denial. That story was that: 'someone else stashed them under Martin's bed', and didn't you say that it was your very own Piggy Paul who under the stark gaze of the headmaster spouted: 'we didn't think they were as rude as they were when we bought them, Sir.' All three of you were banged to rights."

Once again, a thoughtful look with a worried edge crossed Martin's face. He could see the inevitable, yet still decided to fight on.

"You can pop down there. You know the area and speak like a south Londoner. You have a word with him."

"I come from Tooting, different dialect to Deptford."

"Really?" Martin was both sceptical and surprised.

"Your mother would describe them both as common. Anyway, when asked Paul tells his mummy that a young lady turned up to try and convince him to leave, which for the reasons you have already pointed out, he cannot do. How do you think your mummy will react? Come on, Martin, we have all day. It's forty minutes on the train, plus it will be fun meeting all those characters."

As the overground train pulled away from Charing Cross station, Martin had strong doubts that meeting any of the characters his mother had described would be fun.

***

On the rare occasions that Martin took a train, he never felt comfortable. Not that he had ever experienced any traumatic episode on a commuter train; it was just that all those other passengers around him; exactly who they were you could never be sure. Martin was convinced the law of averages would show that at least one person on every train was a psychopath with violent tendencies, which is all very well if you can run faster than them and get away. For Martin, the only way to escape such an attack, would be to leap from the moving train, something which bordered on the side of suicide. He sat anxiously looking out of the window at the industrial units that passed by.

Susan looked at him, saw his unease and decided that now was a good time to ask.

"Remind me, what did you say Paul's odd habit was?"

"I never told you," Martin answered at once, still looking out of the window.

"Well, tell me now."

"It never happened at the restaurant, so I guess he has grown out of it."

"Tell me, tell me, tell me. Please, please, please."

"If that was your attempt at a reasoned argument, it failed."

"I promise if you tell me I will not tell anyone."

From staring out of the window, Martin turned and looked in her eyes. He liked her eyes; if they were the windows of the soul, then Susan always left her windows wide open. What you saw with Susan was what you got, however annoying that might be at times.

"It was very much a schoolboy thing, very immature and silly, so it's best we forget it ever happened."

"I'll just ask him when I see him then."

"Be my guest. If he does want to tell you, just let me know, I want to see your face when you hear what he used to do in class." Martin smiled and turned back to look out of the window.

***

The founder of the Deptford Drop-in, Harry Branston, would never describe his centre as just for the homeless, even though it helped many homeless people. Harry opened the doors to the centre as a place for any local who might need help, advice, companionship, a warm place to have tea n' toast with a chat, without costing you a penny.

Harry worked alongside five helpers, all of whom spent their time chatting, supporting and just being there for people who had no one else to turn to. It was really a social centre for the most vulnerable in the area.

The Deptford Drop-in was situated directly opposite the Southeastern rail station. Martin looked at the red painted building of the centre, he was sure it looked like a converted public house, which in fact it had been for many years until the brewery closed it down. They still owned the building, but they let the charity use it for a peppercorn rent.

"Well, if it was a pub," Susan commented, "then any alcoholics will feel at home."

They crossed the road and the first person they encountered was, in Martin's opinion, a typical tramp, a full-blown man of the road. Sitting on the pavement eating a sandwich, his hands engrained with dirt and fingernails full of filth; his clothes, worn and weary, were layers and layers of second, possibly fourth-hand garments which bulked the thin body of the man who was eagerly consuming his sandwich. His full beard matched his uncut hair, wiry and dirty.

'Maybe,' Martin thought, 'Mother was right.'

The tramp looked up from his sandwich at the two strangers who were about to enter the Drop-in, he smiled with yellowed teeth, "Morning."

"Morning," Susan responded in her chirpy voice, while an uncomfortable Martin just mumbled a greeting, eager to get past the man.

"You do realise," Martin pointed out as they stood in the small lobby of the building, decorated with notice boards and yellowed warnings that no alcohol was allowed inside, "he had things, actual living things in his hair; I saw things moving, like ants or creepy crawlies."

Susan put her hand on the door, but before she opened it, she smiled at Martin, "I bet you are going to love what's on the other side of this door." Without waiting for any sort of answer, she strode through the doorway leaving Martin to follow on behind her.

Back in the eighties, the building had been known as the Mechanics Arms. Today, the original semi-circular bar was still in place, but the partition between the saloon and the public bars had long gone. What remained was a large open space, which was now filled with a mixture of sofas, low tables, and dining tables with plastic bucket chairs. The room was occupied with people of all shapes, ages and colours. Martin estimated there were about thirty or perhaps even forty people crowded in front of them. There was a confusion of sounds that echoed around the room. To his left was the semi-circular bar, the optics gone, and instead tea and toast were being pushed across the counter by three people wearing matching powder-blue polo shirts with the charity's logo on them.

Before they had taken more than a couple of steps into the Drop-in Centre, Susan and Martin were approached by a young man, smartly dressed, with sharp features and a crooked nose which looked as though it had been broken and repaired badly.

"Two new faces," he declared. "Welcome to the Drop-in, I'm Tony and I want to make sure you are appropriately greeted here." Tony offered his hand towards Martin, who gave a firm handshake to the smart young man who was, no doubt, some sort of charity worker.

"I'm Martin and this is Susan. We're here to speak to Paul," Martin requested.

"Oh, you're not a local with that posh voice; bit like Paul, he's doing community service. Punched some bugger, you know, -*fuck it shit*-, almost done his time, -*arseholes*-, shame to see him go, nice guy, -*bitching shit head*-, we'll go an' find him. First you gotta meet Harry."

Martin was not sure if he had heard Tony correctly; parts of his speech were clearly normal but interjected amongst the phrases were swear words combined with a rapid jerk of the head, which he appeared not to notice himself. Martin looked at Susan for an answer to this seemingly odd behaviour.

"Martin, you are so sheltered, he has Tourette's syndrome, he can't help the swearing or the flicking of his head. You must try to get out more."

"Tourette's Tony, -*shit*-, they call me, come on." Without further comment, Tony beckoned them to follow him as he walked off towards the bar calling out above the hubbub of the room,

"Harry, more poshies doin' a visit."

Everyone turned to grab a look at the posh guests, any distraction was a good distraction from the mundane days many of them endured.

A man wearing a blue polo shirt stood up leaving one of the tables and walked towards Susan and Martin. His height was average but the rest of him was very different; his large melon-like head sat on his rounded body. He thrust his hand with its sausage-shaped fingers into Martin's, "I'm 'arry, wan' a cuppa?"

Harry's official title was director of the Drop-in, but he was better known to the local constabulary as Harry Branston, local villain, whose age and experience put him amongst the hierarchy of local crime.

Harry prided himself on being feared by local criminals and respected by some of the toughest villains in London. During any night he might punch a man half to death, plan a robbery, as well as run his night club: 'Homer's', so named after Harry's favourite cartoon character. 'Homer's was a club where only the brave would venture, with its stabbings, fights and shootings; it was a local dive for the villains of the area.

For all the bad that flowed through his veins, Harry had a heart of gold. Once a month 'Homer's' was turned into a place where elderly people could come and enjoy an afternoon tea dance with plenty of free refreshments. They all loved Harry and Harry loved them. He looked upon himself as their guardian angel. Lord help any foolish young boy who might think that grabbing a purse from an old dear was a good idea; Harry would find the culprit and deal with him in his own way. Everyone had an anecdote about Harry, if you didn't, then you were not considered to be a true local.

When the Mechanics Arms was going to close down, Harry pulled some strings with the local council, obtained a large grant to open the place as a centre for vulnerable people in the area and those less fortunate, a sort of Drop-in café for everyone.

"Thanks for the offer of tea," Martin spoke first as he shook Harry's hand, "but we are just here to have a quick word with Paul and then we'll be off and out of your way."

"Well, you're not the cops with a posh voice like that, so I'll tell yer. Paul's out the back making up the sandwiches. He's the only one I trust with a knife around 'ere." Harry laughed and pointed towards a grey painted door in the far corner of the room. "Just go through there, you can give 'im a 'and, if yer want."

As they walked towards the door, Martin looked around the room, it was nothing like he had expected. He knew his mother's description of a dungeon of debauchery was going to be exaggerated, but his own expectation was still of a dirty, smelly and threatening centre. He realised he was wrong. The atmosphere was congenial and with no nasty strange smells. There was a friendly, warm feeling about the place. No one looked threatening, but for one young man, sitting quietly in the corner of the room, reading a Marvel superhero comic. He was dressed in jeans with chains for a belt, and wore a *ZZ Top* black tee-shirt, with a thick leather jacket over it. The young man was overweight and bald, no doubt a razor shaved head. His bald head was tattooed, as was his neck and fingers. Martin guessed that the tattoos extended all over the young man's body. Yes, he looked threatening at first glance, yet his face resembled the look of a lost child.

Before Martin and Susan reached the door, a harsh woman's voice cut above the noise of the room and silenced everyone.

"I ought to tear yer fucking eyes out, you bitch, what are you a copper's nark?"

Everyone turned towards the source of this outburst, which by the tone, Martin guessed, was not a joke and thankfully was aimed at Susan and not him.

"The feds turned me over this morning, took all me gear, 'after a tip off', they said. I guess it was you, yer bitch, you and that poofy copper friend of yours." Flossie slammed her plate of toast on the counter and moved aggressively towards Susan who stood her ground, which was more than could be said for Martin who took a step back, as Flossie moved towards them. But before she could reach Susan, Harry stepped between the two women.

"Floss, don't get griefy, nobody knows where the tip off might have come from. You know you have some jealous neighbours."

"I'll fucking do that bitch," she pointed over Harry's shoulder at Susan. "Comes round thinking she owns the fucking place and loses me stuff. If my man tells me: 'that's it, Flossie, no more selling our gear'. Who's going to pay me rent now I lost me extras."

"Too old to start laying on your back again?" Susan taunted, which did nothing to calm Flossie down, who now tried to push past Harry screaming a torrent of abuse, none of which was related to Tourette's.

"Floss, think you 'ad better go now, take a walk around the block and cool off a little."

Harry guided a protesting Flossie out of the centre. All regulars knew that Flossie's bark was a lot worse than her bite. Flossie was not one to get physical, verbal abuse and a wide vocabulary of derogatory remarks was her stock reaction. Even as she was being guided out, her piercing and threatening eyes stayed on Susan.

"What was that all about?" Martin asked Susan. "Do you actually know her?"

Susan sounded sheepish as she very quietly told Martin that after leaving the café yesterday and even after being told by Colin that dobbing Flossie in would not do any good, she had thought she knew better. She had called the police and told them all: the address, the drugs and the poor childcare. It was that last subject which really seemed to brighten up the operator at the station. So, although Susan had thought they might take a while to pay Flossie a visit, no doubt the mention of a young baby in poor conditions had set off alarm bells.

"Susan, you have got to start listening to the advice people give you. It's no use you thinking you are always right, some of us have a better view of things. Next time you see Colin tell him and apologise."

"You're a fine one to talk. 'Don't tell Jenny', I say and what do you do, the exact opposite, you told her and look where it got you? It's about time you took some of your own advice."

"To be fair, Susan, you are not known for giving out good advice. And I still think that telling her will be for the best in the end."

"You hope," was Susan's only comment as they walked through the grey door.

Paul looked up from cutting sandwiches, a look of surprise appeared on his face when he saw Martin and Susan walking towards him.

"What the hell are the two of you doing here?" Was the greeting that Martin and Susan received.

Martin ignored Paul's protesting tone and began to explain, that as a result of two interfering mothers, he and Paul needed to come up with a reassuring story; one that Paul would not get flustered when telling his mother, some little white lies.

"Are you clear now Paul? You know what we are both going to say to our respective mothers?"

Paul wiped his hands on a grimy tea towel and faced Martin.

"I think so." Paul repeated their planned story line: "You have visited today and assured yourself that there are no dangerous people here, which I could have told you. However, acknowledging my mother's concern for what I am doing, I might give up my charity work, which I enjoy, but I need to complete another two weeks here in line with the volunteer agreement I made with the charity when I first started."

"Good, and no mention of Vicky, only hint that you enjoy it so much that you might stay. Right, that's done, we'll be off. Have fun with the sandwiches."

Martin was keen to leave the place as quickly as possible and get back to the part of London he knew and trusted better.

"Before you go, Martin, you haven't introduced me formally to your assistant. It's Susan, I understand, pleased to meet you," Paul smiled at Susan.

"Paul, Susan; Susan, Paul. Is that OK, can we go now?"

"Not so fast, Martin, I want to ask Susan a favour."

Susan had learnt from past embarrassing mistakes that when a man asks her to do him a favour, it's best to find out first just what that favour might be.

So sensibly she asked, "What sort of favour?"

***

Martin sat alone on the train back to Charing Cross. He had listened to Paul explain how his girlfriend Vicky was a female at the other end of sex chat lines, spending her days doing 'dirty talk to dirty old men'. Martin was about to ask if she offered a discount to friends, when he realised that Paul was truly upset and uncomfortable that she was providing such a service to some of the male population, so had just nodded in a concerned fashion.

Paul's next sentence had pushed Susan's patience to the limit; 'I thought as you come from the same social background, that you might be able to get through to her and convince her not to do it.' At that point Martin stood back a little to allow Susan to explode.

She did no such thing, instead, to Martin's surprise, she had nodded in a motherly way. As Paul was starting to get a little emotional talking about Vicky and her problem, (he always was an emotional boy, who cried the first time he saw Yoda offer sound advice) Susan almost hugged him, only just refraining at the last moment.

If that was not bad enough, Susan, a little too readily for Martin, agreed to have a word with Vicky. This pleased Paul, who quickly added that he was about to finish and go around to see his girlfriend and Susan could go with him. Martin assumed that the invitation included him, but it did not. So now, sitting on the train alone, Martin felt as if his date had pushed him aside for another man, which was a little weird he would be the first to agree but, nonetheless, that was how he felt.

***

Susan felt tense as Paul drove his small red Toyota through the crowded traffic of south London. She would be the first to admit that driving was not her strong point, so for her to feel tense as a passenger was a damming condemnation of Paul's driving ability. He talked continuously, appearing to be unaware that he was in the middle of a busy road.

"There is something else I need you to know before we get to Vicky's. She is in a lot of debt, that is the reason she is doing these sex chat lines, to try and pay off a loan shark. I did not want to mention it in front of Martin, he can be a funny person at times."

"Ah, I don't know; he means well and does his best. So, how am I going to convince your Vicky to give up the sex chat line if she is in such a load of debt?"

"I was hoping you might come up with a solution to that little problem. I try and help out where I can with money, but things are a little problematic for me."

At this point, Susan closed her eyes and prayed as she was convinced that there was going to be an imminent impact with a single decker bus that was turning right in front of the red Toyota. She counted to ten, the car was still moving, she was still breathing, she opened her eyes once again.

"What was Martin like at school? I hear you shared a dorm with him."

"Him and four others, six of us in the dorm. He was alright, everyone thought he was the coolest kid in our year. His parents were kind of loaded with cash. Not that he boasted, he has never done that, it was just he thought being very rich was normal."

"I bet he had some funny habits at school."

"Not really, he did fiddle with his ear lobe when he was a little nervous and he hated being called Dennis."

"Dennis?"

"Yes, a stupid nickname for him. We were often called by our surnames, so when the masters called him, they called: 'Hayden', which the boys translated into 'Hey Den', and from that we called him Dennis, just to annoy him, you know what teenage boys are like."

"What about you, Paul, did you have any habits at school?"

"Why, what has Martin told you?" His voice had become a little more defensive, touching a nerve, Susan thought.

"Nothing, only that all boys have odd habits at school, just wondered if you had any."

"It was a long time ago; I don't recall if I had any. Look, I'll park up here and her flat is just over there behind us."

Susan looked out of the back window to where Paul was indicating. There were two things that caught her eye. The first was a woman's cardigan on the back seat, the sort of thing her granny would wear. The second thing, or things to be more precise, were the row of six shops. The same shops that Susan had stood outside of yesterday morning. They had parked in Turner Road.

CHAPTER SIX

If Susan had to be honest, she was a little wary as she extracted herself from Paul's small yet practical, he said, Toyota. Yesterday morning she had stood here talking to a traffic warden, helping an old lady, and missing the driver of the blue Honda. Susan did a quick visual check in case Flossie was anywhere to be seen.

As well as the café where she had bought her bacon roll, there was a fish and chip shop which Paul pointed out to her together with the door alongside it. With yellow paint peeling on it just above the broken letter box and a little below the glazed arch with its cracked glass, was a handwritten seven. Paul rang the bell and they both waited. A moment later, Susan heard footsteps running down some stairs and the door opened. Vicky stood in front of them, observing Susan with a distrustful eye.

"So, what do you both want?" Vicky's voice was not full of affection as Susan had expected but sounded confrontational.

"Well, Sweets."

Who, Susan thought, ever called their partner 'Sweets'?

"You know how uncomfortable I feel about you talking to strange men over the telephone about sex things. And, I know you think it is OK, but I was just thinking that Susan here might be able to convince you that it is not the best thing for you to do. I'm sure a woman to woman talk would help."

Seemingly begrudgingly, Vicky led them upstairs and showed them into a cluttered room with three grubby windows that overlooked the street.

"So, exactly how do you know Susan?" Vicky demanded; her eyes still rigidly fixed on Paul.

"She is er, a friend of a school friend of mine, Martin. He runs the detective agency I told you about and Susan here is his helper. Say hello, Susan."

Susan wanted to laugh at Paul, she was pretty sure he was on the verge of wetting himself. However, his condescending attitude put the cap on any amusement she might have felt.

"We'll have a chat. I know at times a girl has got to do what a girl has got to do, but Paul does sound worried about you."

"Well, at least you're not one of his posh buddies who think they always know best; try to run my life for me."

Susan was not sure if she should take that as an insult or a compliment; in the end she decided just to agree with the latter part of the sentence. "These posh blokes do think they know it all, which can piss me off at times too." She smiled.

"Too bloody right. Paul, have you told her exactly what I do and why I do it, and how you think by waving some magic wand, everything will turn out right?"

"Sweets, I just want the best for you. I worry that one day you'll get some really creepy guy on the end of the phone and things might turn out bad for you."

Vicky slumped down in a worn-out armchair with a loud sigh, leaving Paul and Susan standing.

"For fuck's sake, Paul, how many times have I told you all the guys I speak to are creepy? They're calling a sex chat line, for Christ's sake, they ain't going to be normal, are they? Don't you agree, Susan?"

Susan nodded as Paul continued, "I just don't like that sort of thing, Sweets, it worries me."

"Worries you? I'm the one doing the talking, remember. I'm the one who has to tell them what I'm wearing, listen to what they would like to do to me and tell them what great ideas I think they have. The longer I keep them talking, the more money I make, simple really."

"You know I would help you with money, but I have told you my money is tied up in various accounts."

"Yes, Paul, tied up in Mother's apron strings. You told me how you need Mummy's permission to spend your money."

"I told you that was a private matter." Paul looked timidly at Susan, clearly Mother controlling his money was not for general knowledge. "Something you should not share because you do not understand the complexity of family finances."

'Well,' Susan thought, 'at least Martin can decide what he does with his allowance. His mother might be controlling, but at least she is not as bad as Paul's.'

Susan decided to sit down on an equally scruffy armchair to the one Vicky was sitting on, neither of which matched anything in the room. Expecting a long argument between the two of them she decided to make herself comfortable and watch the entertainment. The show did not last as long as she thought it might.

Vicky pointed her finger toward Paul, who was standing before her resembling a naughty schoolboy. Susan could see what Martin had meant now.

"You don't fucking understand the complexity of living without any money. Paul Barrington, fucking, Smythe has never in his stuck-up life had to wonder: 'how am I going to pay for that? You just stuck it on yer credit card or asked Mummy to buy it. I have nothing, Paul, when will you actually understand that? I have nothing!" Vicky's voice rose with anger. "I work a measly eight hours a week at Tesco; there are no other hours available, nothing, zilch, diddly squat. I take home as much as you spend on just one of your long, boozy lunches. I get a few benefits off the so-called welfare state which your toffee-nosed Tory arse-holes try and take away 'cause they think I'm fiddling the system. I'm just trying to live. Come on, what am I meant to do? How do I get more money in a week? I get weird men talking creepy to me, I listen, and I get money; it's that easy. And before you ask Paul, I don't like it, I'd rather be in a real job with colleagues and friends instead of listening to a bloke wanking off over the phone."

"I think you are being a little unfair," Paul timidly answered. Susan thought to herself: 'not a wise response'.

"Life is not fair, Paul. Life is shit when you have nothing. Life is shit at the bottom of the ladder, 'cause posh bastards like you and your family are at the top, shitting on us to make sure we stay there at the bottom."

Vicky's demeaner changed in an instant, her head fell into her hands and she started sobbing. Paul leant forward to touch her shoulder and comfort her. She shrugged his gesture away.

"Susan, I think we had better go now, I have to get home and change. There is a reception tonight at the National Gallery and I don't want to be late. Are you ready, Susan?"

"Better if I stay. You get off to your reception thingy, I'll make Vicky a cup of tea. I can get a cab in a bit, no sweat."

Paul withdrew from the room, scuttled down the stairs and out into the street.

"Well, I say a cup of tea, but maybe something a little stronger would be better."

Vicky looked up at Susan and smiled, "Vodka is over there, tonic in the fridge."

***

During the next two and a half hours, Vicky and Susan became vodka buddies. They sat drinking, laughing, drinking, talking and drinking some more, with only the occasional cry. It was the first time, Vicky said, since she had left her council terraced home in Birmingham that she had found someone she felt was not judging her. She did not feel as alone as she had at the start of the day. The vodka clearly was helping her to relax and share her troubles.

Even so, Vicky was not forthcoming to Susan about her problems with the loan shark, so Susan started that conversation.

"Just how did you get yourself tied up with this loan shark that Paul mentioned?"

"I don't want to burden you, it's my problem, I'll sort it in the end. Tell me about your job, sounds real exciting."

"Your problem is a lot more pressing; loan sharks never give up. Tell me how it all started?"

Vicky refilled her glass and started to explain. She recalled arriving at Euston Station, with a large suitcase full of clothes and dreams. That night she spent in a small hostel. The following day she began searching for a flat to live in. By lunchtime her dreams had been dented. Every letting agent or landlord that she spoke to, wanted two months rent upfront as a deposit. She had not considered that. Now she was caught in a dilemma, the longer she stayed at the hostel, the faster her negligible savings would disappear. She could not replenish the savings through work, until she had a permanent address.

"I thought I knew it all when I left Birmingham, I should have known better. Anyway, I met a woman in a café and we started chatting like us girls do. She told me she had a flat in Deptford, never heard of the place. She had just moved in with her boyfriend and had given notice on the flat, but there were three weeks left, and so, she says, I can have the key. There was nothing in it, but I didn't care, slept on the floor. Now I had an address I landed a job with Tesco, but time in the flat was running out fast."

It was then, Vicky explained, fate took a hand in her life. She was passing by the Deptford Drop-in Centre and saw a notice for free tea, toast and helpful advice. She walked in and took the centre up on its offer. She explained her predicament to Harry, who was neither surprised nor phased by what he heard, but said he did have a solution. She sat and listened.

Harry told her that a local councillor owned a lot of properties in the area, some of which were not in the best locations to command a high rent. Plus, the councillor wanted to be charitable and helpful to those not so fortunate. The arrangement was that the charity would allocate six flats above a parade of shops to those who were in a housing crisis and there happened to be one of them free at that time. There was no need for a deposit, all Vicky had to do was to give some details over and the centre could install her in a small flat. She was warned that it was above a fish and chip shop, so there were often odd odours rising through to the flat. Vicky did not care one bit and gave Harry a huge hug. The following day she was sitting exactly where she was now, looking around her semi-furnished flat. Her first home in London.

"Harry had taken care of all the paperwork and stuff, sorted out the electric people, even provided me stuff for the kitchen, you know, kettle, crockery, saucepans, plus some grub to start me off. He was so kind to me."

"Sounds as though you had fallen on your feet, so what went wrong, with the loan shark, I mean?"

"A couple of weeks later this guy turns up, all suited and booted, telling me that I need to pay a deposit. He said he was from the management company of some place. I had to pay two grand deposit. Well, what could I do, I didn't have that sort of money? He suggested that he could lend me the money."

"Why didn't you tell Harry about it, to see if it was correct?"

"Didn't like to, Harry seemed such a nice bloke and he might have just forgotten to tell me. I dunno. But I needed the deposit and I don't suppose that Harry could have helped me with that."

"This bloke, he provided you with the cash for the deposit that he then collected?"

"No, he just got me to sign a couple of things and that was it. It's just that the interest was mounting up, so he suggested that I could do something to pay it all off."

"Did you read the small print or see what you were signing?" Susan asked doubtfully.

"No, he seemed such a nice, helpful guy, smartly dressed, good looking, curly dark hair. I don't read too well, you understand."

Susan did know that Vicky was not the first, or would be the last, woman to be charmed by a good-looking man. She felt sorry for her, she knew some young girls were vulnerable, and she could imagine how Vicky could be coerced into almost anything.

"Hence the sex chat line to pay off the debt?" Susan asked and Vicky just nodded, emptied the last of the vodka from her glass and began sobbing again. Vicky did not want to talk any more.

***

"Are you planning to catch up with Paul at some time?" Martin asked, watching Susan as she paced around the office like a caged lion on steroids.

"You are just not listening, Martin; you really need to pay more attention. Vicky is having to talk to dirty old men to pay off a loan shark, it is really that simple. I think we should find out a bit more about this councillor."

"Why the councillor?"

"Because, as you might recall, Paul said that the flat is in a bad state and the landlord is not keen to do any repairs. Vicky spoke to the estate agent who manages the property about it; he said they had just about no budget to do any repairs on the flats. Vicky could complain to the councillor, but the estate agent advised her not to, as the last time that happened, the tenant was asked to leave. The man sounds like a rogue landlord, offering cheap, no deposit flats to lure vulnerable women into his trap."

"Which man, the estate agent or the councillor?"

"Concentrate Martin, the councillor."

"I suppose you are just trying to impress Paul with your investigative skills?"

"Martin, grow up, will you? This is not about me and Paul, because frankly I think he is an annoying little wimp. It's about injustice; it's about a woman being tricked and manipulated into doing something no woman should do, unless they actually want to, that is."

Susan wanted to ask if he was jealous that there might be another man in her sights, but decided it was best not to say anything. She knew that she was jealous of Jenny. She also knew that it was an unreasonable emotion to have.

Martin, however attractive she found him, was way above her in the social league that frames all our lives.

"Alright, so who is this councillor, the rogue landlord?" Martin tugged at his ear lobe.

"Well I have found out that his name is Derek Primm. He followed in his father's footsteps as a local councillor and inherited a large property portfolio that his father had built up. He owns a restaurant in Eltham called 'Pasta Postcard', which is normally where he can be found. What do you say you and me pop in to see him?"

Martin sat back in his chair and frowned, "Might not be a good idea for me to tag along behind you, weirdly, that's where I took Jenny for our discreet lunch."

"Come on, Martin, you were just another diner, he most likely will not recall you even being there."

Reluctantly, Martin explained how he became a Russian bodyguard called Mikhail. Even quietly-spoken Ernie, out in reception, heard Susan laugh; she laughed so hard that tears ran down her cheeks.

"I can't think which is funnier," she gasped between laugher, "you a Russian or being a bodyguard."

"Well, either way," Martin replied, solemn faced, "I'm not coming with you."

"Don't worry, Martin, I don't need a bodyguard, Russian or not. I'll go on my own."

"Susan," Martin called her, just as she was slipping her coat on, checking she had her phone and about to grab her shoulder bag.

"Yes?" She stood waiting for him to speak. He just sat there looking at his desk, fiddling with his ear lobe. His thoughts appeared to be outside of the office.

"Yes, Martin, what is it?"

"He has a funny habit, Derek Primm, he kind of tugs his trousers up, and his shoulders go higher than his head, looks really odd."

"OK, Martin, I'll bear that in mind."

"Didn't want you to see it, get all surprised and start laughing at him."

"Thanks, see you later."

"Susan," again he called her as she stood in the doorway, still looking at his desk, still nervously tugging at his ear lobe.

"Yes," Susan snapped back. The short silence between them only seemed to sharpen the tone.

Then Martin spoke, "Susan," he sounded uncertain. "Shall I go and speak to the managing estate agents you mentioned? They might know something, perhaps a bit of background on Derek Primm?"

"Yes, that's an idea; find out what you can. The address is on my desk." She knew that he was aware of where her desk was but, even so, she found herself pointing to it.

"Susan," this time he looked up at her. "What are you doing tonight? I have a couple of tickets for the theatre, do you want to join me?"

As Susan stood in the doorway holding the door open, she would have liked to ask a few more questions about Martin's surprise invitation, such as: What was the show? Where was the show? What time was the show? What sort of attire should she wear? Would they meet at the theatre or would he collect her from her flat? Instead, she just said, "Love to, send me a text where we're meeting. See you later." She closed the door behind her as she left. Martin did not see the broad smile on her face.

***

On Lewisham High Street, sandwiched between Greggs the Bakers and Boots the Chemist, was Duffield the Estate Agents. If Martin had known that a trip to see the estate agent would mean another journey to south London, his second of the day, then he might not have offered to visit in the first place.

'Home is but a heartbeat away'; to Martin the catch-line on the shop window made no sense whatsoever whichever way he played it in his mind. In the end, he ignored it and walked in wondering what sort of idiots he might find within.

The dismal interior matched the confusing and slightly bizarre shop window. As any visitor stood in the doorway, having passed through the entrance, they faced three metal-framed desks in a straight row, forming an uninviting fence across the office space. Each desk had a computer screen, a keyboard, a large A4 book, and a black plastic tray. Only one of the desks looked as if it was being used. The whole area was dark and dusty; the least inviting estate agents Martin had ever walked into, not that he was an aficionado.

A smartly dressed man appeared from a doorway on the dark right-hand side of the office, holding a red Manchester United mug.

"Sorry, one was just out the back making oneself a reviving cup of coffee, helps keep one's brain cells buzzing around. What can I do for you?"

Martin did not answer at once, he appraised the voice of the man in front of him, it was nothing like the local accent. Then he had a faint recognition of the face; a face he knew well from his past, it came back to him: his boarding school days.

"Stephen?"

"Well, chase a pheasant around a field if standing before me, is it not the one and only Martin 'Dennis' Hayden, the famous socialite and all-around good guy? What on earth brings you to the dark side of the capital? Grab a seat; fancy a coffee?" Stephen gestured to the desk on Martin's left.

A surprised Martin sat down and refused a coffee.

"What a small world, I was only talking about you the other day, with Paul you remember him. Had lunch with him and we recalled the last time we all met up was at your wedding, you were in some sort of venture capital business with your father at the time. How come the change?

"Everyone calls me Steve now, much more in keeping with the area I now work in. Well, Martin, my man, where shall I start the story of my downfall?"

Steve leaned back on his chair, placed both feet on the desk and smiled at Martin.

"Wedding, venture capital, Father; God, they are all just so historical."

Not one to miss out on someone listening to his life story, Steve spent the next fifteen minutes telling Martin how he had ended up in Lewisham as a simple employee of Duffield Estate Agents.

Their last meeting was when Steve had married Julie in 2012, the year of the London Olympics. The wedding had been a grand, lavish affair: two hundred guests, a marquee in the garden, free flowing champagne and the best cuisine; money had been no object. Steve's venture capital business, supported by his father's money, was making all the right choices. The company was buying businesses cheap and stripping their assets before selling them on at a profit.

"We were Olympic Gold, Martin, Olympic Gold! Then Cross and Sons came along, a large family business that had been operating since the beginning of time. They had played with chemicals all their lives. Anyway, the brothers had developed a small compact battery that charged within minutes. I mean super-fast. It was going to revolutionise the small mobile electronics industry, even electric cars, imagine that, Martin. They wanted cash to expand, we saw the fortune to be had and wanted total control.

"There was a lot of hard bargaining. Finally, we bought out the whole company and wrestled control from the family who scuttled off into the night with our cash. But we had the product that the world and its mother were going to be banging on our door to get hold of. Then came the sting. It turned out that this super-duper battery was already firmly patented by a Japanese firm, which basically left us with egg on our face and a sodding great hole in our pockets."

"So, what did you do, litigate against them?"

"That was the plan until we looked very closely at the paperwork. Turns out there was some clever sleight of hand with the agreements. Our solicitor was not as trustworthy as we might have thought, and the case was not going to stand up in court. Still, so what, knock the whole bloody factory down, sell off the land, worth a few bob on the outskirts of Bingham, for a princely sum, help balance the books, cut our losses. Well, it would have been worth a few million but for the contamination of the land, which the council knew all about, so we had to put right. Apparently, you just cannot leave contaminated land lying around nowadays, bloody regulations."

"What a pain, so your company caught a cold?"

"A cold! Christ, Martin, I wish! It was pneumonia with complications. The complications being: a pile of debt, the Environment agency breathing down our necks, and the bloody Japanese suing us. Still, every cloud has a silver lining, as they say; my wife, with the loud, annoying laugh, left me, which was the good news. The bad news: my firm went bust and I ended up looking for real work."

"What about your father, couldn't he have helped you out?" Martin asked.

"No. It turns out that all of Daddy's vast fortune was just very clever accounting and secretly he was selling all his assets. He died soon after the fiasco, leaving Mother with no property at all, just a small annuity. She is now living with her sister in Devon."

"And you're working here in Lewisham, well, at least the income is regular, I guess."

"Well, it's a job. A shitty job to be honest, Martin, but it pays the rent and occasionally I get to sell a property. Well, the extra commission comes in handy. Old man Duffield tries to grab all the good customers, leaving me with the dross. Anyway, enough of my troubles. What are you after, Martin, planning to move down to these parts? I have some nice property for you if you're interested. I could do with the commission. Or you could buy to let, lots of profit to be made there."

Martin said firmly that he had no intention to move to this specific part of London.

"Well if you're not a customer, to what do I owe the pleasure?"

Carefully Martin explained that he had met up with their school chum Paul, and during their conversation, Paul had expressed concern about his girlfriend, who lives in a flat above a fish and chip shop, one of the flats that Duffield look after. She had got into trouble with a loan shark, who claimed to be from the freehold company. Martin, as a favour, wanted to know a little more about Derek Primm, the landlord with the charitable heart.

Steve took his feet off the table, sat upright in the chair and laughed.

"Fancy you also having lunch with 'porn Paul' as well; still as weird as ever. I took him to Derek Primm's restaurant for a lunch and a catch up, well, I get discount there as I know the owner. Luckily for me there was no sign of his disgusting, albeit entertaining, to us schoolboys, classroom habit."

"Yes, I was relieved as well, it would have put me off my lunch if he had started that up again. So, you do know Derek Primm?"

"I know some stuff about him, he is my client. I should point out that the only reason he is my client is that old Duffield agreed to do him a favour and deal with the management on those six flats without any charge, AKA I get to do the work for no commission. See what I mean, they treat me like the office junior. Anyway, Duffield and Primm are both Rotary Club members so there is not a lot more to be said. We deal with some of Primm's other properties, but I get the dross."

Steve pulled out a file from his desk drawer and opened it out.

"Six flats, Primm finds the tenants via some charity, apparently they are meant to be vulnerable people; we do all the legal bits for them. Any repairs need doing, the tenants speak to me. That's about it really. Primm is a well-known councillor; inherited a lot of the property from his father. As for the freehold company, well, I understand that he owns the whole block, the flats and the shops underneath. Never heard of a separate freehold company, or anyone asking for a security deposit on the properties."

"But," Martin put on a serious voice, "the flats, as I understand it, are not that well-maintained, in fact one person described them as a total car wreck."

"That is just plain stupid, Martin, how can a flat be a car wreck? I thought you were good at English, maybe too much wine. But you're right, they are not well cared for. There is a good reason, I have just about a zero budget for any repairs to those six flats. Unless it is a legal requirement, you know, leaky boiler, risk of the tenant dying, then I have to beg Mr Primm to spare some extra cash."

"Is it fair to say he keeps them in a bad state of repair on purpose?"

"Not exactly, he likes the fact everyone knows he gives out charity, but he prefers not to spend any money on that charitable venture of his. You do realise they are invariably young single women who get the flats?"

"What's that supposed to mean?"

"What it sounds like. If I had six flats that I wanted to put to charitable use, helping out vulnerable people, I would have imagined that there would be some single women there, maybe a couple of single parents, even the odd homeless man, you know, a variety of people making use of them. But every one of those flats, all they ever have in them is young single women. I just think that's odd. But there again, I'm not the one handing out the charity, am I?"

***

Once she had negotiated the challenging entrance to Pasta Postcard, Susan stepped into what she first thought might be some sort of second-hand shop. The walls were covered with frames of all different shapes and sizes, each one containing a selection of postcards. You needed to step up close to the frames to be able to see the postcards in any detail. The menus on the table were designed as large postcards and even the table did not escape. Under the glass top there were still more postcards: vintage, modern, abstract, saucy. There must have been thousands displayed around the restaurant.

Asking to speak to Derek Primm brought a scurry of activity from the waiters and moments later a tall man in a blue suit strode towards Susan. If Susan had not expected it, she would have simply burst out laughing, however, the warning that Martin had given her allowed her to keep a straight face, as Derek Primm pulled up the belt of his trousers.

"I'm here to talk to you about one of your tenants who rents a flat above a fish and chip shop in Turner Road."

He did not answer. First, he took Susan's hand and kissed it like some chivalrous knight. It sent a shiver up her spine. Martin had told her that, apart from the trouser thing, Jenny was drooling as she spoke to Derek. Susan agreed with Jenny's estimation, Derek was good looking with his slightly tanned skin and Mediterranean looks; Susan could imagine him modelling swimwear. The picture she formed in her mind was very satisfying.

"Alas," he looked into her eyes, which gave her another shiver, "I do not know my tenants, of which I have a number; that I leave to a managing agent. I can give you their number if you wish, I am sure they would be more than pleased to help you."

"My colleague, as we speak, is chatting with your estate agent. I'm a private detective and I have some questions." Why she had decided to sound like the arresting police officer in a murder inquiry she had no idea. It was just an easy way of impressing him, plus, hopefully, make her seem more attractive.

"Oh, in that case we had better take a seat. Can I get you a drink?"

Sitting at a table with an attractive man, maybe a little older than she would have liked, a glass of wine beside her, Susan was comfortable. A few compliments would top it all off. As if he read her mind Derek obliged,

"I am a great admirer of young women who step into what must be a very male orientated domain. The world of investigating can only be a better place with such alluring investigators such as yourself. Now, how can I be of help"

Susan made a mental note to make use of the private investigator card the next time she had a man in her sights.

"I could say the same thing. I always thought local councillors were old, balding and fat men. I never realised councillors could be attractive." A little voice in her head, which sounded a lot like Colin's, pointed out that she had serious questions to ask.

"Ah, clearly you have done your homework on me."

Susan finished her glass of wine and spoke as Derek refilled it from the bottle that stood on the table.

"One of your tenants, Vicky, has got herself into the clutches of a loan shark. It began when someone arrived at her door asking for a deposit on the flat, which she never knew she needed. Tell me a little more about those flats, six, I understand." Susan thought all she needed was a moustache and she could have been mistaken for Jim Rockford; no, that was Magnum PI she was thinking of. Maybe she should call a halt to the wine.

"Those six flats you are talking about, are the ones that my father put aside for people who were either homeless or vulnerable and needed a helping hand. I have continued the tradition my father started. As for a deposit, there should be no need for that, it is one of the conditions to help people get a roof over their head. My managing agents know that. I suspect it could possibly be some unscrupulous local person, knowing about the arrangement and basically carrying out a fraud. The area is a little insalubrious." He stopped and refilled her glass.

"But they are in a pretty poor state of repair," she took a large mouthful from her glass. "That must be down to you."

"I cannot be expected to invest large sums of money in property from which I get no return. They are safe, my managing agents see to that. They are even partly furnished, thanks to the Deptford Drop-in who refer people. The flats are a safe haven for people who need a place that they can call their own, while they get back on their feet."

He topped up her glass and continued, "Nevertheless, I understand your concern for what is apparently happening, and I will ask around and speak to some people. I have a reputation to keep. I want nothing illegal going on in any of my properties."

"I wonder if you're married?"

"Pardon?" Derek asked.

Susan thought he looked a little confused by her question. Not surprising, she was convinced she was only thinking the question but clearly, she had spoken her thoughts out aloud.

"What I meant is does your wife help with the business?"

"I see, just an oddly phrased question then. I'm not married, haven't found the right person yet; still looking and hoping, mind."

Susan's phone beeped from deep within her handbag. She dug around and pulled it out into the open as Derek filled her glass yet again.

"It's my boss," she explained. "Sorry, I have to go."

Susan polished off the glass of wine, stood up unsteadily, only just managing to touch the table gently to make herself more stable. Derek also stood and carried out his ritual of pulling up his trousers.

"Next time you come, you must enjoy a meal from our chef, he is Italian and very good at his job. Thank you, Susan, for sharing your concerns for your client. I think it is laudable that you are trying to help find a solution for Vicky."

Derek leaned forward and took Susan's hand kissing it again. He looked into her eyes before continuing,

"Now, although I sympathise with your client, there is not a lot I can do. There is no freehold company, as I mentioned, I own the freehold of those buildings. It is probably someone who is taking advantage of her vulnerable position and it could well be a matter for the police. Although, might I suggest that first I make some enquires amongst some colleagues, to see if that throws anything into the light. I am sure Vicky does not want to get drawn into a police investigation unless it is really necessary."

Once outside, swaying next to her car, Susan read the text that Martin had sent her. It was the address of the theatre that she had never heard of, together with a time that was now only an hour away. She then saw that she had missed four calls from him; mobile phones, she thought, have such funny temperaments and are so unpredictable. She looked at her car once more but decided to make the sensible decision and book an Uber Cab.

***

"Does Dartford have a theatre?" Susan asked the Uber driver as he weaved through heavy early evening traffic on the South Circular.

"Well, that's the address you gave me, so I guess they do."

"I paid for a cab trip not sarcasm," Susan retorted and went back to looking at her phone.

Earlier, when Martin had asked her out to the theatre she thought, not unreasonably, that Martin being the kind of man he was, would have in his possession two tickets to a West End show with seats for the front stalls, maybe even a box. She also wondered about the show itself. Perhaps she should not have just agreed to his invitation without knowing what she might be letting herself in for.

She put her phone to one side, rummaged around her handbag and retrieved her make-up. As she applied extra eye liner, she mused that she really fancied one of those retro dance musicals, one where you can get up and dance in the aisles; that would be her first choice. She might be able to sit through a proper play with plots and stuff as long as it was not going to be too high brow.

Susan thought that Martin did not seem to be a too high brow person. Of course, he was well educated, public school and all that. He knew about Shakespeare, Wordsworth and the rest. He had even mentioned Peer Gynt once, although she was not sure if that was the name of the author or the play. That did sound very high brow and was not the sort of evening entertainment that she would consider to be a good night out.

***

Susan and Martin settled into their seats which were located towards the rear of the stalls. Susan skimmed through the programme that Martin had bought her. She had never heard of the play: 'The Importance of Being Earnest.' The blurb at the front described it as 'a trivial comedy for serious people, first performed in 1895, Oscar Wilde's play has stood the test of time, entertaining audiences across the world.'

"Martin, what exactly is this old play about?"

Martin looked up from his mobile phone and stared at Susan with a questioning face. Ever since they had met each other outside the theatre, he had seemed quiet and preoccupied.

"You haven't heard of this play?" She shook her head. "Well, in a nutshell, it is about people creating another identity to avoid social appointments. It's not hard to follow."

"And why did you bring me all the way out here to see it? I thought it might have been a West End theatre we were going to."

"I had a spare ticket and thought you might like it. It's a bit like a farce: a few laughs and a relaxing evening." He turned back to his phone.

Susan persisted with her questions. "Martin, you have never taken me to the theatre before, in fact, we have only been out on a...." she hesitated over just how to describe the one time he had taken her out, which was not connected with work, "social evening, to that very swish restaurant. You must have had something in mind when you decided to bring me here."

Martin turned towards her and sighed. "Alright, don't get all upset about it but I was going out with Jenny tonight. I had planned this theatre, but she said she could not make it. I thought you would enjoy a night out, a bit of fun."

Susan's first instinct was to reply, 'That makes me second best!' She would also add, 'enjoy a night out, I'm not one of your Spinster Aunties!' But she could see that Martin was quiet and not himself tonight. Even with alcohol still flowing through her veins, she restrained her reply to a simple, "That is good of you to think of me, I don't normally go to plays in theatres; loud music, dances and drinking colourful cocktails is my normal night on the town."

"Well, I hope you enjoy it."

"How come Jenny could not make it? I always thought your dates with her were pretty much unbreakable."

Martin looked at her with wistful eyes; she had not seen him look at her that way before.

"Things change," was his reply.

"What's changed?" Susan was interested to learn more. All the time that Jenny was in Martin's life, there was not much room for anyone else. It was at that moment that the lights dimmed and then the curtain rose on 'The Importance of Being Earnest'.

"That's a well posh room: Victorian?" Susan guessed.

"Edwardian," Martin corrected. "Now sit quietly and pay attention." Martin sounded like one of Susan's schoolteachers, who often disciplined her for not being quiet.

Algernon: *'Oh! . . . by the way, Lane, I see from your book that on Thursday night, when Lord Shoreman and Mr Worthing were dining with me, eight bottles of champagne are entered as having been consumed.'*

"Sounds a bit like us and Colin," Susan whispered. Well, she thought it was a whisper, but the alcohol in her body had muddled her volume control and she had spoken at a normal level.

"Shhh!" Martin responded. Reprimanded, Susan remained silent until....

Algernon: *'Well, in the first place girls never marry the men they flirt with. Girls don't think it right'.*

Jack: *'Oh, that is nonsense!'*

"I'm with Jack on that one." This time Susan managed to keep her voice down a little. Martin just tutted.

Algernon: *'Nothing will induce me to part with Bunbury, and if you ever get married, which seems to me extremely problematic, you will be very glad to know Bunbury. A man who marries without knowing Bunbury has a very tedious time of it'.*

Again, Susan leaned in close to Martin and whispered, "What is, or where is, a Bunbury?"

Martin replied in a hushed tone, "Susan, here's a pen, write down all your questions on the programme and I'll answer them at the interval. For now, please keep quiet and let everyone enjoy the play."

Having been told off as if she was a naughty schoolgirl, Susan sat upright and looked directly ahead. It was then she sensed the man on the other side of her lean closer to her and whisper the answer to her question.

***

The throng for interval drinks was as chaotic as any theatre can be with patrons first searching to locate their orders and then looking for a small space to consume their newly discovered drinks. Martin led Susan through the throng like a seasoned campaigner, snatched up the two large wine glasses, and guided Susan to an intimate corner beside a large poster advertising the Christmas pantomime.

"He told you what?" Martin queried.

"The guy next to me told me."

"He told you that Bunbury is a place in Australia?"

"Yes, and I couldn't understand what they were going on about on stage after that. Are all old plays totally weird?"

Martin sipped his wine and smiled at Susan. Yes, he was annoyed about the way she had started chatting to him at the beginning of the play, but that he put down to her naivety which was something he loved about her.

"It might be a place in Australia; geography was never my strong subject at school. But in the case of Oscar Wilde, it is a way of getting out of something you do not want to do, an excuse. 'I have to go and see my friend Bunbury'; we use it all the time, but we don't always call it a Bunbury."

Susan laughed, "That is something I'm going to add to my list of posh words, impress the girls at the pub."

Susan imbibed some more wine to keep herself topped up as a way of helping her through the second half of the play. She had found it difficult to follow but it might be easier to understand now that she knew there were no Australian connections.

She raised her glass towards Martin and said, "You've done this before, haven't you? I'd still be wandering around searching for my glass."

"Jenny and I often used this theatre for nights out. It's, as you pointed out, a little way out of the capital and so we were unlikely to be seen by anyone we knew. They have some good plays here; productions aren't as big as the west end, but good value and enjoyable."

"If you used this theatre for dates with Jenny, is your sombre mood anything to do with the past tense you seem to be talking in?"

Martin did not want to admit it out loud, but since telling Jenny yesterday that her husband wanted her followed, she had changed. She had called him last night saying she could not make the theatre; maybe she was doing a Bunbury. During that telephone conversation, Jenny had spoken in more glowing terms about her husband, a change from the normal critical words she frequently used. They were meeting for what Jenny described as a quick simple coffee tomorrow. It was just that Martin sensed that the quick coffee could be their last. He had no plans to share those fears with Susan or anyone else for that matter. Even though part of him wanted to tell Susan as her opinion mattered to him, he resisted.

"Let's not worry about Jenny tonight. Do I get the feeling that you are not enjoying Oscar Wilde?"

"Well, it's well posh, so I guess it's just like a typical weekend at your place."

"My mother can be very domineering, as you know, we no longer..."

Without a word of warning, Susan grabbed Martin, hauled him close, very close indeed, with such a haste that his wine spilt onto the floor. Susan's glass turned sideways, and he felt her white wine soak through his shirt and onto his skin. If Martin had thought that was bad enough, Susan then locked her lips firmly on his. She held him tightly against her body embracing him and gave him a long, lingering, ardent kiss. He felt the warmth of her body and his natural reaction was to hug her back, which he gently did. The theatre goers that passed by smiled at the two lovers' passionate embrace. After a moment, or maybe two, Susan let go, stood back from Martin and drank the remainder of what was left of her white wine in one large gulp.

"I would never have thought you would be so moved by Oscar Wilde?" Martin sounded a little breathless or maybe it was from the shock. "I cannot imagine what your reaction would be if you were actually enjoying the play."

Susan drew a deep breath and looked into his eyes, saw the wine stain on his shirt and tried in vain to brush it off.

"It wasn't Oscar, it was Derek Primm and..." She grabbed his face to stop him turning around to look; he wondered if he was going to get more lip on lip action. "...I'm pretty sure it could be the drug dealer who has your number plates."

Martin continued looking at Susan, having taken the hint that he should not turn around and said, "Oh, that drug dealer, I know so many, I'm glad you clarified which one."

Susan ignored his sarcastic remark.

"I'm sorry about the kiss. I just saw them coming towards us and I didn't think it would be wise to introduce ourselves. It was the only thing I could think of doing."

"Please don't apologise, I really enjoyed it. In fact, anytime you feel the need, just let go!"

Susan continued ignoring what Martin was saying as she watched Derek Primm and the drug dealer, who were standing close to a cut-out of some minor TV star she had never heard of. Susan sensed their conversation was serious as neither man smiled but looked at each other with solemn faces.

"What's happening?" Martin asked.

"Shhh, I'm observing."

"Well, if we stand here in total silence we will look like an old married couple."

"Derek is just talking to the younger man, looks to be a normal conversation, wait: the young man is now taking an envelope out of his jacket and giving it to Derek. Profits maybe? Derek has looked inside the envelope; he looks happy with what's in it. They're shaking hands now and going off in different ways. I think the young man is actually leaving the theatre, whereas Derek is now going back into the auditorium."

"Can I look now?"

"No, Martin, we can't risk Derek seeing us. You're a Russian bodyguard, remember. Once they have both gone, you can relax."

"I could be moonlighting."

"Let's not push the false image he has of you."

"I thought you said the drug dealer, the one who has my number plate, in case you know a few, you said he was all covered up with hats and coats and things, so how do you know it's him?"

"I don't know, how could I? But he is a similar height and build, so I'm guessing it is. However good-looking Derek is, I think he is up to something."

"You think he is good-looking as well; what is it with you girls and Italian looking men, Jenny was the same."

"We have good taste. Derek's gone back into the theatre and the other guy has left."

Martin had no idea why he looked around to see where Derek and the drug-dealer had been, as he expected, he saw no one he knew. "What do you think that is all about?" he asked

Susan replied, as the theatre bells rang letting the audience know the play was about to resume, "Clearly Derek is getting his share of the proceeds."

CHAPTER SEVEN

The next morning, Martin and Susan sat drinking coffee and talking about last night's play, which, in the end, Susan was surprised she had enjoyed so much. Plus, after seeing him last night, Susan was now convinced that Derek Primm had some sort of connection with the Blue Honda driver who was supplying pills on the housing estate. Martin was a little more cautious, especially as Susan was not sure it was the drug dealer they had seen with him.

"'A sweet, self-effacing approach is twice as likely to succeed as a bold, bulldozing one'. See Martin, you need to be a sweetheart and kinder to me." Susan continued with Martin's daily horoscope. "'Remember, every little niche in society is different; people from other parts of the globe will not have the same frame of reference that you do. Sometimes these differences can be assets.' That means you're not always right. Do you want to hear mine?" Susan did not wait for an answer, it was going to be irrelevant. "'Very little could put a damper on my high spirits today...'" Susan stopped as the office door opened.

Paul stepped into the office, standing nervously in the doorway.

"No work for you today, Paul, not even community service?" Martin joked as he offered Paul a chair.

"Not Deptford today, my real job, as I told you, just the three days a week, two days and one night. The days vary a little, so this week I am working the weekend. Be honest," he looked at Susan with puppy dog eyes, "I think I made a bit of a hash of my conversation with Vicky yesterday."

"I would describe it more as a complete disaster," Susan told him bluntly.

Martin had already heard Susan's version of their visit to see Vicky. He had listened, but if he was honest, he was more concerned about Susan being with Paul. Now looking at the two of them together, he was not so worried. He knew that Susan liked the stronger male type. Listening to Paul speaking here and now, confirmed what he remembered from his school days with him; even taking into consideration his current criminal record, Paul was, and still is, a wimp. Not Susan's kind at all.

Martin spoke, "I cannot understand how anyone gets into debt, let alone, was it two thousand pounds worth of debt, you said Susan?" Within a few seconds he regretted saying anything.

Susan began, "Cannot understand? Let me explain something for you." That phrase normally meant that Martin, and today Paul as well, were about to receive a lecture.

"You never had to be in debt for the simple reason that both of you are privileged arseholes. There is no way either of you can possibly understand the concept of being in debt.

"Debt starts by living just within your means, getting a salary which is your only income. Once you have paid for rent, food, electric bills and the like, you might, if you're lucky, have a few pounds left over for a rainy day. Sod's law tells us that rainy days turn up before we have enough to cover the cost of that rainy day. So, we must borrow, go into debt, which means we now have less to put away for the next rainy day. As I have previously explained, that turns up before you have enough money to pay for it. If that was not enough, rich bankers and the like, hate giving money to people who might not be able to pay them back.

"Bankers only really like lending to people who have money and assets. People like Vicky, who are poor to start with, get no help from high street banks; she is just too risky. She has little choice but to go to the shady side of money lending to get some money to pay for that rainy day that has arrived. Now, shady loan sharks don't give a rat's arse about the person they are handing money over to, for the simple reason they use threats to ensure they get paid. Hence, once Vicky is in debt, she has few options to get out of it."

"What has the weather got to do with spending?" Paul asked, which sparked an instant response from Martin.

"Bad question, wrong time. Please ignore that question, Susan. How about I pay off Vicky's debt, then she can pay me back a bit at a time. Well, I say me, I'm sure Paul can, in due course, get the two thousand out of his piggy bank if Mummy lets him, and then he can pay me back; it's his girlfriend, after all. How she pays him back is down to him," Martin sniggered.

"Who told you about Mother and my bank account?"

"You were talking with Susan yesterday who is not the most discreet person around. Although to be fair to her, Paul, we do work together and tend not to have many secrets."

"That's exactly what I am talking about," Susan butted in.

"What, being indiscreet?" Martin asked.

"No, just helping a friend with a wad of cash."

"Is it?" Martin asked again, thinking now that he should not have tried to defend Paul.

"You just wave your cheque book and pay the debt, or to be precise, transfer it to Paul and then she is at his mercy. Why not just say, 'here's two thousand pounds, Vicky; I'm spreading the wealth, you can keep it'?"

Both men considered Susan's current mood and decided not to respond to her question.

Susan continued, "Plus, you might well get Vicky out of trouble, but think of all those other women in the same situation. It's better to get to the heart of the problem and take out the loan shark."

Martin thought that sounded a little dangerous given that Susan had already mentioned loan sharks use threats, a fact he also knew from the stories he had read in the newspapers over the years. However, he declined to mention that to Susan.

Paul fiddled with his fingers and looked down into his lap as he spoke, "Look, the reason I have popped in to see you today is to say, don't worry about the loan shark thing. The problem belongs to Vicky and me, so it is just not fair to get you both involved. I'm helping Vicky as best I can, and I think in time I can sort it all out."

"No, Paul, we are involved and more than willing to help; it is the least we can do," Susan volunteered which prompted a simple response from Martin.

"Are we?"

"Yes, we are, Martin, there are times you have to help people; it's called caring for your neighbour. Paul, we'll get to the bottom of this one way or another."

"Well, only if you are sure; I'll help where I can. What about your problem, Martin? Any luck finding your drug dealer using your car, or at least its twin?"

"I would ask just how you know, but you were with 'no secrets Susan' yesterday. Still no idea, I keep telling my faithful assistant that she should just step away, but she will insist."

"It must be hard."

"What, working with Susan? Yes, it can be at times."

"No, I mean detecting and finding things out. It's not as though you're experienced or have completed a college course."

"We get by," Susan interrupted, for no better reason than to remind them both that she was still there.

Paul got up from the chair, "Well, I'm off. Anyway, thanks for helping out with Vicky, Susan, I'm sure it has helped."

"You off to see her now?" Susan asked.

"No, days off are normally at home. Today, I must accompany Mother to her hospital appointment. That's why the charity centre is such a good cover for me to see Vicky."

Susan commented, "A Bunbury charity?"

That made Martin laugh loudly. Paul did not see or understand the joke, neither did he want to have it explained, he just frowned and slid out of the office.

***

Once Paul left, Martin turned to Susan with a broad grin on his face. "I really expected you to ask him what his schoolboy habit was. Most unlike you to avoid direct, to-the point questions."

Susan opened her laptop preparing to check the River Island website for bargains. "Actually, I asked him yesterday in the car and he was not forthcoming, which did not surprise me as I, being a detective, worked out what his habit was and possibly still is."

"You are getting to be the Phillip Marlowe of downtown Regent Street; so, what's the verdict, Sherlock?"

"A transvestite."

"A transvestite!"

"Yes. Be honest, he is a bit of an old woman and in the back of his car was a woman's cardigan, not a fashionable one, but the sort of cardigan a transvestite might wear."

At that moment, the door opened, and a familiar voice spoke out, "Old ladies wear cardigans, transvestites wear highly fashionable haute couture, which accentuates our curves. Who do you think is a transvestite, present company excluded?"

Martin turned towards Susan, "My young assistant here thinks that a school friend of mine has been a transvestite since his schooldays. I'm sorry to say, Susan, you're wrong, totally wrong."

"Oh, do tell," Colin's voice sounded excited as he anticipated hearing what Paul's habit might be.

"Not in front of sweet Susan. I am afraid it will have to wait until we are out of her earshot, Colin, so I'll tell you later."

"Can't wait to hear, sounds very naughty."

Martin put his jacket on and made his way towards the door, "I'm off to see Jenny for a while. I'll be back later so if you two are around I'll see you then, but if not, have a good weekend."

"A bit early for lunch," Susan pointed out.

"We're not doing lunch today, just a coffee." He walked out through the door, avoiding the opportunity for his date with Jenny to be discussed any further.

***

It was not easy for Martin to locate where Jenny was sitting. She had told him to meet her at the back of Leon's at King's Cross station, which was easier said than done. Finding the café on the concourse of the station was not hard, but it took him a while to realise that at the very back of it were a few steps leading down to another obscure seating area, where Jenny was getting exasperated by his lateness. It did nothing to help her mood when he arrived at her table without a coffee and had to return to the counter to get himself one, before finally settling down next to her.

She shied away from a welcome kiss. Martin commented on the location as being okay, but not that cosy for one of their liaisons. He passed the remark in an attempt to justify the frosty welcome he had received.

"I thought it best to be in a very casual place for this chat, Martin. I'm sorry about the theatre last night."

"No problem, there'll be other opportunities for you to see 'The Importance of Being Earnest', if you are desperate."

"That's the thing; there will not be another opportunity."

"What do y..."

"Martin, just listen to what I have to say. Ever since I learnt from you that Ian wanted me followed, I have been giving you and I a lot of thought, as well as thinking about Ian, my husband. He was worried that I might be having an affair and that surprised me; I just thought it was his business that he loved above all else. Then I took some time to talk and listen to him in the evening, hear about his day and frankly, Martin, the old spark that we had when we first got married seemed to re-ignite and flare up into the passion that we once had for each other. It was the business that pulled us apart for the simple reason that I took little interest in it. You see it was my fault, in the main, that Ian and I grew apart."

"But what about the secretary you thought he was having an affair with? Didn't you say that he was planning to divorce you?"

Jenny looked down at her coffee, which she was absently stirring. "My overactive imagination. I took the trouble and the time to meet her and she is a very pleasant person, happily married with two children. In fact, I believe we will become close friends in the fullness of time."

"What about ...?"

"Martin, please let me finish."

Martin sat back into his chair, folded his arms, and looked like a petulant child who had just been reprimanded.

"I want you to report back to my husband that I am not having an affair, for the simple reason I am no longer having an affair."

She stood, bent down, and kissed Martin on his forehead.

"Thank you, Martin, it has been fun, but the time has come to say goodbye."

She picked up the four shopping bags that had been under the table, walked out of the café and out of Martin's life, avoiding any response that he might give. The meeting had been so rapid that all he was left with, was a still hot coffee and several happy memories.

Martin stood on the familiar concourse of Kings Cross station feeling lost. That was it. Jenny was now just an ex-girlfriend. He had a few of those. Ever since his fiancée betrayed his trust, there had been several older women in his life. He had liked the idea that none of them would be searching for a long-term relationship, which was no doubt true, Jenny had proved that hypothesis. It was just that Martin had never admitted that he hankered after a long-term relationship. However he might portray himself, he liked the thought of sharing his life with someone. It was more a question of who to share it with.

It was on a whim that he got off the tube at Sloane Square and walked up the white limestone steps to his bank. Martin had no real plan, just a vague idea that he wanted to do something that everyone would say was stupid. 'So, what', he would tell them, 'I can do whatever I want'.

He walked into the air-conditioned, carpeted and serene reception of the bank. There, holding her clipboard, was Zoe, a tall redhead. Martin first saw her around six years ago, falling in love with her at first sight. No, to be fair, it might not have been love, but it was certainly lust. He knew, from years of observation and study, that there were just two types of redhead. The first would have almost the perfect figure, bust line, waistline, and long slender legs. Their faces would be stunning, and men would drool as they walked past them at a party. The second type of redhead was the polar opposite; odd shaped body, often short, plain, sun-flecked faces, the sort of women who pass you by in the street without you noticing.

"Hello, Mr Hayden," Zoe, who was undoubtedly a category one redhead, moved towards him, a smile full of brilliant white, flawless teeth.

"You should know by now; you can call me Martin." He looked at her knowing full well if she ever changed branch, he would seriously consider moving his account. For him, she was high on the list of 'people who could join me on a desert island'. She gave the impression she found him attractive as well; Martin was sure it was more than just an ordinary customer service he was getting.

"What can I do for you today, Martin?"

Zoe stood close to him, even in the bank uniform she could not help but look sensuous. Yet there was for Martin one small caveat holding back their obviously happy relationship and plans to have two point three children; he had trouble trusting women. Paula, his ex-fiancée, had seen to that. As Martin looked at Zoe, he imagined she would have checked his bank account and possibly decided that she could live with a man whose teeth were not as perfect as hers, the money would make up for that.

"I need to withdraw some cash: two thousand pounds."

"Wonderful! I'll pop you into one of our little rooms and I'll get Mr Earl to come and see you."

As Zoe had competently described it, the room was little. A computer screen, keyboard and mouse sat on the small desk with a chair either side of it. One black ergonomic seat for the member of staff and a plain chair obviously intended for the customer, which to Martin summed up the banking industry.

Mr Earl, wearing a dark, sombre, double-breasted suit, strode in holding a buff folder, shook Martin's hand and sat himself down comfortably on the ergonomically-designed chair, with which he swung towards the computer screen, he punched in his password on the keyboard, and then turned to Martin.

"Good to see you Mr Hayden, haven't seen you in a while. That's the trouble with all this online banking malarkey, never get to see our customers, unlike the good old days."

Mr Earl was close to retirement age, of that Martin was fairly sure. A tall, lanky man, who hunched himself over the keyboard, bashing it violently with a single finger from each hand. Touch typing was something Mr Earl could never get on with and certainly was not one of his skills. He had spent most of his career at the Sloane Square Branch, where for the last fifteen years he held the position of Branch Manager.

"Now, I understand from our attractive Zoe, sorry not PC but true all the same, I'm sure you agree; you want to withdraw some cash."

"Yes please, two thousand pounds in cash, to be precise."

"Well, that shouldn't be a problem, Mr Hayden; you and your family have banked here for years, long before my time. How is your mother?"

"Fine, thanks."

"Good to hear, fine lady. Right, just need to get Bingo Little here to agree and we'll be all shipshape."

"Bingo Little?" Martin asked, recalling the character from a Jeeves and Wooster book he had once read.

"My nick name for this chappie." Mr Earl swung the computer screen round to show Martin as a form of introduction before swinging it back. "Apparently the days of us mere humans giving out the cash to our customers is long gone. Books of rules and unfathomable regulations mean Bingo Little here must make the final call. Seems we gave out too much money to irresponsible customers.

We're in a blame culture; I give you two thousand pounds of your money and you blow it on a horse running backwards at Newmarket and hey presto, it's my fault. Hence, dear Bingo Little does the legal bit. Right, let's get started; can't spend all day here talking to you. Do you have any identification?"

Martin frowned, "But you know me."

"Quite well indeed, but Bingo here doesn't. Well, to be precise, he doesn't trust me to tell the truth. That's what it has come to, banks not trusting their staff. Too many of us giving out money willy-nilly. Passport, driving licence, whatever you have?"

Martin took a bank card from his wallet, handed it over to Mr Earl and watched as he typed in some digits. The two men sat in silence, Mr Earl watching the screen, before he took a sharp intake of breath and confirmed. "Bingo, all good; you are Mr Hayden. Next on the check list, how much. Two Thousand, you said?" Mr Earl typed in the amount as Martin nodded in agreement.

"Reason for the withdrawal?" Mr Earl turned towards Martin, elbows on the table, fingers interlocked, waiting for an answer.

"It is my money, surely I can just withdraw it without giving you a reason," Martin pointed out, not convinced he wanted to share the precise reason for needing the cash.

"Back in the old days, we just wouldn't care two hoots of a donkey's tail. You want to blow your money in a casino, good luck to you, it's your hard-earned cash. Not so today, Bingo Little here needs to understand what you are doing with the cash just in case you do something stupid with it and then blame us for the loss. Compensation Solicitors have a lot to answer for. So, two thousand pounds, where is the cash going, Mr Hayden?"

Martin had never, ever in his life needed to withdraw more than a few hundred pounds. He seldom used cash, so the series of questions he was now being asked were starting to annoy him. It was his cash after all. Having found himself in a situation which was fast becoming a Jeeves and Wooster farce, he decided to play along.

"I am giving it to a woman I have never met."

Mr Earl carefully examined the screen in front of him, referring to the list that Bingo displayed.

"Sorry, not a valid reason, Bingo does not have that one on his list." Mr Earl turned to Martin, leaned forward and spoke in a softer tone, "You do know that most escorts take credit cards nowadays. So, I'm told," he quickly added as he sat back into his chair. Do you have another reason for the withdrawal?"

"Paying off a loan shark?"

Without batting an eye lid, Mr Earl turned back to Bingo's screen, this time running his finger down the list. He dragged his finger down three times in all, just to be sure.

"Closer, I have transferring a credit card balance. Paying off loans is something us banks never like to encourage, loss of interest, you know."

"What would you suggest?" Martin asked, thinking as the bank manager has the list in front of him, it would be a lot easier and quicker to let him choose the reason.

"Can't do that, apparently against some FCA rule. What I can tell you, totally aside from what you are asking, just a bit of general client chatter, you understand, is that paying builders in cash is now a very popular pastime amongst our customers."

"OK, I'm paying my builder."

"Good. Oops, supplementary question, I'm afraid, in case you are a victim of fraud of which there are just so many out there, it is scary. In order to prove you do not have some Nigerian Prince asking for cash, I need to ask you: what are you having done?"

"Really?"

"Rest assured, Mr Hayden, Bingo Little here has your best interests at the heart of his Intel processor."

"My bathroom, I'm refurbishing my bathroom."

"Excellent, just a moment while young Bingo here runs the numbers. Yes, all approved. Teller number three has the authorising code and you can collect your money from her. There, that was easy, have a wonderful day, Mr Hayden and I hope to see you again soon, such a pleasure."

Both men stood up and politely shook hands, leaving Martin to go and collect his hard-earned money from Teller number three.

***

Located next to a fish and chip shop, the door had yellow paintwork which was peeling. Just above the broken letter box and a little below the cracked glazed arch, there was a big handwritten seven. This had to be the place where Susan told him Vicky lived. He held his finger over the bell push. Why he was standing here at all even he had trouble understanding.

Martin always knew that one day Jenny would say goodbye, that she would get tired of him. It was the way of affairs; they faded and petered out. Martin tried to figure out just why he felt so shocked; was it because she had stopped it dead in its tracks? Their passion hadn't faded. She seemed to have just decided to stop doing what they were doing. Snubbed, that was how he felt, his pride had been injured. The brutality of the let-down hurt him the most. Had Jenny woken up that morning and thought: 'I'm going to stop seeing Martin'? Without any consideration for his feelings, she had dumped him; that was the hurt.

It had been a spontaneous decision. Susan had said it was not needed, but he needed to do something that he wanted to do to make himself feel better.

Now, standing outside of Vicky's drab and tired looking door, he wondered if he was doing the right thing. He had read about housing estates, seen news items, heard people talk about them, but to stand in the middle of one was something he had never done before. He was starting to regret having a large sum of cash in his jacket pocket in such a dubious area. Driving onto the estate had been enough for him to begin to fret.

He had seen groups of men and teenagers just standing around on the pavement, or beside doorways, sitting on walls, talking and looking, he thought, at him. None of them were well dressed, most were wearing jogging bottoms with stained tee-shirts. All appeared to be smoking, a few had a can of beer in their hands.

The solid brick buildings looked tired and unkept; some had windows that were broken and boarded up, others had bed sheets covering up whatever was going on inside. Martin felt nervous.

He had parked as close as he could to the fish and chip shop that Susan had mentioned. He wanted his car to be near him, his only escape route. Was it his imagination, were people looking at him? A mother swerved around him as he exited his car. She pushed a scruffy buggy laden with shopping bags; a small child sat back in it, biting on what looked like a naan bread.

Even along the few steps from his car to the door, he walked past torn black rubbish bags, their contents spilling across the pavements engrained with discarded chewing gum. All around him Martin sensed the feeling of despondency that hung over the estate. It both alarmed him as well as opening his often, narrow vision of others who lived in a London that was not the same London he knew.

His finger pushed hard on the bell push and he waited.

"Who are you?" A female voice spoke behind him.

Martin turned around and was surprised to see a young woman, maybe in her late twenties. She was tall with lips covered in bright red lipstick. Her hair was spiky and short and had been dyed red, not a bright red like the lipstick, but more of a maroon colour. Her eyes looked Martin up and down suspiciously. They were eyes that your mother would suggest you should not trust, as they would look too shifty to her; however Martin thought they looked more sensuous than untrustworthy. She was heavy in build and he doubted that she ever left much food on her plate.

"I'm Martin, and who might you be?"

"I live here, so out of my way; if you're selling stuff, you can piss off."

"You must be Vicky, Paul's girlfriend?"

Her eyes dropped the suspicious camouflage and looked warmer. She put her shopping bag on the pavement and moved to the side of Martin, placing her key into the lock.

"Paul's mentioned you a few times, all good stuff. Come up, unless you're going to tell me to stop my work on the phones, in that case you can stay right where you are."

Martin, walking on the threadbare treads, followed her up the poorly lit, steep stairs. At the top was a small square hallway lit by a bare light bulb, where there were two doorways. The first had no door, all he could see was a cluttered cupboard of coats, an electric meter, three empty wine bottles and a pile of shoes on the floor. Vicky opened the door to the second doorway and invited him to follow her. It led into a room that was both untidy and more than just a little dusty, which Martin found a little uncomfortable to be in. As well as an oppressive humid heat, there was a stale odour of fried food. Martin thought if she had spent some more time cleaning the flat, then she could at least have burnt off some of her excess calories. However, he diplomatically declined to make such a suggestion to her.

"Paul does not know I'm here."

"What about your moll? That Susan girl who came round, she can drink, you know. Do you want one?" Vicky called from the kitchen area of the room where she was unpacking her shopping.

"No drink, thanks, and no, she does not know I'm here either."

"What you here for, fancy a bit of rough like Paul?"

"That is a little unfair on Paul; he does like you a lot. After all he is doing community time for you."

"He just got a little carried away; I don't think he ever thought he could thump someone. I don't know who was more surprised, him, or the bloke he punched." Vicky took a drink from her mug, Martin had never seen anyone drink vodka from a mug; maybe it was the only clean vessel she could find.

From a corner of the room, Martin heard a phone ring. It was one of those rare types nowadays, that had a length of wire that plugged into a wall socket.

"Sex line?" Martin asked.

Vicky nodded as she closed the cupboard where she had stored some of her shopping and walked across the room towards the phone, still holding her mug of vodka. Martin raised his hand.

"Allow me, I've always wanted to be on the other end of a sex chat line."

"You a regular for phone sex then?"

"Once, with some friends, of whom all had drunk a little too much wine, just wound the young girl up at the other end. I guess she still got paid."

Martin picked up the receiver, which felt a little sticky, and spoke,

"I am sorry, but all our operators are busy satisfying other clients. Please hold yourself until an operator is available."

He placed the receiver next to a small portable radio, which he switched on; it played easy listening eighties music into the mouthpiece.

Martin and Vicky both laughed, went to the other side of the room and sat down, leaving one of her clients listening to music, and the shopping half unpacked.

"Tell me," Martin started, "this loan shark, the one you owe the two thousand pounds to, who is he exactly? Perhaps we can sort him out for you?"

Vicky poured herself another vodka. "Big guy, broken nose, bald as a bat, not the sort of person easily scared. I just do me chat lines and pay him off; it's no hardship. It's Paul who thinks I should not be doing it, but what does he really care? I'm happy and some of them blokes are a laugh."

"Paul has never told me how you two met up in the first place?"

"Him posh and me common, that's what you're asking really. Everyone says that, even down at the Deptford club they say: how comes you got yerself a posh geezer? Well, it's a sweet story, really. I was doing some shopping down the road a little way, the next estate actually, and I was running out of the shop with a bottle of vodka under my arm. The reason I was running was I had no plans to pay for it, and the shopkeeper had seen me stuff it in my jacket.

"I dashes out right into this bloke, who turns out to be Paul. He grabs me, I think: shit, and the shopkeeper, out of breath, is now standing beside us. I'm thinking: I'm well screwed here. Then your mate Paul says: 'Darling, you forgot your purse, I was just coming in with some cash.' The bloke from the shop gets all flustered looking at Paul and no doubt thinking this is a posh bloke, he ain't gonna steal anything.

"Paul hands over a score, tells the bloke he can keep the change for the trouble caused." She saw the confusion in Martin's face and translated for him, "A score, twenty quid. Paul then guides me into his car and we drive off. You know that was about the only time anyone around here had shown me any real kindness. I know the charity and that help, but that's their job. Paul just did it without thinking."

"Nice story and then you started going out as a couple?"

"A couple, you're an old-fashioned sort of guy. But sort of, he brought me back here, I invited him in, and we got it on, if you know what I mean; it was my way of saying thanks."

"Romantic."

"Yeah, I thought so." Vicky had missed the cynicism in Martin's voice.

"I would have thought the shopkeeper would have made more of a fuss. You'd still attempted to steal a bottle, and I never would have imagined that Paul could be described as intimidating."

"Me too. I'd been too that shop before and nicked stuff, never caught, got close once, so I thought the police would have been called. But, oh no, Paul stepped in and the shopkeeper was more than happy to let things ride. I know it will not last forever, you know, me and Paul; we're just from different ends of the world, but it's fun for now."

Martin reached into his jacket and pulled out an envelope, it was the cash that he had withdrawn from the bank. He offered it to Vicky.

"Look, Paul and I want to help out, get the loan shark off your back and give you a chance to get yourself on your feet again."

Vicky took the envelope from his hand and looked inside; the sceptical look returned to her eyes as she saw the contents. Martin could see her hesitating; the temptation was there. Even so she passed the money back to Martin.

She walked across the room, replaced the receiver and turned off the radio.

"That's nice of you both to offer, but it'd be pointless."

"Pointless," Martin repeated, "it will pay your debt off; what is so pointless about that?"

"Look Martin, I've only just met you, but I can see you're a nice bloke, a lot nicer than Paul. But one payment would not really help me. I have a crap little job, one day a week, maybe two if they are short of staff and need me. It barely pays my rent here, let alone the electric bills, food, plus all the other stuff you need to live. I do get some benefits off the state, but barely enough to live on. The fact is, I need to spend to live, and I cannot get enough money to live, so I'd be in the same spot of debt in a few months' time. The sex chat line and a bit of thieving helps me keep my head above water. Paul helps me out from time to time with a few pounds here and there, so I get by.

"One day I'm sure I will meet a nice bloke from my side of the tracks. He'll have a job and we'll live together and get by, just the same. Not have much but have each other. Thanks for the offer, Martin, but you can keep your money."

Martin returned to his car, his money once again in his pocket. Susan was right, getting out of debt if you have nothing is harder than he had thought. Well, he had offered, what could you do for someone other than offer to help. He hoped that it would work out for Vicky in the end, which was more than he could say for the officious traffic warden who had placed a ticket on his car; angrily he stuffed it in the glove box and drove off.

CHAPTER EIGHT

Two sets of eyes turned towards Martin as he walked into the office. Susan and Colin were huddled around a laptop. It was Susan, as was her habit, who spoke first.

"That was a long coffee break; you and Jenny make up?"

Martin did not speak, but took off his jacket, sat down at his desk and sighed. He ignored Susan's question and instead asked, "What are you guys up to?"

"Suzie Baby let me explain for you. Martin, we're evaluating the case."

"What case?"

Colin brought the laptop over to Martin, pushed aside three out of date newspapers, a polystyrene cup and a Mars bar that Susan had earlier bought for Martin, despite the fact he had told her on a number of occasions that he did not like them. Colin sat beside Martin and explained the situation.

Half-heartedly Martin listened and tried to understand what Colin was getting at. Colin pointed out some of the facts that they had collected over the last few days. There was someone driving around south London in a car the same make and model as Martin's and with the same number plate, accumulating parking tickets. This had led them to Flossie's flat who was known for her ability to procure and sell prescription drugs to women on the estate where she lived. They also knew that Paul's girlfriend, Vicky, had to be at the end of a sex chat line in order to earn money to help pay off a loan shark. The flat where Vicky lived belonged to a Derek Primm who appears, according to Suzie Baby who Colin described as a star witness, to be in contact with the suspected driver of the car who is supplying drugs.

Martin nodded, so far he was with Colin.

Colin continued with the fact that Derek Primm owned a restaurant which, Colin said, can often be a useful business to have in order to launder money from drug deals. Plus, there was no reason to assume that Flossie was the only person selling drugs around south London, as it is an area where Derek has lots of property, so there could be many more women like Flossie around.

Martin frowned; he was not so sure of what Colin was getting at.

Then Susan took over, "We have a plan of action to find out as much as we can about Derek Primm, which should shed some light on what he is actually up to."

Martin did not like the sound of a 'plan of action', but he remained silent and continued listening to Susan.

"It's not too late in the day for us all to shoot off to south London. We can drop Colin at the local library, where he will search through as much information as he can find about the business interests of Derek Primm, get all the facts. Then we can pop in and see Vicky; I want to ask her more about the loan shark, what he looks like, how she first made contact, that sort of thing."

Martin was about to say that he already knew what the guy looked like, then held his tongue, he did not want either of them to know what he had just offered Vicky.

"Afterwards," Susan continued, "we can pop in and see your other school mate, the estate agent Steve, and see what more he knows about Derek Primm. Colin also said that if we can find out the premium number that those men ring to speak dirty to Vicky, we can get a clue as to who runs it. My bet is: it is going to be Derek; he's just too good looking to be a councillor."

"Are you happy with all this Colin?"

"Something is not right so it makes sense to try and discover what is going on. Plus, you know what Suzie Baby is like when she gets a bee in her bonnet."

"Let me get this clear." Martin was still trying to understand the plan. "We suspect that Derek Primm is behind the drug dealing, the loan shark and the sex chat line. Can't we also accuse him of causing world hunger?"

"That's stupid," Susan answered, "he runs a restaurant if anything he is helping cure world hunger. But he is doing something underhand."

It was then Colin's opportunity to take Susan's abstract plan, Martin's reluctance and his own experience, and meld them together into an operationally effective plan.

"I can get as much information as I can about his business interests, that will help determine if he has sources of income that are not fully explained. As I said: a restaurant is a perfect front to launder money you might have acquired illegally. We also need as much information about the loan shark that we can gather, so Vicky is our only source for that at the present time and Suzie Baby is best placed to wheedle information out of her, so best let her do the talking.

"When you go and speak to your school pal, whom I guess you trust, you've got to tell him that we suspect Mr Primm of not being as pure as the driven snow. If you share your suspicions first, it will surprise you how often someone will say: 'funny you should say that, I have been wondering about ...' then they tell you their own suspicions.

"All this might turn out to be for nothing, he might be legal and above board, but until we ask the questions, we will not know."

***

Up until last week Martin had only once driven along the Old Kent Road, which he felt was a remarkable achievement given his age. The first time he was passing the Elephant and Castle was when Susan had introduced him to the south London tradition of pie and mash. Now, he felt like a local driving down the Old Kent Road, pointing out the pie and mash shop he had recently eaten in. He was sure that his accent would not blend into the local shops or pubs that well, when in fact his cautious driving was also making him stand out from the locals.

He was listening to Susan recount a long evening spent moving from pub to pub around the area, describing, in a little too much detail for Martin, what two men showed her as she left one of the many establishments she and some other girlfriends had visited that night.

They passed by Peckham Park Road, where this time it was Colin's turn to reminisce. He pointed to a dull block of grey flats where, he said, a pie and mash shop had once stood, if that was meant to be progress, then in his opinion, it would explain the reason there were so many vegetarians around nowadays.

Martin wondered what the pre-occupation was with south Londoners and their pie and mash; in his humble opinion the dish was nothing special at all. He decided that maybe it was akin to the Scottish and their obsession with haggis.

Susan was sitting beside Martin who was continuing to drive cautiously, when Colin, sitting at the back without his seatbelt on, leaned forward, placing his head in between them, his fragrance, a sweet-smelling flowery scent, preceded him.

"Ahead," he pointed to a car a little way in front of them, "the blue Honda, it has your number plate."

"Shit, yes!" Susan excitedly called out almost deafening both Martin and Colin. "Catch it up and ram it or something to stop it"

"Calm down, Suzie Baby, we're not on an L.A. Freeway, plus we have Martin driving, so let's not expect too much. Martin, just follow the car and see where it goes."

"How do I do that?" Martin asked. He was mildly confused, having earlier believed that he was at ease driving in south London, he now felt he was fast slipping out of his comfort zone.

Colin reassured him, "Simple really, if he turns left, we turn left, if he turns right, then we turn right, if he drives straight on, we drive straight on. That is how we follow someone; the clue is in the title. It's not rocket science."

"If he reverses," Susan laughed, "you can shit yourself."

Martin was glad that he had Colin talking in his ear, despite the perfume. Telling him to: 'pull back a little', 'accelerate closer', 'he looks like he is going straight ahead at the traffic lights'. Colin seemed to be able to anticipate the moves Martin's twin car was going to make. When they were close enough, they could see the back of the driver, but were unable to make out who it might be, or even if they were a man or a woman.

As they moved into the New Cross one-way system, there was just one car between Martin and his twin car, both were moving slowly through the congested three lanes of traffic. Susan was all for jumping out, pulling open the driver's door and dragging the occupant to the floor. Astutely, Martin thought, Colin advised against such a path of action.

All three of them were now so intent on the car in front, that they didn't notice the police car that closed up alongside them, until they heard the two-tone horn. The policeman signalled for them to pull over and stop, and then moved forward a little and pulled over the driver of Martin's twin car.

"Result!" Susan called out.

"Not if he asks to see my driving licence," Martin pointed out. Neither Susan nor Colin commented, as they were both focused on what was happening to the car in front of them.

The police officer got out of his car, stood beside the driver's door, spoke briefly to the driver in the twin car, nodded his head a few times and smiled; the smile disappeared when he started to walk towards Martin's car.

"Good afternoon, Sir. Just a quick routine check, is this your car?"

"Yes, Officer," Martin answered.

"Your name, Sir?"

"Martin Hayden."

"Martin Hayden, you say. Do you have any form of identification on you, driving licence for example?"

A silent anticipation filled the car. Martin's heart was beating faster than it should have been. He hoped he did not look guilty.

"Would a bank card do?" he asked as innocently as he could. If it was good enough for Bingo Little, he hoped an officer of the law would accept it.

The policeman nodded and watched as Martin ferreted around in his jacket for his wallet. Unfortunately, he first pulled out the white envelope that he had offered to Vicky. The wad of bank notes were visible to everyone inside and outside of the car.

"What exactly do you have there?" The policeman could not fail to notice the cash. Martin looked at the envelope as if he was surprised that it was even in his pocket.

"Money for my builder, he's doing some work for me. Ah, you think I'm a drug dealer of some sort with all this cash?"

"It did cross my mind, Sir."

"No, Officer, nothing illegal here, the builder offered me a big discount for cash, no VAT, that sort of thing."

"Yes, that's called tax fraud, still not exactly honest. Let's get back to my first question, any chance of some identification?"

Martin, who felt that he was now perspiring, put the envelope full of money on his lap and thankfully found his wallet, only to have this short-lived relief shattered once more when he heard Susan speak,

"You never told me you were having any work done."

"Thank you, Susan, I'll handle this."

Susan lowered her voice hoping to be discreet. She failed as everyone heard her say, "Badly, if you ask me."

Martin passed over his bank card to the officer and waited while he examined it carefully. He had a dark feeling that this was not going to go well. He was sure the police had some sort of database which would flag up the fact that he had no driving licence, and he was now starting to regret not having bothered to take the test. The police officer made low murmuring sounds as he turned the card over and looked at it. Finally, he delivered his verdict:

"Sir, this is a bank card that has the name Mr M. Hayden on it, but I'm not happy at all."

This was it; Martin thought and began to wonder what it might be like to be arrested and taken to the local police station. He only hoped he would not have to spend the night in the cells. Exactly how much of a crime was not having a driving licence? Not a major felony in Martin's opinion. Not that he was going to point that out at this moment in time.

The police officer, still holding the bank card continued, "You see we had a tip-off earlier this week that a car matching your car was involved with drug dealing not too far away from here."

Susan interrupted the police officer, "Yes the other car, that's the drug dealer, not us. That was the car in Turner Road delivering the drugs to the flat with the old lady and the naked child."

Martin turned towards Susan. "Please tell me that when you called the police to tell them about Flossie, you did not give them the registration number of the car."

"Of course, I did. How else would they catch him?" Then there was a flash of recognition on her face, "Ah, you have the same number, so they think you are the drug dealer." She turned to the police officer, "But it is the bloke in front, he's the real drug dealer, Officer."

"That may be the case, Miss, but real drug dealers often have large wads of cash on them just like your friend here, and you seem to know a lot about what's going on. Do you know Flossie?"

"Yes, I went to her place and ..." Susan stopped, only now thinking about what she was saying.

Then just when Martin thought things could not get any worse, he was proved wrong as Colin spoke,

"Of course, you're not a happy officer, since when were the traffic division ever happy?"

Martin interrupted Colin before he could say any more, he was beginning to feel as though he was a teacher with two naughty schoolchildren in the car. "The kind policeman is interviewing the driver. It would be extremely helpful if you could both keep quiet."

"I will not," Colin continued, ignoring Martin. "Traffic division are just boring. The only reason you're giving us the run around is because there are three of us in the car and the only one of the two cars with the same index with a transvestite in it. Bloody discrimination if you ask me."

"Colin," Martin pointed out, "please, you are not helping one little bit."

"I'm just indicating the obvious for the humble traffic officer."

The police officer frowned as he heard the comments that came from Colin, whose head was still poking forward between Martin and Susan.

"I know you?"

"Our paths have crossed previously."

There was then a flash of recognition across the policeman's face, "Colin the cross-dresser, or cosmetic Colin."

"I hated that second nickname, makes me sound like a superficial person, but cross-dresser is fine."

"Good to see you again, Colin. Must say I didn't recognise you, having never seen you dressed as a lady. Your two mates here still look to be a little on the dodgy side. Who carries such a wad of cash around with them unless they're dealing?"

"No, far from it. In fact the car in front we think are the real drug dealers; you know the other one you stopped before you then decided we were the most likely crew to have committed a crime."

"Honest error, Colin, but the bloke in front reckoned he was Martin Hayden, who is the registered owner of the car."

"I would suggest you go and ask him again," Colin pointed through the windscreen, "but that might be difficult, as you might have noticed he is just driving off."

All four watched as the Honda pulled away fast, weaving in and out of the traffic.

"Shit!" Was the only comment the policeman made.

"Martin, can I suggest that we make off too. I doubt the kind police officer is still interested in seeing your non-existent driving licence." Colin sat back in his seat sniggering as he watched the police car try to pull away, no way was he going to catch the other blue Honda.

***

Having, as Susan described it 'given the cops the slip', they drove towards the large library in Lewisham. There they dropped off Colin, who disappeared into the building attracting a few dubious looks from those who were exiting the library.

Martin edged his car through the slow-moving traffic as the Friday afternoon rush hour began to slow everything down. Today was not turning out to be anything but a pain. All he really wanted to do was to get home and have a large glass of wine; something he had come to expect at this time on a Friday afternoon. In his mind he ticked off each awkward encounter he had had so far today. Jenny in the coffee Bar, sitting in a disgusting flat with Vicky, learning about the history of Pie and Mash and not forgetting being stopped by the police. And now he was having to drive through congested streets to see Vicky again. Today had been rubbish so far. He was hoping that it would not get any worse when he heard Susan tell him.

"I've been thinking."

That phrase for Martin was a bad omen.

"Really, Susan, there is no need to share any thoughts you might have; I am more than happy to live in ignorance of any opinions you might have."

"We need to find out more about Derek Primm's finances, how much money he has and where it all comes from. What do you reckon to asking Becky to help us out?"

"Not your loopy friend who works at the bank?"

"Yeah, why not? She has helped before and alright she is a bit weird at times, but you have to admit she does know her stuff when it comes to banking and things."

"The trouble is she would still, I am sure, be risking her job by digging into people's bank accounts and passing on the information to us, it just cannot be legal. A bit like this stupid white van in front of me trying to turn right when you are not meant to."

"Good point, Martin, but it's only wrong if he gets caught, if not, he has got away with it, and I know that Becky has a habit of getting away with lots of stuff."

"Well if you think it can help."

"I'm certain it will; I'll give her a call tonight. I'm sure she'll be eager to help us, just to be near you. But be warned, Martin, she is a bit of a floozy."

"That's not a nice thing to say about a friend of yours. Here we go."

Martin stopped outside the fish and chip shop, pulled up the handbrake and turned off the engine. He pushed the envelope containing the cash further down into his pocket, just in case, you could never be too sure in an area like Turner Road.

Susan turned to Martin and asked what she thought was a good question based on her deduction of the situation. "How did you know where Vicky lived?"

Martin unclipped his seatbelt, looked at Susan for a moment, then said, "you gave a good description of where she lived and you told me the name of the road, so it wasn't hard to find. Shall we go in?"

"Martin, I know you've been to south London before, but knowing this road, it's not a well-known place."

"Shall we go in?" He repeated opening the door to get out of the car and hopefully stop this conversation and the direction it was going in.

"And that wad of cash that you flashed to the copper; would I be right in assuming that there might be two thousand pounds in there? The same amount that Vicky owes."

Martin did not answer. He got out of the car and walked towards Vicky's door leaving Susan to catch him up. There was no reply to the doorbell. They stood outside considering the best thing to do, which Susan guessed would be to leave a note informing Vicky that they wanted to speak to her about the loan shark and to ask what the phone number was that men must call to speak to her. Susan found a scrap of paper in her cavernous handbag and used Martin's back as a writing desk, which he found to be a little erotic, although he had no idea why. They pushed the note through Vicky's letter box and returned to their car. Susan was going to return to the subject of the two thousand pounds and the miraculous internal sense of navigation that he had found, but the parking ticket on his windscreen distracted her.

Susan yanked it off the glass in anger. She was about to throw it into the glovebox when she saw another parking ticket already there. She took it out and examined it.

"Oh, look Martin, not only do you have a twin car, you also have twin parking tickets. This one is from earlier today. I thought you were with Jenny all morning, am I wrong?"

Martin turned towards her; she detected that he was not as amenable to her humour as he usually was. He decided a confession was going to be the only option.

"Yes okay, I popped in to see Vicky and offered to pay off her debt. She refused for whatever reason, so I still have the cash in my hand. Satisfied now? Can we get back to London and start our weekend? I'll see Steve another time; it's late and I'm fed-up now."

It was clear to Susan that he was irritable, so she asked the question that had been nagging at her over the last couple of days. Although, in view of the way that Martin had been acting, she believed she already knew the answer.

"You and Jenny not going to plan?"

Martin toyed with his earlobe, turned the engine on and then hesitated before turning it off again. He sighed.

"Jenny and I are," he spoke gently, "no longer having an affair. The relationship, I understand, has now concluded." He turned to look at Susan. "At least I can be honest with her husband and say that she is not having an affair; I'll just leave out the word anymore."

Susan leaned toward him and put her arms around his shoulders pulling him closer to her. It was an awkward embrace in the confinement of the car. "Poor you, that is so sad. I know you liked her lots, but to be honest Martin, she was married, so it was kind of doomed from the start."

Martin pulled away. "Thank you for the kind words of sympathy, which sounded nothing like kind words of sympathy."

"I think, for the most part, it is always best to be honest. Besides, you're too good a catch to be wasted on some married woman. Let's go back now; we'll catch Vicky and Steve next week. Fancy a drink tonight to talk about her?"

Martin started the car and prepared to drive away, glad to be returning to his side of London. He shook his head, saying, "Thanks for the offer. She's not dead and I'm not worried, so I'll manage. I'll drop you off home on the way."

"No, Martin, I have a better idea."

At once Martin began to feel anxious. Susan often had ideas, but they weren't usually well thought out.

"Shopping that's what you need, a shopping spree."

Martin was not convinced that shopping was exactly what he needed. But Susan would persist in highlighting all the advantages of wandering around shops, beholding shop window displays and indulging in selfless acts of consumerism. He guessed they were not her words and he supposed she had read them in some style magazine. As enthusiastic as she sounded, he pointed the obvious out to her.

"Susan, I do not do shopping. I make purchases when I want some things. I do not place myself in random shops with the sole intention of walking out with bags of stuff, that an hour previously I had no need of, only to find out an hour later I still have no need of."

"Then you'll have to learn. It's the only way, or at least it is one way, of getting over a broken relationship. Bluewater shopping centre is open until about nine tonight; I'll direct you."

***

Martin was not one for shopping centres, the very mention made him wary. His experience of shopping was limited. If he were food shopping, on the rare occasions that his mother was not around to do the weekly shop, he would turn to Waitrose with their online shopping service. He would have welcomed the additional provision which saw the delivery driver putting your shopping away into the correct cupboards as well, but he understood that such a service might be a little complex to organise.

For his personal shopping he had simple needs. Clothes entailed a simple stroll along Saville Row to his favourite shop: Norton & Sons. For Martin it was his one-stop shop for formal, casual and special occasions; they could supply his every need. Why hike around endless shops when you could walk into just one where the staff knew your size and taste, and if any items were not in stock, well, wait a couple of days and they would have your size there in a luxury carrier bag just for you.

For everything else, there was a single shop. Just a short walk from Norton & Sons was his favourite wristwatch shop: Watches of Switzerland, his cologne shop: Jo Malone, a new car: Honda dealer. For his every need there was a single address he could attend, from which he could purchase exactly what he wanted.

At Christmas things became a little more difficult as choosing gifts became more complex. One year he had purchased all his seasonal gifts online from Peter Jones, only to discover that the result was not as he had originally planned, having missed the microscopic tick box which indicated that his purchases were going to be gifts. Each had arrived at their individual destination neatly packed in a plain brown box with the invoice tucked inside. That year was not a good year, as many of his aunts and uncles were a little put out.

The following year Martin reviewed his Yuletide strategy and decided to go to a shopping centre. Well, not so much a centre, more of an arcade, Burlington Arcade, Piccadilly, to be precise. Martin would set aside an afternoon in which to meander up and down the ornate gallery with his list of people to buy gifts for, as well as spending some time choosing a special gift for himself, which invariably he bought from Crockett and Jones.

Nothing had prepared Martin for the mammoth shopping complex that was Bluewater. He felt as if he had driven through some sort of time warp. He observed bright colours, shiny marble surfaces, as well as ornate sculptures hanging from the glass roof. An upper level and a lower level were something he had only previously associated with management jargon. Then there were the people everywhere, all shapes and sizes as well as children of all ages, and all producing sounds at what he considered to be an excessive decibel level.

"Now the key to shopping to alleviate emotional stress is not to have a plan, we walk, we meander, and we peruse the shop windows, looking for the perfect or near to perfect purchase. Do you fancy walking around clockwise or anti-clockwise?"

Martin gazed at Susan, he looked confused, he needed to raise his voice as a screaming child was dragged past him by a mother who looked ready to deposit the child with any unsuspecting passer-by.

"What on earth do you mean?" he asked.

"It goes round in a big circle, well a triangle really. Bluewater has three sides, so we start here and end up here," Susan explained pointing at the map. "The direction is up to you but clockwise always seems more natural to me. A boyfriend once told me that you tighten a nut up clockwise and undo it anticlockwise; that's why I always like to go clockwise if I'm doing things. OK?"

"Is there a bar I can wait in until you have finished shopping?"

"No, Martin, you're here to heal your wounded emotions, shopping is the healthy way of doing that, drinking is not. So, follow me, I'll show you the way."

As Martin accompanied Susan, who seemed to stop at every other shop window to gaze and then point at a few objects before moving on, he questioned himself as to just why he had agreed to this excursion in the first place.

He would tell you he was doing it to humour Susan, a generous gesture on his part. The truth was, and Martin knew it, he was pleased to be out with Susan: distracting him, teasing him, making him smile. The alternative would have meant sitting at home, either in the living room with Mother watching some mindless TV programme where excited amateur experts rushed around purchasing odd-looking antiques, only to see the items sell for a lot less than they had paid, or to sit alone in the study with a large glass of red wine feeling sorry for himself.

Maybe there was never going to be any long-term future with Jenny, but he had hoped it might have lasted a little longer. Martin thought he was probably more ego-bruised than heartbroken.

"What do you think?" His thoughts were interrupted by Susan tugging him back towards a shop window where shoes were elegantly displayed. "The black ones on the left," she added excitedly, pointing towards a pair of shoes which looked to Martin to be a cross between a boot and a high heel. Martin knew he was not an expert on ladies' shoes; Colin would have been far better placed to venture a judgment.

"I think they look a little weird and given the name of the shop, why am I not surprised? Who calls a shoe shop: Office?"

"What is it with you and names? I suppose you buy shoes from Crabtree Matthews Pilkington and Sons, established long ago when Queen Victoria was on the throne and we still had an Empire."

"Crockett and Jones, if you must know, established in 1879."

"So, Victoria was on the throne, right?"

"You really should have paid more attention at school, and yes, we still had an Empire."

"That's why I like shops with modern names. All the others have too much history which I was never much good at. Let's go in and try them on."

"I'll wait here."

"No, you're coming in with me, I need a second opinion when I have them on."

"But I know nothing about women's fashion."

"Don't worry, you look gay enough to have an opinion, which I'll ignore anyway, so it's a win-win situation. Come on," she pulled on his arm drawing him into the shop.

It was not all bad news in the shop: Martin got to sit down, there were no noisy children, plus there was that luxurious smell of leather which Martin always found oddly comforting. He watched as Susan slipped on the shoes. They had a triangular look to them; the heel resembled a pyramid; they were shaped to a point at the toes with the instep cut away, again in a triangular shape. Susan stood up in them looking down as she moved her foot around to inspect the shoe from as many angles as possible.

"What do you think?"

From bitter experience Martin knew his answer was critical, honesty was not always the best policy in this situation, diplomacy normally won out.

"They do have a unique design and they're black; they'll go with anything." He stopped, deciding that to add anything else would be risking too much.

"You like them?"

"They would never suit me," Martin parried with a humorous quip, a useful alternative to diplomacy.

The shop assistant, an unusually tall lady who when helping Susan on with the shoes looked awkward, with legs that did not seem to fold in as they would on normal people smiled when she said,

"I think your husband is a little nervous to give a view. Husbands I have found prefer to remain neutral."

Susan sat down and without any form of hesitation told the assistant, "he's not my husband, he's my sugar daddy, so much more fun than a husband."

"I'm not her sugar daddy," Martin at once corrected, "I'm her boss." Which did nothing to help the situation or the implication that the assistant clearly made judging by the look she then gave Martin.

"I'll take them," Susan spoke handing her credit card to the shop assistant, then turned towards Martin, "I'll pay for these, darling, you can pay for the meal tonight." She smiled at Martin who could feel his cheeks warming and colouring up.

***

They continued their clockwise tour of Bluewater's lower level, Susan hanging proudly onto her colourful Office carrier bag with her new shoes inside. Having made one purchase, she continued to stop and peruse shop displays, the night was young yet.

"Do you take pleasure in embarrassing me in front of people?" Martin asked, as they stood in front of a travel agent's window, where Susan recounted some of the holidays that she'd had with the girls.

"It's fun to see you squirm; you look so cute."

"That may be so but telling that shoe shop woman that I was your sugar daddy, well, it just made me feel cheap."

Susan turned away from the pictures of sun-drenched beaches and brushed an imaginary piece of fluff from the shoulder of his jacket. "Come on, it's a laugh. We'll most likely never see her again, it does no harm. Plus, I would say when she gets home, we'll be one of the topics of the day as she tells her family about all the peculiar customers she has put up with. Didn't you ever wave to random strangers from the top of a bus leaving them wondering, 'do I know that person?' You need to loosen that Crockett and Jones tie of yours."

"They make shoes," he corrected her, as she moved onto the next retail unit.

"Now that is a party dress," Susan stated as she looked at a very skimpy plain red dress, that apart from being short, had a plunging back.

"I'm sure you would look wonderful in anything," Martin responded, hoping that she was not planning on going inside and trying it on. He knew from bitter experience with Jenny that deciding on a dress is a lot more complex and time consuming than trying on a pair of shoes.

"Hello, you is Paul's mates."

They turned in unison to see just who had recognised them. He was taller than either of them and twice the width of Susan. His smile was boyish and coy. He wore a well-worn black leather jacket together with dilapidated jeans which could easily be mistaken for highly fashionable distressed ones. Neither Susan nor Martin could see the motif on the back of his jacket, but passers-by could as they stared at the young man. 'Hells Angel Chapter' written around a skull, encouraged shoppers to give him a wide berth, while hoping he was not giving grief to the respectable couple he was talking to. Even if he was doing so, they gave just a brisk glance before continuing with their shopping.

Martin recognised him at once, well to be precise, he noticed the bald, tattooed head. He took one step back and bumped into the glass of the shop. Susan smiled.

"You're from the club in Deptford. Fancy seeing you all the way over here, never took you as an avid shopper."

"Nah, can't afford to shop in this posh place," he laughed, reminding Susan of her young niece.

Martin guessed that if he wasn't shopping then he was perhaps shoplifting, that seemed like a feasible explanation. Susan continued the conversation.

"Well then, what brings you all the way over here?"

He looked ashamed, "I come over here for the free food."

"Free food," Susan repeated, "how does that work?"

"Come the end of the day, some of the places that sell food give it away. I have my regular spots where I wait to collect out of date stuff." He proudly held up a shabby Poundland plastic bag. "Last night I got some sandwiches, plus a large slab of carrot cake, it's my very favourite. And they gave me a large latte. I shouldn't tell you 'cause they might get into trouble, but you look kind."

"A bit like a lucky dip. Let's hope they have more carrot cake for you tonight."

"Hope so, you know it is my best cake." He turned to look at Martin, who still had not spoken.

The initial apprehension Martin had felt had now eased just a little. Mugging appeared less likely now. The young man spoke as his eyes examined Martin's jacket,

"Nice jacket, Mister. Whip stitch on the lapel is a nice touch, hand tailored, you must be rich?"

No longer feeling afraid, Martin felt as if he was looking across a wide gap that defined social worlds. He had always been aware that his life was privileged. In the same way he was aware that many people struggled with their daily lives and were not so well off. Yet this young man in front of him, who could be no more than in his mid-twenties, was standing there with a plastic bag in which he was going to collect discarded food. That seemed to accentuate the chasm between them, but he could see a bridge being laid across the gulf as the young man clearly recognised a handmade jacket.

"I think my tailor did mention something about a whip stitch, not that I know what such a thing is."

"It is a simple stitch for joining two pieces of material together. Normally it gets covered over, but it can be a decoration. Looks good on your lapels," he added.

"You seem to know a lot about sewing. Have you read about it?" Martin asked.

"Nah, I was a tailor. I did a three-year apprenticeship, then started with a tailoring firm, mostly cutting, plus doing trousers. They said I was good."

With a tone of hesitation in his voice Martin asked, "but you are not a tailor now?"

The young man looked down at his scruffy trainers; he looked embarrassed to answer the question, yet he did anyway. He had been taught that if someone with a posh voice asks you a question, you must always politely answer them. He learnt that from cutting and sewing trousers for people who spoke with a plum in their mouths.

"The tailors I worked for closed down. The father dies, and the sons didn't want to carry on. I was out of work but couldn't get anything, couldn't pay me rent so ended up in a hostel. They are not nice places; people kept nicking my stuff and hurting me. Had to look hard, had loads of tattoos," he pointed to his head, in case Martin had missed them. "I'm not really tough, but now I look it."

"Can't you get a job?" Susan asked the question.

"Not after decorating my head, I'm stuck now. Can't stay, I had better get round to Costa, see if they have any more carrot cake, it's my best cake, if you didn't know. Nice to see you."

He turned and began to walk away but Martin called after him, "I'm Martin and this is Susan, what's your name?"

He continued, answering as he walked, "Brendan, might see you around." They watched him fade into the crowds.

"Blimey, that's put a damper on the shopping spree," Susan commented.

***

"You really remind me of Jenny at times," Martin observed looking at Susan.

"Tall, beautiful, attractive personality, with a sensuous sense of humour which has men craving her company?"

"No, I mean sitting at a restaurant table surrounded by designer fashion shopping bags. Do you really need all that shopping?"

Susan placed the menu down on the white linen tablecloth. They had decided that as the shops began closing it was time to curtail the extravagant shopping spree that Susan had embarked upon. Given the hour of the evening they decided that a meal was called for, Martin had chosen a corner table in Cote Brasserie, a pseudo French restaurant that he felt comfortable in.

"I did it for you. As I told you a shopping spree can help with emotional distress."

"Susan, I think you will find that earlier it was deemed that I was the one suffering from emotional distress. Therefore, how do you explain that it was you on the shopping spree, I, being a mere observer? Plus, sitting here, I now realise that as my car is waiting for me in the car park, I will be the one unable to drink alcohol to alleviate my emotional distress. I am sure it will come as no surprise to you that you will be the one drinking wine on my behalf, to alleviate the emotional distress that I am feeling."

"It's a sacrifice I am prepared to make for you, Martin, be thankful."

Martin was amused to see Susan work her way through three courses. Pate followed by steak all polished off with a crème brulee. He imagined that her enlarged appetite was also a consequence of his emotional distress.

They had chatted about many subjects during the meal, none of which concerned the current problems with Paul and Vicky. They were both relaxed when Martin asked a question he had been meaning to ask for a while, in fact ever since Susan had told him her mother died after an accident three years ago.

"The last time we were having a meal which included linen tablecloths was at the Papillon Restaurant."

"Ah, the posh one I thought looked like a greenhouse."

"That's the one. We talked about you losing your mother after the accident she had on her bike and your father turning off the life support machine. Have you really never spoken to him since?"

Susan pushed her empty coffee cup away and took a sip of the brandy that she had ordered as a digestive.

"I told you before, my two sisters and I have not forgiven him, why should we? Her daughters had faith that she might recover, he went his own way."

Absently Martin brushed a few crumbs from the white tablecloth. "Maybe it is time to forgive, he was, no doubt, only doing what he thought was for the best. No one can predict the future; decisions have to be based on present circumstances."

"The way we view it is that he took our mother from us when there was still a faint chance that she might have come through it all. Even if she ended up in a wheelchair and unable to speak, she would still have been our mother."

"All I'm saying, Susan, is that one day your father will die. And when that day comes, you'll regret the time you never spent with him. I know I did. My father and I never really agreed on much. I was a big disappointment to him and when I said I had no plans to take over the family business, although he accepted it, I know deep down it hurt him. That pain only deepened when he sold the company to a bunch of investors from Hong Kong.

"My father had always been there, and I assumed he always would be. We were civil but never close, then one day, he was gone. I had said goodbye to him that evening before going off with the guys for a drink. It was a massive heart attack. When I arrived at the hospital just after midnight, he just laid there, unconscious and clinging to life. He could never be my friend, because he wanted to make me the best person I could be, that's what fathers are there for. Me, his son, should have repaid that by respecting him and acknowledging that I was pleased he wanted me to fulfil any potential I had.

"He died the next morning. That was it, the end. I could never tell him; never ask questions about his life. What I'm saying to you, Susan, is while you have time, speak to your father. You do not have to forgive him, but you can engage in conversation, tell him about your life, that you are happy or sad. Let him know, I am sure he is missing you and your sisters. He no doubt sacrificed a lot to bring you girls up, helping to make you the best person you could be. Let him know, the sacrifices he made were not made in vain."

"I understand what you are saying, Martin, but you must realise, you and I are different people."

As Martin drove her back to central London, he could not help but notice Susan was unusually quiet and pensive. He knew they were not that different from each other.

CHAPTER NINE

If Mondays were not bad enough for Martin, then the sight of Ian Shillingford with a big smile on his face striding into the office clutching a Costa coffee cup did nothing to lift his mood. He would be the first to admit that after his shopping spree with Susan he had still brooded for the remainder of the weekend, unable to focus on doing anything. He had turned down several offers to go drinking with friends. Had not bothered to shave on Sunday, which only resulted in his mother saying she hoped that he was not growing one of those ludicrous beards like the man had on the Senior Service cigarette packet. Martin thought he knew the old-fashioned logo she was talking about, but it was very historic and abstract. He kept telling himself his fling with Jenny was fun while it lasted, that there would be others, but he could not convince himself however much he tried.

"Ah good, we're alone, now about our little arrangement." Ian sat down on Susan's vacant chair.

Susan's call to Martin earlier had done nothing to help his melancholy mood. She said something about an inset day, school, and her little six-year-old niece. Martin had no real idea what she was talking about and cared even less; all he knew was that she would be in around lunchtime.

"Ian, I'm sorry I have not got back to you yet I was just making sure of a few facts. I was planning to give you a call during the week."

"No problem. I can call you off the whole thing; everything has changed."

If it was not bad enough for Martin to be told by Jenny that the affair was over, it looked as though he was going to get the same gloating speech from her husband.

As it turned out it was nothing of the sort. More of an admission on Ian's part that he had overreacted by suspecting his wife was having an affair. He blamed the business with its ups and downs and not spending enough time just talking to his wife. He could now understand that she had wondered just what she was supposed to do; sit at home for hours on end waiting for him to pop in in-between business meetings. His conclusion was that he had been very inconsiderate to his wife.

He told Martin, with the excitement of a schoolboy hitting puberty and having his first girlfriend, that the two of them had just looked at each other one night and said almost the very same thing, that they had grown apart and both wanted to change things. He admitted that the evening turned out to be a very special one.

Martin was not bothered about what Ian was saying and was not really listening to him. Instead he had been studying Ian's shoes: brown leather brogues that had a blue section around the heel. He liked the style and wanted to ask Ian where he could get them from, however he did not, men do not exchange fashion tips, or at least they were not meant to.

Ian continued to witter on, leaving Martin just hoping he would be on his way soon.

"Now, there is just the matter of a cheque for your charity by way of gratitude."

Martin looked up from the brogue shoes and smiled at Ian. "You give me an office, so we'll call it quits."

"No, I insist, Martin. The charity thing, I'm told by my right-hand man, is some sort of tax-effective arrangement. Who shall I make it payable to?"

Martin felt uncomfortable about accepting money for something he had not done. Although in a way he had been complicit in having an affair with Jenny, which had in a roundabout way, led them to get back together again, but he was never going to explain that to Ian.

Martin thought about Susan's theory and her extraordinary distrust of Derek Primm. Maybe there was a way they could get something out of Ian.

"Ian, there is something that you could do for me without writing a cheque. Do you know a Derek Primm, he owns some property around south London?"

"Ah, Ian does indeed know Derek Primm, that prick who is forever pulling up his trousers. Yes, I know him, well, I say I know him; I have met him on a few occasions at various functions. Why do you ask? Are you investigating him?"

"Can't say too much." Martin tapped his nose with his index finger, he had no idea why; it was just that he had seen the gesture in a couple of films and thought it would be cool. No sooner had he done it, than the idea that he might be turning into another Susan with her playacting crossed his mind. He wanted to say lots about Derek to Ian, but he thought it sounded a little more professional to pass no comment. "I just wanted to get an idea of what he is like as a man."

"It would seem that for some weird reason he is attractive to women. In fact, he is odd all around. As well as the syndrome with his trousers, he collects postcards, bloody stupid thing to collect, I think. Then he sticks the bloody things all over his restaurant, as some form of decoration, which I think sounds terribly tacky. Never been there myself, but I have heard about it.

"His dad was a councillor, as is Derek, following in his father's footsteps as well as inheriting the property portfolio from his father. It all makes him a little arrogant. He acts as if it was him that built the empire, but really, he just took over control. Also, being a local councillor and owning a load of property in the same borough, I do not think such a connection is that healthy.

"No one in the business really likes him; part of that is down to his Midas touch for picking up cheap property. The latest gossip is that he owns some property on Turner Road right in the middle of a council redevelopment zone. As lucky as ever, he'll make a handsome profit out of that one, especially as he has, no doubt, some friends in the council.

"In conclusion, I would not trust him and now I trust him even less knowing that your charity is investigating him. I can imagine him having a string of women being used and abused."

"You do not seem to have a good impression of him."

"I told you, the man's a prick I hope you get him." Ian stood up, threw his empty coffee cup into the waste bin, then offered his hand to Martin. "Good luck getting Derek. If you need anything else on him, here's my card with my private number on it."

As Ian left the office, Martin gave the business card a fleeting glance before throwing it into his top drawer to join all the others he had collected. He felt his phone vibrate but he ignored it.

That was it, Martin fully understood now that Ian and Jenny were once again a happy twosome, there was nothing left for him. Could Jenny and he ever have become a long-term couple? Susan was right, it could never have happened, and even if it did, he would always be wondering if she was being unfaithful and having another affair. Not the best foundation for any relationship.

As ever, Martin concluded, Susan knew what was best for him, better than his mother at times. Maybe he should have continued the shopping spree into the weekend. It could have done no harm and though he would never admit it openly, he always felt relaxed and at ease around her. Somehow, he could just be himself with Susan, not that he understood just who he was.

His phone vibrated again, this time he answered it and heard Colin's voice.

"I understand that you two did a 'foxtrot oscar' without doing a single thing and leaving me to the mercy of an insane librarian who asked me the most stupid questions. Questions like: 'Do I not get embarrassed going into a women's shop and buying female clothes?' I told him, its only embarrassing when I can't get into a size twelve dress without holding my breath."

"You're not a size twelve," Martin retorted, irritably.

"Part of the skill of wearing women's clothes is not to dwell over the size of the garment you're wearing; it's all about the colour and the cut. But that is beside the point, the insane librarian did in the end dig out a lot of information about our Derek Primm, which I shall now relay to you verbally. Pen at the ready, Martin, I know you have a sieve for a memory."

Martin did exactly as he was told and made notes on a pad as Colin spoke.

"Derek took over a whole portfolio of property from his father, who died five years ago. Against all expectations from those around him, the portfolio continued to grow and is considered by some to be successful. The six flats and shops that your friend's girl lives in was part of the father's acquisitions, bought from the council for pretty much nothing, on the understanding that the flats would be let to vulnerable people and the shops should be local shops, whatever that might mean. I could never see IKEA squeezing a furniture store into one of those poky units. I digress.

"Currently, the whole estate, including Derek's parade of shops, is due to be knocked down and rebuilt, so there are ongoing negotiations with the council of whom Derek, like his father, is an elected member. Something my insane librarian banged on about a lot; he didn't approve.

"Along with the various residential properties he owns and rents out, he also, as well as the restaurant, owns three chemist shops. Not only does he own the freehold, but he is also a director of the company that runs the three chemists. If we're looking for a connection to prescription drugs, there it is."

Martin looked over what he had written, it was almost a mirror image of what Ian had already told him.

"Plus, I hear that you've been dumped."

"How come everyone knows my business?"

"That'll be for what should be an obvious reason to you, you told Suzie Baby. I guess plenty of people now know. Still onwards and upwards, Martin. If you want to move on from the married kind, I'm sure there will be a queue of both eligible and single young women queuing at your door before too long."

***

Susan slammed down the phone receiver, turned to Martin and told him in a very firm angry voice, "That bastard low-life!"

It had, up to that point, been a relatively quiet morning in the office for Martin, apart from the fleeting visit from Ian and then the call from Colin. Otherwise, Martin had relaxed with the newspaper until Susan arrived. She then proceeded to share too much information with him about children playing games, colouring, and watching You Tube; none of which interested him.

It was during her description of something called 'Baldi's Basics' that the telephone rang. Susan answered in a calm voice, while Martin returned to a news item about men living with their parents.

Susan's voice quickly rose in volume and took on a frustrated attitude, disturbing Martin's reading and forcing him to fold up the paper and drop it onto his desk. He was not going to be able to focus on any news item while Susan was talking on the phone, as her voice had now reached shouting point.

"Vicky, we are trying to help you, can't you see that? Some things you can't do on your own."

Martin watched Susan's face which showed her growing frustration.

"We need to know more about him. .... He's done what?" Her voice had now reached fever pitch.

"No question, whatever you say we're coming down to see you now. .... I don't care, Vicky; he's a bloody monster and we are going to get this sorted. No arguments, we're on our way."

Hearing the crash of the receiver and Susan's expletive that followed, Martin was tempted to ask the reason for the exclamation. Then he decided against it as he was going to hear it anyway, so he might as well save his breath.

"That was Vicky calling to tell us not to bother; she'll sort it all herself, in her own way."

'That works for me,' decided Martin, but wisely he kept that particular thought to himself.

"I tell her no; we're going to help you anyway. Then she tells me, that loan shark has just beaten her up, warning her to stop talking to us. I gather only a couple of punches and a few slaps, but that is not the right thing to do. I've told her, we're coming down to see her and to get this sorted, once and for all."

"Are we?"

"Are we what? Going to see her, yes, of course. You'd better drive down there with me, in case he comes back. Vicky said she didn't want us down there, but I'm not having some fat-arsed pig hit a woman, we're going to see her and then find him."

There was a time in Martin's life when he would have happily argued that it was maybe not the best thing to confront a loan shark with a clear penchant for violence. Even if you ignored the request from Vicky not to see her, there were far better places to go and more civilised people they could speak to. However, knowing Susan, he understood that nothing was going to stop her. Hence, he found himself obediently driving towards south London, once again passing a selection of pie and mash shops, eating at one of them would have been a lot more preferable than the prospect of facing an aggressive loan shark.

***

Susan was no less persistent when they arrived at Vicky's, who quickly succumbed to her insistence, even though the welcome was still only half-hearted. Vicky sat in one of her forlorn sofa chairs, her eyes reddened from the tears she had no doubt shed earlier. To Martin's relief, she was not caked in blood and bruises, although she had a red, sore looking left cheek, plus a few nasty looking scratches on her left arm. There was no sign of the loan shark.

At first Martin had not noticed the total chaos of the flat. Given the state of the place before, he had expected it to be unchanged, which largely it was. It was only when Susan pointed it out that he noticed all the light switches, well three of them, had been smashed, the broken white plastic strewn over the floor. Plug sockets had suffered the same fate and were either broken or cracked. Some of them had wires showing through. The light bulbs and fittings appeared to have gone unscathed, maybe the loan shark was short and could not reach them.

Susan sat on the threadbare arm of the sofa and put her arm around Vicky, who had now started to sob. Martin stood opposite the two girls feeling at a loose end. Handing out emotional support was never his strong point; he always worried that when confronted with a distraught person, anything he might say would make things worse. He therefore felt it easier and safer just to stand in silence doing nothing. Susan, as ever, had other plans for him.

"Best call your school mate and get him down here to sort out these plugs and stuff; we can't leave her like this."

As instructed, Martin called Steve, a conversation which started off politely by Martin giving a description of the damage to the flat. It was just that Steve did not seem to be very keen to make a visit. He offered to get an electrician around as soon as he could, but for Martin that seemed a little too vague as things needed to be sorted out sooner rather than later. Their conversation moved onto confrontation, until Martin decided it was time to step up a gear.

"Steve, the thing is you will be leaving a vulnerable person in an extremely dangerous flat, stumbling around tonight in the dark. She could easily trip and electrocute herself. I want you down here now, see for yourself exactly what is going on, and if need be, get her rehoused until the repairs are done. Either that or I cause a right stink with the authorities, which will include the local council and councillors. I am sure your Mr Primm will not want his properties seen to be the subject of subsequent discussions."

The threat was enough to cajole Steve into agreeing to make a visit to the flat. Martin put his mobile away smugly, that felt good.

"Blimey, Martin, you can be a right hard nut when you want to be." Susan smiled, before turning to Vicky who wiped the tears from her eyes. "This loan shark, where can we find him?" Susan asked.

"You just don't get it do you?" Vicky snapped back. "I told your boyfriend the other day, this is the life I live, there ain't no escape. I'm trapped in debt and always will be. There is no way out. Even if there was, what work can I get? Nuffin' much. Any wages I get will be nothing like enough to live on. So just leave me to get on with my life and you two live your own life."

"Maybe you're right," Susan answered, inwardly liking the thought of Martin being considered her boyfriend. "But this loan shark bloke, he has no right to knock you about and smash your place up. It's bad enough he is draining tons of money out of you. It is not only illegal but morally wrong as well, and that's what really gets me."

"But it's legal for big business to get me to work for peanuts and only give me hours when it suits them. It's always been that way, one rule for the poor and another for the rich. Just leave me alone and let me get on with my life."

Vicky then burst into tears again. She was still crying when the doorbell rang. Martin went downstairs to answer, hoping it was Steve and not the return of the loan shark.

"Come on Vicky, crying is not going to help. We have to be strong if we're going to get back at this guy," Susan said.

Vicky wiped her eyes with a now soggy tissue. "He just scares the shit out of me, it would be better if you just left me alone."

"No one is that scary, Vicky. What's he look like?"

"Big guy, ugly and fat as well, looks as if he was a boxer once. Blue eyes and brown unkempt hair, curly brown. Not the sort of bloke you'd want to date."

"You say that, you don't know how desperate I've been in the past," Susan joked. That put a moment of light relief into the conversation as together they laughed.

***

Martin was so relieved that it was Steve standing in front of him and not some hulk who was going to beat his brains out. Steve did not look happy though, standing there on the doorstep, in fact, he looked decidedly nervous.

"About time you got here; come up and I'll show you the damage." Martin turned to walk back up the stairs, but Steve remained on the pavement.

"I'm not coming up, Martin, there is no point. I am not qualified to do anything electrical, that is simply not what I do, whatever you think. I've only come down because you're an old friend and I wanted to speak to you face to face."

"Well, as you're here…"

"No, I have already spoken to my electrician, who I know very well, he does a lot of work for me. He is going to drop everything he is doing today and come over and sort her out. He should be here in the next hour or so. He'll make it all safe at least for the night. Then return in the morning with new sockets and stuff to get it back to how it should be."

Martin was going to speak, but Steve raised his hand to silence his old school friend, then continued,

"Let's not forget, Martin, I am doing you a bloody big favour here. If one of Mr Primm's tenants damages their flat, then it is down to them to get it all fixed. Old man Primm does not like spending money on these flats, or any of his flats for that matter, let alone if they have been vandalised. I am having to pull a fast one on him to help you out. Twist some figures, hide some costs and tell some white lies. Don't forget that this is a special favour because we are old friends."

"Your bloke had better turn up tonight or else I'm on the phone to Mr Primm."

"I'm sure you would be, Martin, but hand on heart, he'll be here later and get it all sorted out."

"What about this loan shark person who has done all the damage, if we find him do you want to know who he is?"

"Primm will know nothing about this, neither will old man Duffield. To be honest, I can't see me taking action against a violent thug unless I'm forced to. I'll leave you to it, Martin. Maybe catch up for a drink in a week or two."

Without waiting for any reply, Steve turned and walked away, crossed the road and walked towards the block of flats opposite. Martin could not understand why he chose not to close the door and go back upstairs. Maybe it was the shortness of the meeting and the bluntness Steve presented, but for some reason he waited and watched.

A few moments later, from behind the block of flats, he saw a car appear, turn right and drive away into the distance. He could not make out the registration number, he did, however, see that it was a blue Honda.

***

"You're kidding! You mean you have never, ever eaten fish and chips out of paper before?"

Not only that, Martin thought, but he had never sat at a small Formica table with a ghastly floral design, in the window of a fish and chip shop. Apart from the generous sprinkling of salt that was already on the table before they sat down, the shop just did not seem to have the room for one table, let alone the two tables that were set right up against the window. They were both giving passing pedestrians a grandstand view of the diners and what they were eating. The frail looking man who sat at the table behind Martin, did not seem to care. He wore very dark sunglasses, which matched his jet-black mop of unkempt hair.

It was while Martin stood at the counter beside Susan, waiting for their order, that he had first noticed the sunglasses man. Looking out of the corner of his eye, Martin watched the man eat. He was interested to see just what the locals actually ate.

Sunglasses man had an open can of ginger beer on the table in front of him and laid out on his sheet of paper were: two saveloys, four pickled onions, one egg, - which Martin presumed was pickled - as well as three large gherkins. Martin surmised the man was not too worried about his digestive system.

"I think the closest I have come to eating out of paper is at the sea front where you get a paper cone full of chips, then walk along the promenade talking to friends and fighting off the sea-gulls."

Susan passed him a brown plastic fork and then started eating. She was hungry, which was the real reason she had suggested to Martin that they have some fish and chips. She had thought they would go back to his car and eat them there, but he was not enamoured by the idea of fish and chip odours in his car. She wondered if he now regretted that decision as he looked uncomfortable digging into the white fish with his small plastic fork. Yet another reason was that every time the man behind him with the wild looking hair, took a swig of his ginger beer, he followed it with a loud burp.

"Remind me, what was your mate Paul's strange habit at school?"

"I could only remind you if I had told you, which I have not, and I have no plans to do so."

"But you told Colin."

"He's a man who can keep a secret and then taunt you with the fact that he knows it. Paul's habit is something only men should be told about; ladies like yourself are excluded from knowing such things. Do you really need that much vinegar on your fish?"

"Yes, I do. It helps break down the oil they fry it in. Your other friend, Steve, he was not very social was he, didn't even come up and see what the problem was."

"There are a number of things with Steve that I am starting to have concerns about. I agree it was odd that having arrived at Vicky's flat, he clearly had no intention of coming in. Logically, I would have thought he would at least want to see the damage, for no better reason than to ensure his electrician does not overcharge him. Then there was the time he told me about, when he was going to her flat and saw the police there, he just carried on past. He just does not sound like a responsible estate agent to me.

"Finally, and I have not told you this part, I watched him leave earlier. He walked across the road to those flats, walked into, I guess, what is the common area, that sort of courtyard bit between them; I presume he must have parked his car there. Now, to be fair, I did not see who was driving, but moments later a blue Honda Civic, the same model as mine, drove out. I am beginning to think he is not as honest as he should be."

Susan's jaw dropped. She held a lone chip on her fork close to her mouth awaiting its entry, but spoke first, "The same car, Martin, he could be our dealer, which would make so much sense. He knows the area, has all the contacts and is in touch with Derek Primm and his string of chemist shops, a great place to get his supplies." Finally, she pushed the expectant chip into her mouth.

"I realise that. Steve was once a wealthy person; he always loved money and all the trappings of wealth, so it must have hurt him to see his bank balance disappear overnight. Maybe he is planning on building another fortune. I know he has never been averse to bending the rules or even making them up as he goes along."

There was a loud burp from behind Martin as the man in the sunglasses stood up, crumpled his paper and placed it carefully back on the table. He then took a sideways step and was now beside them. "You posh folks looking to buy up a new flat? Not the first," he continued without waiting for an answer. "There's a lot of interest in this redevelopment that's happenin' soon. Knocking the 'ole bloody lot down an' building posh tall towers. Not for the likes of us here, but you posh'ens will be queuing up, I guess."

"Too far south for my friend here," Susan answered, pointing at Martin with her fork which had a skewered chip on the end. "We're here to find somewhere to buy some pills, nothing risky, just stuff you get on prescription. Do you know of anyone who can help?"

Martin gave Susan a quizzical look which she ignored. The sunglasses man answered as if he had been asked what the weather was like.

"You'd need to have a word with Flossie, over the road there," he pointed out of the window in a vague manner. "The red door, she'd be the one to help you with that."

"I thought she had been shut down?"

"Nah, not Flossie, when her ticker stops then maybe. Until that day, she'll be doing her stuff. The old bill turns up once a year, clears 'er out, slaps 'er wrist, then the next week she's back selling 'er stuff."

"It's good to know you can rely on some things in life. What about somewhere to get a quick loan, nothing too great, say five hundred quid, where'd I get that from?"

Sunglasses man looked down at Martin, paused for a moment, then turned to the counter.

"Terry, where would one get a quick loan nowadays around here?"

The man behind the counter was tall and appeared slim in his white overalls; he held a batter-covered fish over the boiling fat. He stared at the strangers sitting at the table and decided they did not look like police.

"There's a few around here that would help you, but none of them are honest or kind, so I'll not be telling you. I'd suggest that you think of another way to get your money. Those around here are all low-life. Just get your bloke to pawn his Rolex watch, that'll see you through for a couple of months."

Timidly, Martin tugged his sleeve down over his watch; clearly, he should think twice about what he wore around this area.

Terry served another customer as sunglasses man sauntered out of the shop. Susan wiped her fingers with a tissue she had taken out of her handbag, then offered it to Martin to clean up his own hands.

As they left, Susan turned to Martin saying, "I have a plan. Tomorrow, with Colin, I'll visit Flossie first thing and see what else we can get out of her. If she's that good at keeping her business going, then I'm sure she will help point us in the right direction for the Honda dealer. Huh, see what I have done there, Honda dealer, but not a car dealer, a drug dealer."

"Very droll, Susan, and what do you have in store for me? I imagine you have a task planned to help me occupy my time."

"I think you should go and see Steve once again, ask him about his car. Hopefully, by the morning, Becky will have got back to us about Derek's finances and that might throw some more light on a situation that is starting to confuse me."

"Oh, by the way, in all the excitement of having fish and chips off a sheet of blotting paper, I forgot to tell you something. There was a torn-out newspaper advert beside Vicky's phone, an advert for a sex chat line, I am guessing it may be the one she answers. Colin said that he could, if he had the number, find out the company operating it. If you can give it to him in the morning, see what he can find out, we might start to get somewhere."

"Call it out and I'll put it in my phone. I'm the worst organised when it comes to bits of paper."

As Susan typed the number into her phone, she became aware of someone standing next to her, it was the man from the chip shop, she could see her face reflected in his dark glasses.

"If you two are lookin' fer a quick loan, the bloke you want is Gerry, works out of the snooker 'all in the 'igh road. Tell 'im Blackie sent yer."

"What, he'll give us a loan?" Martin asked.

"Nah, but 'e'll point yer in the right direction. Don't forget Blackie sent yer." He then wandered off down the street leaving Martin and Susan a little mystified.

***

The Snooker Hall was easy to find in the High Road. It was the only double-fronted building with blacked-out windows and the words 'Snooker Hall' in large red letters that had been stuck on the glass. Even though someone had added two eyes in the middle of the 'o's, priding themselves as being detectives, they guessed it was the right place.

"Are you sure about this?" Martin asked, but Susan did not appear to hear him as she pushed open the door. He followed her into a dim room where sitting behind a small desk on the left was a large black man smoking a pipe as he read a newspaper.

"We're here to see Gerry," Susan told him. There was no reaction at first, he appeared to want to finish the news story he was reading before looking up. Once finished, he eyed them suspiciously.

"Ya not invited, ya no come in." His deep Jamaican accent was warm and not in the least threatening, Martin thought, which encouraged him to point out that Blackie had sent them.

"Him know ya?"

"Had lunch with him," Susan added.

"Ya should 'ana eat wid him, him eat funny. Take dis," he gave them each what looked like a red casino chip. "See da man by da bar." He pointed to the double doors in front of them.

Once they were through the double doors, the room they found themselves in was as big as an aircraft hangar, or so Susan likened it to. Martin pointed out the error of her judgement, but he agreed that any room that could house ten snooker tables, could be considered on the large size. The rectangular tables were all occupied by players. A single pool of light above each table illuminated the green baize and the colourful snooker balls. The gaps between the tables and the edges of the room were lit by the reflection from the table lights. They spotted a small functional bar at the far left-hand corner of the room. To the right of it stood a man who appeared to be guarding the door beside him. They made their way towards him. Martin could feel his heart beating; at that moment he would rather have been on the street of any council estate, at least he would have been able to run off. Escape here did not look to be easy.

"Here to see Gerry," Susan told the brute of a man by the door, offering her token as she spoke. He collected Martin's casino coin, then knocked twice on the door, opened it and waved them through. They stood in a compact office. A tacky office in Susan's opinion, although she made no comment to that fact. A large dark wooden desk dominated the room. The walls were decorated in a grotesque – Susan's opinion again – red flock wallpaper, which reminded her of being in an Indian restaurant. The lighting source was a single bulb contained within a very ornate chandelier.

To the right of the desk was another thug of a man, dressed in a smart suit. He had the word love tattooed on one hand and hate on the other. His collar and tie did little to hide the tattooed cobra that wrapped around his broad neck. Behind the desk sat another man who could have been in his forties or possibly older; the dim lighting made a more accurate assessment difficult. He looked up, waved them forward towards the desk and spoke,

"Blackie sent you. You just messengers or do you want something?"

"We're looking for a loan shark," Susan told him. His reaction was a raised eyebrow.

"Do I look like a f'ing cash machine? Blackie has had too many of his pickled eggs if he thinks I drop loans around. Mind, you two don't look like you need any loan."

"We're after a name for one who works the Turner Estate, picks on vulnerable women."

"Why is that important to you, neither of you look like old bill, what's your interest?"

"Can we take a seat?" Martin asked, looking at the two velour dining chairs in front of the desk.

"No," was the curt reply. "Why do you want to know?"

"A friend of ours is in trouble with him and we want to help out." Susan then added, "we're just after a name."

"Now, I already told you I ain't a f'ing cash machine; I now have to tell you that I ain't no f'ing grass either. So, piss off and leave me alone."

"I want a name," Susan demanded, which was not the sort of question either Gerry or Martin, for that matter, wanted to hear.

Both Gerry and Martin looked at her, even the hulk of a man took a sideways glance.

"Stupid cow, that's a name I'm giving you, how's that?"

Susan moved up to the desk, put both hands on the polished wood and leant forward towards him. The thug moved to protect his master, who held up his hand to stop his 'attack dog' for now.

"No one calls me a stupid cow, however much of a dick head they are." Susan made her voice as threatening as she could. Martin chimed in with,

"Let's leave it."

"No," Susan told him without taking her eyes off Gerry. "I want the name of the loan shark who is screwing around with girls on the Turner Estate. You know the name and I want it."

Gerry flicked his hand in the direction of the door, the universal sign in his life to instruct the brute next to him to eject whoever might be annoying him.

"Come on, love." Using his hand with the hate tattoo on it, he grabbed Susan's arm.

She looked up at him and told him, "You got to be one of the dumbest looking apes I ever saw."

At this point, Martin wanted to run fast through the door, past the snooker tables and then out onto the street, all in as little time as possible. However, he thought it was not very chivalrous to leave Susan behind. Although part of him did think if she was dumb enough to say that to a man who looked like he had spent his life fighting for a living, then maybe running was the right thing for Martin to do.

Gerry looked at the anger that was rising in his bodyguard. "You aren't afraid of him, are you?" he asked Susan.

"You damn right, I am," Susan responded, which Martin thought made no sense at all.

"Hold on, Charlie, leave her alone. Well, young lady, do you know who you sounded like just then?"

Susan looked back at Gerry, "Jim Rockford."

On reflection she had no idea why in a moment of sheer panic she had recalled an obscure Jim Rockford quote. A quote which was not the best one to make given the circumstances that she found herself in.

"You must be a real fan of the Rockford Files to recall that. Another fan of the great man, sit down, young lady. What did you say your name was?"

As Susan introduced herself and Martin, Gerry got up from his chair and scuttled over to a large set of drawers, which resembled and in fact was a surveyor's bureau from around 1905 that had belonged to his grandfather. Gerry opened the third drawer down, shuffled through some papers and came back to the desk with several sheets of paper tied together.

"It's not often I stumble on a fellow fan of the Rockford Files. In my mind, James Garner was one of the greats of TV detectives, better even than Columbo. Jim Rockford had humour, violence and it always ended well; that's my sort of TV. Here, look at this, I got it off eBay last year, my prized possession, a script from series three, episode four, 'Drought at Indianhead River'. Paid a lot for it, but worth every penny. Here, have a butchers," he handed it over to Susan, who began to read the script.

"Even got handwritten – handwritten, I tell you – notes by the man himself. Look at that one there," he pointed to a note about halfway down the page, "'pause a little longer'. That's what I like about him, sense of timing, man's quality."

"Well, I am a fan," Susan admitted, "but you seem to be a super fan."

"It's my little indulgence. Thursday night at home on the sofa, large Irish whiskey and soda with back to back episodes. Makes me forget all me worries and makes me f'ing laugh as well. I suppose you have all the episodes on DVD?"

"No," Susan felt a little inadequate in the fan club stakes compared to Gerry. "Just a few, never got around to getting any more."

Gerry took the script back from her, looked at it as if it was his lover and returned it to the safety of the drawer.

"This is what I like about my job, habitual criminal, if you must know. What I like is the people you meet: killers, thieves, drug dealers and Jim Rockford fans, all in one day, makes it all interesting. Anyway, you wanted to know something about a loan shark?"

"Yeah, on the Turner Estate," Susan reminded him. She glanced at Martin; he had been so quiet she thought he might have fainted.

"Well, to be honest, young lady, I only know a couple of those low-lifes, not the sort of thing I like to get involved with, you understand. Years ago, it was a profitable little sideline but not anymore. What with pay day loans and pawn shops, the whole loan shark industry has become legit, which is not where I operate, you understand. The couple I do know work over the Brixton/Streatham part of town, none round here, if there were, I think I would've heard."

"Well, it was worth a try," Susan said, her voice disheartened. She began to doubt ever finding the loan shark without just sitting and waiting in Vicky's flat for him to turn up. When added to the drug dealer, Martin and she seemed to be going around in circles.

"Nice to have met you, lady, and you, fellow. Stick around if you want, have a game of snooker, on the house."

"Thanks, but we're working and still hoping to find the loan shark."

They walked out, crest-fallen but relieved that they at least still had all their limbs intact.

"Let's go home now," Martin suggested, "I have had far too much excitement for one day."

CHAPTER TEN

Sitting in the office alone again the next morning, Martin turned on his laptop and started to research Steve Ellis. He wanted to find out as much as he could about his old school friend. Since their shared schooldays, he'd had little contact with him. The web produced precious little about Steve, apart from some legal stories about his family business going into administration. Companies house had some basic stuff about Steve but nothing too revealing. Everything else that popped up on Google was for all the other men in the world called Steve Ellis.

Martin stopped, something had occurred to him, that he was working. This had not been the plan at all when he started the detective agency. What were the advantages of working? The office door opened and there stood a six-foot four blonde, with blue eyes, long legs and a short skirt. Now he recalled one of the advantages.

"Becky, come in, good to see you again. Sorry, Susan's not around." He was pleased to have some company for a while prior to his leaving to see Steve.

"Hello, Martin." Becky walked over to him, kissed him on both cheeks and hugged him a little longer than would normally be accepted. "I wasn't sure if she was going to be around, but you're here anyway. I thought you'd want the dirt on Derek Primm as soon as possible."

She sat down at Susan's desk and pulled out a manilla envelope from her large handbag. She paused with the envelope in her hand and looked at Martin in a wistful manner.

"I'm so, so sorry, Martin. Life can be so cruel at times to such a loving and kind person; my heart truly goes out to you. Mwah!" she blew a kiss across the desk to him.

"Sorry, Becky, you have somewhat lost me there."

"You and Jenny, divorce can be such a terrible thing."

"Still not totally clear about what you mean exactly, but I am now getting the gist."

"Jenny leaving you for her husband, so terrible! Frankly, I think she is being totally disloyal to you and doing womankind a disservice that taints our reputation."

Martin rubbed the back of his neck as he tried to interpret what Becky was getting at. "Becky, you do understand that she was having an affair. Taking that into account, technically, she is regaining her loyalty. And she would need to have married me first before she could divorce me."

Becky pulled some papers out of the envelope and laid them carefully on the desk in front of her, then she spent a moment arranging them into some sort of order. An order that she alone understood.

"Just man-made barriers to true love. She clearly loved you but decided, rightly or wrongly, to go back to her husband. I guess it all ends happily ever after, all except for you that is. Where is Susan today, what's she up to? Or is her arrival expected soon?"

Martin delayed responding, simply to take time to make some sort of sense of what Becky was saying. He just could not keep up with her reasoning, so decided to just answer her.

"She is visiting a woman, all to do with this case. I use the word case; it is more a set of odd circumstances I find myself in."

"That is so much like Susan, always trying to help. If anyone can convince Jenny to return to you, Susan can."

"No Becky, the situation is connected to Derek Primm, the guy I asked you about."

A deep frown formed across Becky's forehead, interrupted by wisps of her blonde hair. "Is he involved with Jenny as well? I am starting to develop an exceptionally low opinion of Jenny, maybe you are better off without her after all."

"No, let us put Jenny to one side for the moment and talk about Derek Primm's bank accounts."

"Trust me, Martin, it is hard to put to one side someone you have loved. I too have been hurt in that cost centre of life. The accounts just did not balance, and my heart was left in deficit."

Martin was fast becoming convinced that it would have been a lot easier to ask Derek himself about his financial situation. Then, as if a switch had been turned on, Becky looked intensely down at the sheets of paper she had laid out. Martin anticipated he was now going to get some answers. He was wrong.

"Do you know that these Manilla envelopes come all the way from the Philippines. They must make an awful lot there."

"Derek Primm?" Martin did not want to begin an abstract dialogue about stationery.

"Oh yes," she picked up one of the sheets. "Interesting, the accounts that you get from Companies House paint a rosy picture of his business, 'Primm Properties', sweet name, but the reality is he is nearly bankrupt. He just spends and spends, drawing off a fat salary for himself while the company is struggling to make ends meet.

"How bored do you want to be? People I know get very bored once I start drilling down into the nitty gritty of accounts and talking about accruals, pre-payments, creditors, debtors' assets and the like."

"Does he launder money?"

"No, he just has a couple of chemist shops, a restaurant and a number of properties that he rents out. No laundries."

"What I meant was, does the restaurant appear to be acting as a front for money laundering?"

"Oh, I see what you're saying now." She switched the sheet of paper in her hand, considered the columns of figures then looked up at Martin. "If he is, then he is doing a really bad job. The restaurant is not taking much money at all, and the chemists have such strict stock control, I doubt they would be a viable vehicle for money laundering.

"I would add, looking at the portfolio of his properties, and I am no expert, a lot of them look to be exaggerated in value. This helps his accounts to look better than they really are. I can tell you and I should not really tell you, but accountants are the very worst. Ask them what two plus two equals and they will say, 'what do you want them to equal?'. In a nutshell Primm Properties is on the verge of collapse."

"What about if he sells a chunk of his property to the council for redevelopment. Would a large cash injection help the company?"

"It would be interesting to see if he gets what he has valued it at in his accounts. It could be awkward for him if he gets less. But I see what you are saying and yes, it would help. Although he does not appear to be very good at business, so in my opinion, he would only be delaying the inevitable."

Becky put the sheet of figures back onto the desk, then started to gather them all up as if she had finished her report on Derek Primm. Then she added,

"You need to ventilate, Martin, that's what you need. It will help you get over Jenny."

"Ventilate?"

"Yes, let's go for a drink and a laugh. It'll do you good and it will be a nice way of saying thank you to me for getting the low down on Derek Primm."

"Go for a drink? It is only ten-thirty, a little early, don't you think?"

"I never took you as a law-breaker."

"What?"

"Well, Martin, technically the law allows twenty-four-hour drinking in the UK, so all I am suggesting is that we act like good law-abiding citizens and have a drink."

"The law might allow it, but that does not make it compulsory."

"Martin, you are a private investigator not a lawyer, don't try and understand the law, just go along with the spirit of it. Grab your coat and we'll pop along to that 'All Bar One' that is fortunately around the corner and we'll get Jenny out of your system."

***

"You look smart, new coat?" Susan asked Colin as they walked up the single flight of grubby stone stairs, and onto the stained walkway that led to Flossie's red front door. Colin was wearing a honey-coloured Boucle coat over his skinny jeans. The coat was unbuttoned and revealed the lilac floral print top that he wore underneath.

"Do you like it? I got it in the Dorothy Perkins sale, bit of a bargain if I do say so myself." He twirled around as they arrived at the door. "Wasn't sure if it was a bit too old-fashioned for me, then I thought, sod it, I'm in my sixties, better to look old-fashioned than look like mutton dressed as lamb."

Flossie was not pleased to see them. They could see that clearly from her face and the way she greeted them, using three 'not nice words' as Colin pointed out to her. Despite the hostility, he pushed his way past her and walked through the hall into what would have been described as a living room when the place was first built. Flossie described it as her day room; the room in which she spent all day watching television, smoking and calling friends. The discarded takeaway containers were testament to the fact she ate all her meals in this room as well.

Colin and Susan wisely stood and looked down at Flossie as she sat on her scruffy, cracked faux leather sofa which would have appeared stained were it not disguised by its dark brown colour. She lit a cigarette, leaned back and asked,

"So, what now, is yer moll arranging another raid on me?"

"From what I've heard, Flossie, you are up and running again. I know nothing much stands in the way of you and making a few quid on the side. You are clever and resourceful enough to find another supplier should you be careless and lose one. I, and my kind friend here, Suzie Baby, now accept that unless you end up marrying a millionaire, which is highly unlikely given the shortage of them on this estate, you'll be selling little pills until they take you out of here in a wooden box. What we want to know from you is just who it is that turns up here once a week and hands over a quantity of prescription pills to you, 'sans prescription' so to speak."

"Sands prescription?"

"Don't worry yourself, Flossie, we just want a name and should it turn out that he has broken the law, then there might be a little hiatus in your operation here, but I am sure you'll soon have it back on track."

"Why should I help yer?"

"Because, Flossie, I can make life extremely hard for you. Regular visits from my friends in uniform will not help your business and they will point out things like the parcels over there." He nodded towards a group of maybe six or seven brown cardboard boxes, all with address labels on. "I doubt any of them are actually addressed to you at this flat, possibly an empty flat around the corner, but certainly not your address. Trust me, Flossie, haven't I always done the best for you in the past. Now I want a favour back; who is giving you the pills?"

Flossie stubbed her cigarette out in a foil takeaway container, which looked as though it still had some rice in it. She then picked up an open can of Red Bull from under the sofa, took a large gulp from it and started to speak.

"I ain't no grass Mr Higgins, but yer dun me good in the past, so I best help yer. He calls himself Gary, but I bet yer it ain't his real name. Posh sounding geezer. Pops in once a week and hands over a few boxes of pills to me. Too bloody early in the morning, if yer ask me, always before nine, I mean I 'ave to set me alarm. I pay him for the stuff and off he toddles. That's all I know about him. Yer know what it's like, Mr Higgins, best not ask too many questions of these people."

"How did you meet him in the first place?" Susan asked, feeling a little left out of the conversation.

"You can have a seat, if yer want?"

"We don't want," Colin said firmly. "We want to know how you met this Gary."

"I'd been doin' me pills for a while; telling the doctors a few porkies about me bad back and they give me the pills. I then sell 'em to me friends. Now yer know that's only gonna last so long before the doctor begins to ask questions, and yer can only go to so many of them before they start talking to each other. As I couldn't get all me stuff, I had to do some other bits and bobs to get a few quid, help me benefits. That's when this Gary guy turns up."

"What other stuff are we talking about?" Susan asked innocently, feeling she was missing the point.

"Suzie Baby, if I tell you, try not to picture it. I am guessing Flossie hands out relief to local men."

"Urgh!"

"I told you not to picture it. Right Flossie, this guy was presumably one of your customers. Posh speaking so not local then. How come he ended up selling you pills? Was that some sort of post-coitus pillow talk?"

Susan shuddered, still unable to push the mounting images of Flossie and her men to one side.

"Not really, Mr Higgins, he sees the empty pill boxes in the waste bin and says to me, 'you in a lot of pain or selling the stuff?' Well, having just given him his doings, I thought he can't be a copper, so tells him I sell the stuff and ask if he wants some. He says, 'no, but I can get you as much as you want'. Well, it was like Christmas. The next week he turns up with a plastic bag full of stuff; he even gives me the first batch on credit. He's been coming here ever since."

Colin began to button up his coat. "Interesting, this guy must have read one of your postcards in the newsagent, if that's how you advertise your service." Flossie nodded in agreement. "Popped in to see you and then a stroke of luck, if you'll excuse the pun, sees a way of making a few pounds himself. What does he look like?"

"I dunno really. He's a bloke. Never really look at me customers, and in the morning I'm too knackered to really notice him. Youngish, average height, normal sort of bloke, not fat or thin, just a normal bloke."

Colin and Susan stood at the bottom of the grubby stairs pleased to be out in the fresh air again. They looked at each other, then Colin spoke, "Well, a posh, average bloke who likes a bit of rough, not a lot to go on, but it is something."

"Maybe Martin has found out a bit more about Steve. I'll text him see if he's finished; he can maybe give us a lift back to the office. I can't imagine him getting the train to Lewisham."

***

The sound reminded Becky of a teaspoon being tapped on the edge of a tin, in fact, it was the metallic chime that emitted from Martin's mobile phone as it lay on the table beside his glass. She watched as he collected up the telephone and read the message. She saw his cute eyes move over the text, the phone in one hand, the fingers on his other hand fiddling with his ear lobe.

"Susan is wondering how I got on with Steve and wants a lift from Lewisham." He placed his phone on the table, picked up his glass and took a sip of the cocktail, which was a little too sweet for him. He had planned to have a simple beer, but Becky had convinced him he should be more adventurous and try a cocktail, which she assured him would count towards one of his five-a-day, thus helping him to keep healthy. He quickly realised that the

Candy Pink Fizz was not for him, even if it did contain some fruit-flavoured syrup, he was still not fully convinced doctors would consider it to be part of a healthy diet. "She will be a little disappointed on both counts, I suspect," he added.

"Pass your phone over here, Martin; I'll be your P.A. for a while and reply to Susan."

He would have turned down Becky's offer, had it not been for the two Ginatonics, the first being raspberry and peach, the second: watermelon and orange, that he had consumed before the Candy Pink Fizz. Martin's judgement was now clouded either by the sudden consumption of surrogate fruit or the genuine alcohol, he was not totally sure which. Foolishly, he handed his phone over to Becky.

Becky spoke the words as she typed, "There has been a new development. Becky on the job with me -smiley emoji- following up on a legal thingy in All Bar One."

"Becky, I do not use those emoji symbols and would never say the word thingy in my texts."

She pressed the send button and handed the phone back to Martin. "Well, you are just going to have to learn."

"Tell me, Becky, have you always lived in London or do I detect a slight hint of a west country twang in your voice?"

She was surprised, and at the same time, flattered that Martin was asking about her life. She had always thought that he was not interested in other people and their lives. She waved her arm at the waitress and ordered two Peach and Mint Julep cocktails. Martin made no comment as he waited for her to answer his question.

"Any accent I have will have been picked up from my Grandpappy; he was from Truro. I was born just outside Truro; my parents divorced when I was six. I also have two brothers, so when my parents split up, they took a brother each. As they couldn't divide me up, I was handed over to my Grandpappy, who at the time lived in London and he brought me up. I think there must have been some sort of family rift, as I never saw my parents or my brothers again. And Grandpappy, who was a really good substitute dad to me, never mentioned them any more. I arrived just after the death of his wife and following that he could not settle down with anyone else. He always had a lady friend hanging around the house, but they didn't stay long. Whatever people might have said about him, I loved my Grandpappy and he was always kind, loving and considerate to me."

Martin tasted his Mint Julep cocktail, which he rather liked on account of the large measure of bourbon in the glass. "Your parents and brothers, you've never ever seen them since you were a child; have you ever tried to trace them?"

"Mmm, I'm liking this mint tulip thing. No, never bothered. I was six, Martin, when they let me go and neither of my parents ever once came to see me, so naturally I didn't see my brothers either. Grandpappy always avoided talking about them. It's not as though I was close to any of them, I was a little kid when they split up, I barely recall what they even looked like."

"Do you still live with your grandfather?"

"No, he died when I was sixteen. I had just finished my exams and he dropped dead. Me, being the only relative or friend that he had, I had to get to grips with all his affairs, which fortunately were not a lot, we were pretty poor."

"Well, at least you had his house to fall back on."

"Come on, Martin, we don't all have money and houses. I lived with him in a rented flat above a grocery shop. All he left me were a number of debts and a collection of Doris Day records, neither of which were any good for me."

"Sixteen and homeless, what happened, were you taken into care or something?"

Becky leaned across and held Martin's hand, she smiled broadly. "Ah, Martin, you are so sweet and caring; I didn't think you had it in you. Thankfully, I did not end up in care. I stayed with a school friend for a while; her parents were kind to me. My luck changed when I was at the bank sorting out Grandpappy's debts, which the bank was not keen to write off. The bank manager was impressed with my grasp of figures, always been good at maths I have, so he offered me a job, would you believe. Plus, he helped me secure my first flat. My own place, I was really proud of that."

"He sounds a nice chap, the bank manager."

"Not really, he also helped me lose my virginity, but that didn't last long. I mean the affair with him, not my virginity, although I suppose...well, moving on. He got the sack for dipping into people's savings. But he had given me a good job at the bank, I had my own flat, what did I care?"

The metallic notification on Martin's phone chimed out. Martin picked up the mobile, he smiled, emptied his glass and held the phone towards Becky.

"I think Susan has worked out it was you writing the message. I told you no smiley faces; I stick to pure English. Susan says, 'Becky, can't you do anything without drink and screwing around?' We're not screwing around, are we?"

"I wish," Becky whispered to herself.

Martin put his phone back into his inside jacket pocket. He felt a touch lightheaded, he now regretted not sticking to beer. "It is just not right, Becky, a horrible old man taking advantage of you, forcing you to do things against your will, you must feel like a victim?"

"Grow up, Martin, and stop being so naïve. He was young, good looking, and terrific in bed, for me a result all round."

"You do have an interesting viewpoint on life. For now, I think I should get back to the office and get a cab down to see Stevie boy, my mate, as I am in no fit condition to drive." Martin stood, placing his hands on the table to steady himself a little

"Sit down, Martin, just one more before you go. Have you ever tasted a Long Island Iced Tea? If not, you have not lived, it totally lights up the whole afternoon."

Martin slumped back onto the chair, "Well, if it is tea then just one won't hurt."

***

Colin carefully examined his plain red nail polish. He was very much a traditionalist when it came to his nails; simple nail varnish applied with a simple brush. He would not be caught dead in one of those ostentatious nail bars, where women spent hours and pounds to have appalling creations affixed to their nails. He hated such places. The downside of shaping and protecting your own nails was that invariably one gets chipped. Today, it was the one on the middle finger on his right hand and it had left a jagged edge on it. He was sure that Suzie Baby would have an emery board in her handbag. He would have asked her for it, but for the fact that she was in the middle of an entertaining argument with Becky.

It reminded him of those domestics that he often had to attend when he was a police officer. Now, as it was then, alcohol was a major contributory factor. Colin had to laugh, when Becky and Martin walked into the office, clearly having had a little too much to drink. He held back when he saw the expression on Suzie Baby's face. She was not a happy bunny. He could not be totally sure if she was getting 'out of her pram' because both her and himself had to get a train back from Lewisham, or if it was because Martin and Becky had been out drinking together; Colin suspected it was the latter. Suzie Baby, he knew, could be the jealous type, especially where Martin was concerned.

"The trouble with you, Becky, is you're a vulture. A dyed blonde vulture who preys on vulnerable men. I tell you all about Martin and then you pounce when he is not himself. Martin is really down about Jenny, which I know might surprise someone like you, but I know he is hurting inside," Susan shouted across the office, ignoring the fact that Martin was listening.

Colin liked the way Suzie Baby just spoke without thinking. She spoke from her heart, pure honesty and no room for any sort of diplomacy. Recalling their first meeting, he was glad he had intervened outside that night club when she was being harassed by a drunken lout. It was the first time he had used everything he had learnt as a police officer since the force decided a detective dressed as a woman was not what they really wanted.

Leaving the force and his wife leaving him had been dark days for Colin. Even when he tried to occupy his time volunteering or helping in the community, his dress code was not as widely acceptable as he had hoped. Then he had gone to the aid of Suzie Baby. Suzie Baby, who was facing a choice of getting a job or sleeping with her landlord to keep a roof over her head. He helped her, that was what he liked to do, help people. That was the reason he had joined the Police Force in the first place. He had helped her to get the job with Martin's detective agency and suddenly he had a chance to bring his experience and help out with that too. Once again, he was getting up in the morning and having a purpose to his life.

"Well, at least I make an effort to help," Becky retorted. "You just holler at people and tell them to get on with it, whereas I am compassionate and caring."

"The only thing you care about is getting laid, getting pissed and getting on people's tits."

Colin thought that Suzie Baby should try and slow down a bit and think a little before she spoke. The downside of that was she would be nowhere near as entertaining.

"At least I can get laid, and in any race to lay a man, I'd win hands down, as I have done in the past and will do in the future." Becky bluntly and unkindly reminded Susan.

Colin decided that it was time to step in, cool things down a little and let everyone get on with their lives, or at least try to sort out the two problems they had: Vicky and her loan shark, Martin and his twin car. He stood up and placed himself between the warring women.

"Ladies, Ladies, Ladies, I think we should all focus on the job in hand. Helping Vicky get clear of this loan shark is a lot more important than who is sleeping with who and in what order. Can I also bring to your attention that tomorrow Flossie gets her delivery, that will be a good time to confront the drug dealer once and for all. What I am saying is, it will be a good time to put this all to bed instead of each other." He paused for a moment, there was silence in the office. He then continued, "I have also found the address of the phone operator of the chat line Vicky is earning from. I suggest that Suzie Baby and I go off and visit the said operator to see if he matches the description of the loan shark. Martin should wander back home and have some black coffee; cocktails clearly are not your thing. And Becky, I know Martin wants you to look into the bank accounts of Steve the estate agent, well, if you could toddle off and do that, I think we, as a team, can make lots of progress."

Colin had a presence, even dressed in a floral blouse. Becky did toddle off, Susan and Colin left Martin in the office alone. Martin promised he would have the coffee first then wander home.

Martin finished the black coffee that he had made, promising himself that cocktails were, as Colin had pointed out, not for him. He even considered, at one point, that if Becky ever invited him out for a drink again, he would take a rain check on her offer. He might have told himself that today, but he knew that on another day, he would find it difficult to turn the offer down. He was washing his cup in the kitchen when he heard the office door click open. He turned and there in the doorway stood Jenny.

CHAPTER ELEVEN

Susan and Colin stood outside the address that Colin had written down as belonging to Brandt Information Telephone Services. It was plainly a dry-cleaning shop with windows that were screened by condensation. Colin examined the scruffy door alongside the steamy windows and there, affixed to the door frame, was a tarnished brass plaque that had seen better days. Brandt Information Telephone Services was located above the shop. He pushed the door, which was unlocked and walked up the dimly lit stairs. Susan followed him up, helped by the butterflies in her stomach.

Once at the top, they found themselves on a dusty landing with a grimy threadbare carpet, which had a distinctly sticky feel as they walked on it. Three doors led off the dimly lit landing, two marked private and the third indicated by way of a plastic sign that the 'Chief Executive' resided within. Colin and Susan looked at each other, a look that asked the silent question, 'shall we go in?' Colin knocked once then without waiting for an answer, he opened the door.

The Chief Executive's office at Brandt Information Telephone Services consisted of a single rectangular room. Along the left-hand wall were six dark-grey filing cabinets. The right-hand wall was dominated by a large grubby window that looked out onto the street. Below the window was a table on which stood a kettle together with all the paraphernalia required for teamaking as well as an open packet of chocolate Hobnobs. Hanging in the air was a strong chemical odour which seeped up from the dry-cleaning shop below.

"Can I help you?"

The voice came from the other side of a large mahogany desk that was directly in front of them. The desk had a computer screen on the left and another on the right; in between the two screens was the source of the question. A man stood up. Well, Susan assumed he had stood up, he was short, noticeably short. He came out from behind the desk; Susan doubted he could stretch across it to shake hands. He stood in front of them and yes, Susan was correct, he was short. He was also fat, his girth almost equal to his height. His shape reminded Susan of a chocolate creme egg. He wore faded jeans and a washed-out AC-DC, 1975 High Voltage Tour tee shirt. He had yellowed teeth and wore small rounded frameless glasses. His hair was grey, very thin on top, but grown long at the back where it emerged a little thicker from his head. This grey straggly hair was pulled and tied behind him in a ponytail, not a good look for a man in his sixties, Susan decided.

"We're looking for the person who runs Brandt Information Telephone Services?" Colin asked.

The short man in the ponytail with the fat body and unusually thin legs offered his hand to Colin and smiled.

"That'll be me, Aldi Brandt, my company I call BITS, not so much of a mouthful. What can I do for you?"

"Aldi," Susan repeated, "like the supermarket?"

He gave her a creepy look before he answered, "Yes, although I should point out to you that it is only a nickname. It was given to me by my school chums back in Germany where I once lived. My real name is Aldus, German for older boy. But they thought it hilarious to call me by the name of a supermarket; it has just stuck with me ever since. Looking for work, Miss? Please take a seat." He pulled two very upright wooden dining chairs from the tea table and placed them in front of his desk, before scuttling back to his own swivel chair.

Once they had settled themselves Colin spoke, "Well, Mr Brandt."

"Call me Aldi, no point being formal," he interrupted with a smile as he started to roll himself a cigarette.

"Aldi," Colin continued, "your company, BITS, am I right in thinking it is a sex chat line?"

Aldi licked the edge of the cigarette paper and then finished rolling it before finally tapping the end on his desk. "I would describe it as a premium line providing a valuable service for gentlemen and some ladies, I should add. I am completely legal and run, I like to think, an honest and fair service. I even deal with complaints from some of my customers, which overall they do not often make. One example from the other day was when a gentleman rang up to complain that he had been put on hold and ended up listening to music for ten minutes before he put the phone down. I, of course, refunded him his money. You see I am just an honest businessman earning a living." He lit the small roll-up and blew the smoke high above his head, which was at eye-level for Colin and Susan.

"But your girls, tell me, how do you find them?" Colin asked

"Generally, word of mouth. Occasionally, when I am running short of freelance employees, I put an ad somewhere. Are both, or either of you, thinking of volunteering your services? The percentage of the call I offer is generous compared to other providers. Plus," he eyed Colin up and down, "I am intrigued to wonder just how a transvestite line might go down, unless you're gay as well that is, that could seriously increase your earnings."

"Neither of us want to work your sordid telephone lines." Susan decided it was time to step in. "We're here to ask you about Vicky Connell and exactly how much she owes you, and when she'll pay back her debt."

Susan had no real idea that the short man in front of her was the loan shark; he certainly did not match Vicky's description, but such inconsistencies never held her back from speaking.

"Ah, Vicky Connell, which is a strange coincidence because she was the one who put the caller on hold and played him music for ten minutes. She was not forthcoming about the reason she did that. Are you here to stick up for her, because if you are, then I think you are being inconsiderate? I told her I would overlook it this time, but next time I would deduct the call from her payment. You can't be fairer than that."

"But what about what she owes you?" Susan continued.

"Owes me? No, I pay them. She came in about a year ago and signed up. To be honest, she has a good number of paying regulars. She gets sixty percent of the call and I take the other forty percent, which is very generous by industry standards. I can tell you Vicky is on a nice little earner."

This time Colin asked a question beating Susan, who had been about to voice the same one. "Vicky came to you?"

"Yes, as I told you. About a year ago, one of my other girls pointed her in my direction and hey presto, she now works for me and makes a reasonable income. If she's not declaring it then that's up to her. I tell all my girls to tell the benefits people and the tax man, but to be honest, I doubt they all do."

"But what about this loan shark she is indebted to?" Susan asked, trying to make sense of what he was telling them.

"No idea. If the silly girl has got herself into trouble with a loan shark, then I can't be held responsible. Let's not forget, I need those girls as much as they need me, so it is in my interest to treat them well. Are you both friends of hers?"

"You could say that" Susan replied. "But why should we take your word for it?" she asked, her head starting to feel a little light from the fumes that seeped up from the shop below.

"My dear Fraulein, I am German, we like to do things the right way, correctly. And look at me, a man in my sixties, not a physical giant, do you think I would ever consider getting involved in the seedier side of life? No, I am happy to pay my way, pay my taxes, and happiest of all when my girls and boys are making some extra cash for themselves. As we say in Germany, 'alle sind glücklich', everyone is happy."

***

Jenny walked towards Martin's desk, set her two Bruce Oldfield shopping bags down and slumped into his chair. Martin looked at her as if she was a mirage.

"Sit down, Martin, we need to talk."

As instructed Martin sat down opposite Jenny in Susan's chair.

"To what do I owe the pleasure?" he started with a smile.

"Trust me, Martin, this is not going to be a pleasure, far from it. Have you been drinking? Your breath reeks."

"Yes, a liquid lunch. So, what is not going to be a pleasure?"

Jenny unbuttoned her coat. She regretted wearing such a heavy one, but the wind had been bitter in the morning when she had left her house and the weather had now tempered.

"Martin, as you know this prestigious office space that you currently occupy was acquired by me for you as a favour, as at the time you and I were awfully close. I had to pull several strings and cash in a few favours in order to secure this office space without my husband being fully aware of what I was doing, which was of course, giving you rent-free office space.

"I achieved this no mean feat, by working very closely with my husband's personal assistant, an obnoxious little man. Nevertheless, he played around with the paperwork and managed to portray this office space as some sort of charitable donation which offered some tax relief, pleasing my husband no end, I would guess.

"Part of the arrangement I made with the obnoxious personal assistant was that I would, from time to time when Ian was not around, sign cheques without looking too closely at the paperwork, which overall was complex and I understood very little of anyway. Obviously, I imagine he is fleecing my husband and fraudulently taking money out of the company which I now, given my refreshed relationship with my husband, want to stop.

"What I need you to do for me, Martin, is to write to Ian, my husband, and tell him that your so-called charity needs to move to larger premises elsewhere, or whatever excuse you would like to come up with. Thank him for his help allowing the office rent-free and wish him well. Once you've gone, I'll out the little shit who is stealing money from my husband's company."

"You want me to move out of here?"

"Yes, Martin, that is exactly it. Look at it like our relationship, it was good while it lasted but now is the time to move on. It is not as though you have a thriving business here after all it's only a refuge to escape from your overbearing mother."

"Do I have a choice?"

"No, Martin, you have no choice. I want you to write the letter tonight giving up your tenancy of this office. I'm sure you'll find somewhere equally suitable to carry on avoiding your mother and your recreational detecting."

He watched Jenny rebutton her coat, collect up her bags, and make her way towards the door. She stopped as she opened it and turned back to him. "It was fun Martin, while it lasted, but times change, and people change. I wish you well." She closed the door behind her. Martin sat alone in the office, knowing that the end of Martin Hayden Investigations was on the horizon.

CHAPTER TWELVE

Martin recalled a time, not too long ago, when his days would include ambling around the house for most of the morning before catching up with some friend or other for lunch. In the afternoon, maybe a bit of shopping before an evening event somewhere in town: a pre-theatre drink, an art gallery launch, or just a simple dinner with friends. Never, in his wildest dreams, did he ever imagine sitting in his car at eight o' clock on a chilly Wednesday morning with a transvestite in the back and a female alongside him reciting his horoscope.

If that was not bad enough, he was parked in a part of south London he had never even heard of until last week. Apparently Susan was, through the medium of astrology, assuring him things were going to get better. He hoped they would; they could not get any worse, could they?

The plan of action had been concocted last night. He suspected that Colin and Susan drew up the plan and just hijacked him when he was off-guard at home moping with a bottle of red wine. He guessed that Susan would be the acting general-in-charge laying down the strategy.

It was going to be a two-pronged approach. Susan had already called Vicky, telling her they were going to pop in as they had some news about the loan shark, which she explained to Martin was not true. What with the early morning and all the alcohol he had consumed yesterday, Martin was struggling to keep up with what that was supposed to accomplish. Prior to seeing Vicky, the second prong of attack was to wait outside Flossie's flat ready to ambush the other Honda car with its drug dealer and catch him red-handed. Through his fog, Martin thought that sounded a reasonable idea.

Last night he had not considered the implications of what eight o' clock in the morning might feel like and certainly had not worked out that he would need to pick up Susan at six forty-five in the morning, and Colin just after seven.

"The ears of your co-workers may prick up when you express your plans for ambitious new ventures that rapidly make your business grow." Susan looked at Martin as she shared his daily horoscope. "Well that sounds like bad news for you, as I know you're not keen on finding new business, but it's in the stars, Martin, expect lots of cases to investigate."

Martin had not told anyone about Jenny's visit yesterday. He had written the letter as she had requested and emailed it to her husband last night. He wanted to find the right time to tell Susan that she was going to be out of a job and he knew that was not going to be an easy conversation to have with her.

"Your turn, Colin, looks a good one: 'Scrutinize the current company you're keeping and decide if this is a pattern you want to keep or throw to the curb.'"

"The pattern of early mornings you can bloody well stuff for a start." Colin, like Martin, was clearly not a morning person.

"Shut up and pay attention; I'm not finished yet. 'Dig deeply and the truth will burst like a geyser from the earth. Consider what philosophies and values matter most.' I think the company you're keeping is among the best."

Martin remained sombre as both Colin and Susan bantered. Finally, he changed the subject.

"What if the drug dealer and the loan shark are one and the same person. It is not beyond the realms of possibility that they could be. I, for one, do not want to get up close and personal with a violent bloke who sounds to be a right villain."

"From my experience, I doubt it is the same person," Colin offered.

"He does sound pretty hard," Susan agreed with Martin. "Vicky reckoned he might have been a boxer once. She said he has scary, blue eyes and a mop of brown, unkempt hair. I bet he looks like an ape."

"You're wrong, Susan, he is bald."

"No, Vicky told me he had a mop of brown hair."

"Sorry Susan, you must have misheard her; too much of the fire water does that to you. She said, and I was sober at the time, bald as a bat, broken nose, a big guy."

"Well, she told me: big guy, brown hair, blue eyes, a bit on the fat side."

"I'm telling you; you are totally wrong."

Colin butted in, "Calm down, Girls. I presume that neither of you have actually seen this man in person. That being accepted, so far, we agree he is a big guy, we are just a little mixed up about the hair situation and possibly the broken nose. You need to ask Vicky when you see her later, and just please both of you listen carefully when she tells you. Remember you need her to verify not only the description of the loan shark, but also her relationship with the little German telephone operator, Herr Brandt."

"Talking of officious people, look who is coming along the road," Martin pointed out, "your friend, the traffic warden."

"Civil enforcement officer," Susan corrected as she lowered her window and greeted the traffic warden like an old friend.

"We're only waiting here for the illegal Honda that turns up each week," Susan offered as she watched the ticket whirl out of the machine before being neatly folded and placed into a plastic envelope.

"In my eyes, you have arrived, and your weekly parking ticket is about to be issued."

"What about the other one that tuns up here?"

"I'm not sure, but your blue Honda is always here about this time, just unusual to see three inside and talk to them."

Then without a further word, the civil enforcement officer affixed a parking ticket to the windscreen, took a step back and photographed the whole car before turning and walking away with a wry smile on his face.

"Your friend seems to be a little jealous that you already have a boyfriend," Colin pointed out.

"More likely a man dressed as a woman in the back of the car spooked him out; I think he might be of a nervous nature," Susan said as she leaned out of the window and removed the ticket, before handing it to Martin. Martin took the ticket and looked at her, a tired look in his eyes, it was still early for him.

"Why is it, Susan, that since you decided to try and stop the flow of parking tickets to my office, there has been an increase in the number arriving?" Martin asked knowing he was not going to get a sensible answer from her. In fact, it was Colin who spoke first.

"If you two are going to have a lover's tiff, then I'm out of here. I'm off to see Flossie; I have a funny feeling that our man in the Honda has already been. You two need to pop over and see Vicky and sort out the fog that surrounds her sex chat line and the loan shark. A description that you both agree on would be helpful.

"Plus, take your time, I'm grabbing the bus after I have seen Flossie and do a bit of shopping in Lewisham Market, they have some great fruit stalls there."

***

"How many fucking times do I need to tell you both I don't want help? I told you last night, just piss off and leave me alone!" Vicky was obviously not pleased to see Martin and Susan standing on her doorstep once more.

"You're not happy, that I understand." At first Martin sounded sympathetic, then the tone of his voice changed to one of exasperation. "But I should point out that I got up incredibly early this morning to come and see you. This is not the first time I have been here. Previously, I offered you financial help, and chased up your landlord to get the electrics fixed. I listened to my friend talk about you and your money problems, as a result of which he ended up with a community order. Now I find out that you might have volunteered to talk on the sex chat line and not been forced into it as you told us. You see, I am in no mood to walk away. I've come this far, this early. Now we are all going upstairs, and you are going to tell me the truth, the whole truth, and nothing but the truth about your sex chat line."

Clearly, Susan thought to herself, Martin's mood does not warm up until after eleven.

The three of them sat around the squalid flat. Vicky, sitting and sulking, taking large gulps from her cracked tea mug emblazoned with a large smiley face, which was the opposite of the atmosphere in the room.

"That's exactly what he told me, so one of you is lying," Susan concluded, having explained in detail the conversation she'd had with Aldi Brandt. Vicky silently clung to her mug, acting like a child who had been caught with their hands in the sweet jar. "Are you the one lying?" Susan asked, trying to prompt a response. It worked.

"Alright, I did sign up to do the sex phone thing; I was just embarrassed to tell you the truth about it. I needed the money and it was an easy way of grabbing a few extra pounds to help me through and pay back the loan shark. I told you before, it's bloody hard being on my own, paying the rent, buying food, having some nice clothes to wear; it all costs money and the benefits aren't much at all.

"I have never been given a chance to better myself. Every time I try, I get knocked back. So there comes a time when you just think to yerself, sod it, this is my life until I die. There is no magic formula, no knight in shining armour who is going to come and rescue me; I'm here for the long haul. So, a few extra quid goes a long way to help."

"Thanks for being up front at last, Vicky, we are only trying to help you. About the loan shark, can you run over what he looks like again? Martin and I have different versions of what you have told us."

Vicky banged her mug hard on the coffee table. The lukewarm, milky tea shot up out of the mug and splashed over the wooden table. Vicky ignored the mess.

"What's this, a fucking interrogation? You're not the feds; you're just a couple of do-gooders having a laugh at how the other half live."

Susan wanted to get up and slap Vicky. Martin had a more measured response, which Susan appreciated given what time of the morning it was.

"Vicky, you have lied once; I suspect you are being untruthful again. If you are, I wonder why you feel the need to lie about loan sharks and being forced into chat lines."

"Why would I lie, smart arse?"

"Because fortune has sent you a knight in shining armour called Paul who I am guessing, after hearing your made-up sob story, helps you make ends meet."

"Paul's a weak prick; I asked him to tell you not to come today and he couldn't even manage that."

"But being weak, I am sure you convinced him to offer a few pounds to help you out."

Vicky stood up and turned away from them looking out of the window. She watched the street, alive with people going about their business. She started to speak as she continued to stare out of the rain-stained window.

"I told you, I signed up for the chat line last year and it helps me out. It doesn't make me rich, but it helps. Then I bump into Paul, and he with his posh voice and nice clothes starts chatting to me, takes an interest in me. He helped me avoid getting done for shoplifting; that makes him a nice chap in my book. But he has loads of money and comes from a posh family. He has no idea about finding some cash to charge up the electric card or pay for something more than fish fingers and chips. So, I just mentioned that I owed some money to a not nice person and he helps me to make the payments to the loan shark."

"I presume we are talking about an imaginary loan shark?" Martin asked.

"Yeah. I only take fifty quid a week off him. I told him it's best not to pay the shark off in one go or they'll come back for more. As you said, he is a weak prick, so it's easy to weasel some cash out of him."

"Is that why you refused the two thousand pounds I offered you?"

"It worried me; I thought it might be some sort of trick and I didn't want to be greedy. I was happy with Paul's money, at least it was regular. What would I have done with a couple of grand? Blown it in a week or so and be right back here by the end of the month. I told you, I'm a lost cause; nothing good will ever come of me. I suppose you're gonna tell him."

"Of course we are, he's our friend and you're a leech. Come on Susan, I think it's time we left."

CHAPTER THIRTEEN

"This is not a restaurant, Susan, it is a box, an overrated box at that."

Martin looked up at the peeling sign above of what was a ridiculously small shop unit alongside Catford Bridge station. In the colours of the Jamaican flag, the shop name: 'Jamaican Inn' was colourful and patriotic.

Susan had promised to treat Martin to lunch at a restaurant she knew, having dined there once after a raucous night out with the girls. It was her way of saying thank you to him for getting up so early. He should have known that Susan's recall and description of the restaurant would have been seriously clouded by the amount of alcohol she had likely consumed prior to eating there.

Things became even more confused for Martin when he asked what he considered to be a reasonable question, 'what sort of menu do they have?' Of course, he meant was it an extensive menu with a lot of choice or was there a special lunchtime menu, also if they served wine. Normal questions he would associate with dining out. He was tired, so had not really thought the question through with as much vigour as he should have done. Standing outside an overrated box, which Susan had earlier described as a pleasant restaurant, he hoped that the frontage was merely the small entrance to a larger restaurant that lay behind the peeling sign. He should have known better.

"There is no menu. It depends on what the bloke is cooking today."

This reply from a relaxed Susan did nothing to endear Martin to the Jamaican Inn, but he followed her through the door.

Martin's hope of a larger, concealed dining area was soon dashed when it turned out to be even smaller inside than it had looked from the outside. As he stepped into the restaurant, which he now would describe as a poky take-away, he almost walked straight into the chest-high counter that partitioned the shop in two. The customer side had just enough room for a Bob Marley poster, a large chilled drinks cabinet and a small table with two chairs against the window. Martin had thought the fish and chip shop was cramped, he now realised how wrong he had been. There was just about enough room for about three or four people to stand in the shop waiting to be served, but there was little chance of a horde of customers piling through the door.

Behind the high counter, wearing a big smile and a woolly Rastafarian hat, stood a man with large biceps that strained against the cook's overalls he was wearing. Susan, as ever, stood up to the mark while Martin looked around with an expression of bewilderment on his face.

"First time in a Caribbean restaurant?" she asked.

Martin turned to her, "What do you think?"

"I'll do the ordering then." Susan now sported a bigger grin than the Rastafarian waiting to take their order.

They sat eating at the one table where passers-by could see them. Martin wondered if eating in a shop window was normal across all south London or just the places Susan frequented. In front of him on a polythene plate was a pile of what looked like a lamb stew. It was accompanied by, what had been described by Susan, as rice and peas. Now Martin felt he had a fair knowledge of the vegetable family and could identify most species. He looked at the rice and peas and knew with a degree of certainty that it was rice with red kidney beans, not peas. If that was the case, the rice dish being misrepresented, then the chances were that the stew was not going to be made with lamb either. Next to his polythene plate was a brown bottle of Supermalt; he wasn't sure if he should drink it or if it was a sauce to pour over his meal.

"Susan, did you not say this was rice and peas?"

She finished her mouthful before answering. Susan never hesitated when it came to food, whatever the country of origin. "Yeah, rice and peas with meat curry."

Martin poked his meal absently with his plastic fork. "Ah, it is a curry then, not a stew. But these are not peas, they are red kidney beans."

"Yeah."

"So why is it called rice and peas?"

"I don't know, why is toad in the hole called toad in the hole? There are no toads in it, are there? If it tastes good, I don't really care what it's called. Eat up, Martin, enjoy it, it's my treat." She stopped talking to take a large mouthful of curry and rice.

Susan watched Martin load his fork and sample the curry. She waited. He moved the food over his taste buds, then nodded at her and swallowed.

"Nice and spicy, a lot better than I thought it might be. Should I ask what sort of meat this might be or is that not a question I want answered?"

Susan lubricated her throat with the Supermalt. Confirming to Martin it was a drink, glad he had not sprinkled it over his food.

"Well as I said, every day he does something different depending on what is looking good in the market. I reckon this is goat's meat, common enough in these places."

Martin took another mouthful before he concluded, "This is good! The last time I had curried goat was at some foreign embassy event I attended with my father. That curry was bland and insipid, although to be fair the rice came without any veg."

"I guess on real plates as well," Susan added.

"And cloth napkins."

"You could always ask, but I am guessing all his cloth napkins are at the cleaners."

Martin laughed and that was why he did not really mind where Susan took him. Wherever they ended up there always seemed to be a laugh or two along the way. He was going to miss her. The notice period on the office was just thirty days. He would, of course, make sure she was financially secure until she found herself another job; that was the right thing to do. He liked to do the right thing and now that meant telling her about Jenny's visit. Before he could, Susan asked,

"Martin, do you think it will be better coming from you? You know, telling Paul that his sweet girlfriend has been stringing him along to get cash out of him. Don't suppose he will be too pleased, although you never know, if he's getting his leg over a few times a week, he might just continue, he's got the money after all."

"I have not told you yet," Martin ignored Susan's question, "Jenny paid a visit to the office yesterday after you and Colin left."

"Has she changed her mind?"

"Far from it. She has decided that the arrangement I have with the office must come to an end. I have given them notice that I am leaving. I'm so sorry Susan, but Hayden Investigations will no longer exist. Without a base, we can't really carry on. I will, of course, ensure that you do not lose out money wise, and I'll give you stunning references and do everything I can to help you find another job. I'm just sorry that it is all over."

Susan beamed. "Yeah right, you're telling me this 'cause you're fed up of all the strange places I take you to eat; I'll let you choose next time. Somewhere with cloth napkins, I guess."

Then she looked at Martin's face. It was not a joke. In her head she repeated what he had said to her: 'Hayden Investigations will no longer exist'. Whatever way she replayed those words, the meaning ended up the same. Her sudden change of expression told Martin she was now taking him seriously.

"What was meant to be just a ruse to ensure I continued to receive my monthly allowance, turned out to be a lot more fun than I ever imagined. Fun only because you joined the firm," Martin smiled out of politeness, not emotion.

"Wow!" Susan broke her silence. "That is a bombshell. But does it really mean the end of Hayden Investigations and us? There must be other cheap offices around we can make use of. After all, you still need a ruse to hoodwink your mother. Not that I'm pleading for my job, well, I am really, I know, but not in a greedy, selfish way. I just want to keep working with you. I'm sure there is lots more we can do, investigating and that sort of thing."

"Maybe, but we still need to have a base to work from."

"Or not work from, depending how we feel." Susan chuckled again.

That was just why he liked her so much. Martin was thinking doom and gloom, but Susan still could see a humorous side to the situation. "And bases cost money," Martin added.

"Yes, I guess working from home would sort of defeat the objective. Unless you locked yourself in your bedroom like some teenager."

"Locked in with you doing my dictation."

"Martin, just stop there! You have presented me with so many opportunities to be rude. I will only say, there must be lots of teenagers who would not mind being locked in their bedroom with an older woman."

"That sounds very weird indeed." Now even Martin laughed, but immediately he felt guilty. "Come on, Susan, this is serious; you will be out of a job."

Susan finished her Supermalt and leaned forward closer to Martin. "Something will come up I'm sure. Let's get your parking ticket man sorted out first, then we can turn our attention to finding an office that we can use."

"Do we need to bother; parking tickets are the least of my worries?"

"Martin, it is the principle of the matter. Plus, we should never give up just because the going gets a little tough or, in this case, confusing."

They left the Caribbean take-away and walked towards the centre of Catford, talking as they navigated the busy roads. Between them, they reviewed the little they knew about the driver of the blue Honda. Flossie had given them only the vaguest description of what he looked like: in his mid-thirties, posh voice, but apart from that, an average man. They knew he drove a Blue Honda and called once a week on Flossie to hand over a plastic bag full of prescription drugs. She had, or so she said, no phone number or any method of contacting him. That was the limit of what they knew about him. Martin decided that they should offer up candidates, but Susan pointed out it could be just about any male in the country.

"Not really, Susan. I have been thinking. Yesterday, when Steve called around to see Vicky's flat, he was not keen to come up. I thought, and you agreed, that was strange."

Susan nodded in agreement as they walked into the Catford Shopping Centre, with its mix of shops that were open and those that had ceased trading long ago. Martin continued as they sat down on a graffiti strewn bench, "I know I saw a blue Honda leave a block of flats, which I am sure Steve walked into, although I cannot be sure it was him driving. Now add those facts to what I know about Steve, who speaks posh, although I think it sounds normal, but you seem to think it is posh. I know Steve came from a rich family who liked to flaunt their wealth. So, when he lost it all as a result of being greedy, I would imagine he was not happy and would be looking at other ways to regain a small fortune. And I know that he has never been one to shy away from bending the rules to get what he wants.

"Add to the aforementioned facts, that he works in an estate agent which manages properties across this area. He'd know a lot about what goes on and might well see an opportunity for himself to make some cash. Finally, he told me that he was planning to visit Vicky the day the police were there arresting Paul. He admitted that he quickly left the area, not wanting to go into the flat. A guilty conscience?"

Susan shooed a pigeon away that was taking an unhealthy interest in her foot. "Can I add something?"

"Go ahead, what have you got?"

"Becky sent me a message about Steve's bank account which either you or Colin asked for, I forget who asked."

"Wait a minute, Becky called you. Why you, I asked her about those accounts?"

"Don't get shirty, it was actually Colin who asked her on your behalf, you having drunk a little too many cocktails with Becky. Anyway, I told her to let me know as you're a busy man. Well she told me..."

"More like you're jealous when Becky is around me."

"No, not jealous. It just seems that every time you two come anywhere near each other, you both make off to the nearest bar and get pissed."

"We have been for a drink twice, both employment-related. You're just jealous."

"Anyway, that is beside the point. She told me that Steve gets regular payments from Derek Primm, he with the loose trousers and rising shoulders."

"You're jealous," Martin pointed out again.

"If you must know, I am sure you recall that you employed me as your personal assistant, it is part of my job. Focus on the investigation, Martin. Hopefully, you will recall that Derek Primm, as well as flats and stuff, owns three chemists, a ready source of prescription drugs, I would say."

"You're still jealous." Martin smiled as he repeated his allegation.

"Martin," Susan's voice sounded exasperated, "I am not jealous of you and Becky. Why would I be? But if you are asking me for my opinion..."

"Which I am not but will nonetheless get all the same."

Susan glared at him before she continued, "...she is not your type, too much of a loose woman; your mother would certainly not approve of her."

Martin laughed, grabbed her hand and kissed her on the forehead. "God, you are such a pain in the arse at times. But not an uncomfortable pain," he added.

"I'm pleased to hear that. Now back to business, what do you propose we do about Steve?"

Martin's proposal was simple, he once again planned to go and see his old school friend, whose office was just a short drive away in Lewisham. He also added to the mounting evidence, that it would not take much effort to find out the registration number for his car. Such a move by Steve would ensure that his car would make him immune to parking tickets and the like. Steve would also know that Martin was never that bothered about such things and would just pay them assuming that he was the guilty party. Martin did not elaborate to Susan, but he did add that there was something else that was bothering him, something he hoped Steve would be able to clear up. Who paid Vicky's rent?

Susan walked back to Catford Bridge station. She planned to join Martin in the morning when they intended to break the news to Paul that his girlfriend was not as nice as she had at first seemed.

CHAPTER FOURTEEN

Martin walked into Duffield Estate Agents. The three desks that were in front of him looked the same as they had the last time he had visited. Two of them were still unoccupied but at the third, Steve sat having a telephone conversation. He gestured for Martin to take a seat.

Martin continued to stand and listened as Steve explained about the size of the security deposit required, no doubt for a flat he was hoping to let. From the side of the conversation that Martin could hear, he guessed that Steve's customer was having a great deal of difficulty understanding the concept of a deposit and the fact that he might not get it back when vacating the property.

Realising that the conversation would not be ending very soon, Martin stood and ambled over to a display of properties to let. Amongst them was some office space, or as it was described against a photograph of a contemporary looking office, 'an exciting affordable business centre for entrepreneurs.' Martin wondered if a space would still be suitable for a selfish someone hiding away from his mother. No exact rent was mentioned anywhere on the glowing overview of all the facilities the centre had to offer. Martin doubted it would be cheap enough for him.

Such was his dilemma; he had to have a job in order to secure his generous monthly allowance from the family trust. If he had to rent an expensive office, it would make a sizeable dent in his allowance, thus devaluing his income and curtailing his lifestyle, and certainly would not allow him to continue employing Susan. That is unless he actually tried to become a private detective and get paid for investigating. Whichever way he turned it meant work, something he had tried to avoid for most of his adult life.

"Sorry about that, Martin. If you're here about your friend, Vicky, my electrician called round last night and sorted her out, plus he is going back today to finish off. Have a seat; can I get you a coffee? And before you say anything, I'm sorry about yesterday, I was bang out of order. It was just old man Primm hates spending money on those flats and I was sort of stressed as to how to balance things out."

Martin refused the coffee but took up the offer of a seat. They sat looking at each other across the desk. Steve looked tense and nervous, tapping his pen against the desk. Martin wondered just where to start the conversation, finally, he decided to take the mate approach.

"Let's forget about that; I think we were all a little tense. Thank you for getting it done for me. Are you always on your own in this office?"

"Normally," Steve replied, putting the pen down and intertwining his fingers. "There are four other branches dotted around south London. The main office is based in Bromley; that's where all the big boss men are located. I just run this branch most of the time on my own. I think there used to be three staff here at one time," he looked towards the two empty desks, "but the markets aren't as buoyant as they used to be when old man Duffield started up the business."

"So, what's your connection to Derek Primm?"

"He is a customer of ours, a good customer. I look after his properties and offer advice if he needs it. I get all the complaints from his tenants, which they all seem to do, even for the smallest thing. At times you would think they owned the place that they rent. If they did own them, I bet they'd ignore most of the defects they complain to me about. Why do you ask? You know he is a client."

"Yes, you told me before. It was just at the time I was not aware that he pays you a nice little sum each month, well not him directly, his restaurant pays you to be precise. I just wondered what that might be about."

The tension resurfaced on Steve's face; he picked up the pen again, this time twisting it between his fingers.

"I don't know how you found out about that, but it is simply none of your business."

"Does old man Duffield know you are getting a regular payment from one of his prime clients?"

"I told you it is none of your business and nothing to do with my estate agent job."

"Come on, Steve, you said yourself Derek Primm is not a charity, he must be getting something in return for his money."

"And I told you, it is none of your business."

"It is, if you're dealing drugs on his behalf."

Steve looked surprised at the mention of drugs and dealing in the same sentence. Martin watched Steve's eyes look around the office, he could see he had touched a nerve.

"I have no idea how you found out about the payments; I never imagined you to be that good a detective, but it has nothing to do with drugs."

"What is it to do with then?"

Once more Steve refused to tell Martin, citing it was none of his business as it was a purely innocent arrangement. He tried to deflect Martin's questions by asking a question of his own: just how did Martin find out about the payments? You cannot just poke your nose into someone's bank account, that is illegal, he pointed out. There was now tension between the two of them which only served to increase Martin's persistence.

"Put it this way, Steve, I will at some time need to report all this to the police. If I'm sure you're not involved, then I need not mention your name."

The thought of police being involved softened Steve's resistance to clarifying the reason for the payments he was getting.

"It's not drugs, that's the last thing I would ever get involved in."

"Really," Martin added.

"Okay you remember, a bit of weed while we were all teenagers at school, but that was more of..., well it's not the same as doing real drug dealing."

"And the payments from Derek Primm?"

"I help him out with some of his deals. Let me be honest with you and clarify exactly what I do for Mr Primm.

"I act as his eyes and ears. If there are any cheap flats going up for sale, small plots of land, the odd house ready for demolition or being totally gutted and rebuilt, then I let him know. Give him the heads up as to where the bargains are to be had. He is then able to get in before any estate agent sign goes up, and that saves him and the vendor a hefty commission as well as having no one else putting in bids and pushing up the prices.

"I'll admit, old man Duffield would not be happy, but he pays me shit wages and gives me all the manky jobs. I'm just topping up my income. I get a monthly retainer from Primm, or as you rightly pointed out from his restaurant, for," Steve mimed bunny ears with his fingers, "culinary advice and menu suggestions. That's all there is to it, nothing criminal, just sharp business practice."

"Well, that sounds plausible, I'll admit, more credible than imagining you as an epicurean. Although I still do not understand just why you did not want to come up to Vicky's flat yesterday?"

"Susan was there, or so you told me. You might not know, but I saw the two of you at Dartford Theatre, and I was sure that she had seen me alongside Derek Primm when I was giving him some documents regarding the purchase of three self-contained flats that were about to go on the market. I did not want her to recognise me and hence get asked some awkward questions, which now, I see, was clearly a waste of time. That simple, Martin, nothing devious or sinister about it."

"And is that why when the police were busy arresting Paul, you just walked right on by? Susan wasn't there then as far as I know."

"Martin, why are you acting this way, like some jerky private eye attempting to shut down a speakeasy a hundred years ago? I'm just getting a couple of backhanders from a bloke; no one is getting hurt."

Martin said he now felt thirsty and wanted to take Steve up on his earlier offer of a coffee, which Steve was happy to go and make. While Steve was in the kitchenette waiting for the kettle to boil, Martin changed the subject to Derek Primm and his chemist shops. Steve called out that he knew nothing about them as that was Derek's business-type stuff. The only part of Derek's property portfolio that he dealt with was the residential side. Martin had stood up and once again was surveying with envy the office advertisements dotted in between residential properties along the wall display.

When Steve returned and placed the coffee on the table Martin remained standing, making Steve feel nervous. He might not have seen Steve much since their schooldays, but even so he could tell that his school friend was still holding something back.

"One more thing you could clear up for me as you are in the business of letting property. It is my understanding that all the six flats above the parade of shops, including the one that Vicky lives in, all belong to Derek Primm, and that they have been provided under some sort of covenant, which means they are given rent-free to vulnerable people."

"Why question after question, Martin? What is this really all about?"

Martin raised his voice, "It's about some low-life who drives a Honda Civic like mine and has cloned my plates, giving me not only parking tickets, but getting me connected to some common or garden drug dealer. What car have you got?"

"A crappy Ford Focus, a company car would you believe. I don't actually own a car, I have no need for one, public transport in London is not that bad. So, just finish your coffee and leave. I'm off the hook, I guess."

"Back to my earlier point. Vicky tells me she pays rent, or to be precise, gets housing benefit to pay it for her. Yet I thought that the flats were rent-free under the covenant I mentioned. I think someone is lying and I doubt it is the innocent piece of paperwork that sets out conditions for the flats, which was written years ago by Derek's father."

"Shit! Martin, why do you always have to do the right thing? You were such a rebel at school; we all got into some grand scrapes and had fun. When did you become a boring, middle-class fuddy-duddy?"

Martin sipped his coffee. "When I think someone is doing the dirty on someone else. Does Vicky pay rent?"

This time Steve threw the pen down on the desk; it bounced and landed in his paper tray, he was not having a good day.

"Alright, you want the full story, here goes. You're right, Vicky's flat is rent-free, it is part of the agreement made when the council passed the properties on to Derek's dad. Vulnerable people rent-free, and the rents on the shops are fifty per cent of commercial rents. Everyone is happy, except you it seems.

"But look at it this way, Martin. With the advent of housing benefit, it is the tax man who is in fact saving the money. If Vicky was living in a normal flat, then she would be able to claim housing benefit and the government would pay her rent.

"I felt that it was not fair that poor Vicky is struggling to make ends meet and the jolly old tax man is saving cash. I suggested to her that if I provided all the paperwork to show she was paying rent, then she could claim housing benefit and we split it fifty-fifty; can't get fairer than that. She gets a bonus, I get a bonus, and the tax man is not really losing out.

"And before you ask, that was the real reason I walked on by when the police were there. I was just going to pop in to see Vicky. Of course, when I saw the police, I assumed that she might have been in trouble for something, so I was ready to run back to the office to lose all the paperwork I had here. In the end she called me later to tell me what had happened. There you have it in all its dirty glory, Martin. Now are you going to report me?"

Martin stood up, still holding his coffee which by now was tepid. He looked around the dreary office, the tired desks and the uninviting carpet. To Martin, it seemed the perfect place for Steve, who had always been keen on making money, whatever the cost.

"No, you'll only find some new scam to swindle someone out of a pound or two. I have no plans to dob you in. Middle-class fuddy-duddies have other means to make our point."

Martin leaned forward, poured his coffee over Steve's head, soaking him and his desk, then he turned and walked out with a wry smile.

CHAPTER FIFTEEN

It was safe to say that Flossie was not pleased in the slightest to see Colin standing in her doorway. It was not his outfit that rankled her, in fact, she quite liked the simple navy pleated skirt and court shoes that he wore, and even the navy and white yoke ruffle top, although she could not see herself in it. The reason for her anger was the time of day she had to open the door to him. When she finally did open it, she looked at Colin and said,

'For Christ's sake! You're the second caller today and it's not even nine o'clock."

Well that, in fact, answered his question, he had wanted to know if the drug dealer had already called. He looked at her and hoped she was not telepathic as he was thinking, who would ever wear a pink, panda print onesie to answer the door? Clearly, Flossie would.

"Come on Flossie, getting up early is good for your health. I thought I'd have another quiet word with you. Can I come in?"

She had learnt from bitter experience that if a police officer or even an ex-police officer asks, 'Can I come in?', there is no point denying them entry, they will come in anyway. Flossie led Colin into the kitchen where she was having her breakfast. He sat down at the square kitchen table opposite her, turned down an offer of tea and watched as she dipped her bread soldiers into a boiled egg. In all the years he had known her, he had never imagined her as a boiled egg and bread soldier breakfast person. If he'd had to put money on it, he would have said Flossie was just a tea and a fag breakfast person. It showed how wrong you can be at times.

Colin looked around the kitchen. He had seen worse during his career in the Police force, a lot worse. Even so, the square kitchen with beige units, off-white cooker and washing machine with its door open and some underwear hanging out, could all do with an hour or two of elbow grease and copious amounts of bleach and kitchen spray. Thankfully, he had no plans to either eat or drink in it.

"This must be your gear?" He leant forward and picked up a large white plastic bag that was leaning against the fridge. Flossie just looked at him as he rummaged among the contents. She carried on eating and finished her egg before she spoke.

"Bloody seven-thirty this morning he starts banging on the sodding door. I ask you, he dragged me out of bed. Didn't warn me. Just turns up, saying 'he had fings to do'. Still no reason in my mind to turn up that bloody early."

"Lucky you had your onesie on then."

"Nah, baby doll nightie, got it as a birthday present a while back. It was alright, he'd seen it all before. Anyhow I'm not a shy person."

"Pity," Colin said in a hushed tone. He took one of the boxes out of the bag. "You have a lot of Oxynorm here."

"Popular with the girls around here, makes 'em feel good, forget all the shit that's going on."

Colin examined the other boxes, Diazepam, Benzodiazepine, Codeine (there were several different types), all potential killers, all of them in an innocent plastic bag. They were all packaged in branded boxes, just as you would get them with any prescription given out by a doctor. The difference here though was there was no need for a prescription, Flossie would give them to whoever could afford them.

"I would never have thought of you as a person who would jeopardize the lives of those who live on the same estate as you."

"Mr Higgins, I see me as helping out, giving the mums and girls a break from their lives. It ain't fun living on a sink estate with your old man unemployed, four kids and no money. I just help 'em get through it."

"But you still take some of their money. I presume you have not registered as a charity yet."

"It's the way of the modern world, Mr Higgins. Not like in the good old days, the men would be out doin' a bit of nickin'. Take my old man, he was in the docks until he got chucked out. No drug dealin' for him. A bit of armed robbery helped us make ends meet."

"Still illegal, Flossie."

"Maybe, Mr Higgins, but it hurt no one. The banks lost a few quid; they got it back on the insurance, so everyone was 'appy. Today it's all drugs and stuff. We're robbin' each other on this estate. It can't be right, Mr Higgins."

"No Flossie, it's not. But if I said to you why don't you stop, you'll say to me, 'if I don't do it, then someone else will'."

"Too right, Mr Higgins."

"So, who else sells around here or nearby? Who's your competition?"

Flossie walked over to the sink with her egg cup and its empty shell, putting it all in the sink together. She then grabbed what looked to be a used glass tumbler from the draining board, filled it with tap water and gulped the whole glass down in one go. Flossie turned back to Colin and looked at him with a questioning look, as if she were debating if she should tell him or not. She had known him for years; he had done good by her; he was one of the good cops. She lit a cigarette and inhaled deeply, blowing the smoke up towards the ceiling.

"Her name's Natalie. She lives down on Fellow Street near Brockley station, so not much of a threat to me. Flogs the same stuff, pretty sure we have the same supplier. I can give you her address if you like. What have you got against this guy anyway?"

"Well apart from selling illegal drugs, he's upset my boss. We just want a word or two."

"I suppose if you put him away, I'll have to find another supplier or do a bit of me extras to help me with a few extra quid."

"Talking of extras, you said that was how you met your supplier, on his back without his clothes. I'd like to ask a few more questions about that Flossie if you don't mind?"

"Mr Higgins, I never took you to be the kinky type."

Colin smiled and listened to Flossie as she gave a graphic description of the first time she had met her prescription drug supplier.

CHAPTER SIXTEEN

"Is this a date or purely business?" Susan asked as she found herself once again being driven by Martin towards the streets of south London. Martin did not answer at once. He was trying to negotiate a BMW in front of him, whose driver was not sure if he should turn left, right, continue on, or just simply stop.

"Take your choice," Martin said to Susan, having passed the indecisive BMW. "It can be either or maybe even both," he teased.

Martin did not in the least believe Steve when he said that he was not a drug dealer and drove a clapped-out Ford Focus.

If Steve was lying, then the next logical step was to speak to Derek Primm and see how he reacted to being told about back-handers and benefit fraud. He too would no doubt lie and cheat, of that Martin was sure. Even so, between the lies sometimes you can see the truth. Well that was what Martin hoped.

He had called Susan; told her he was picking her up and they were going to Derek's restaurant. The reason for the visit he explained only as they drove towards Eltham. He told her all about Steve, the backhanders that he was getting from Derek, the housing benefit fraud, which appeared to apply not only to Vicky, but also to the other five flats above the shops which were designed to be for vulnerable people.

"You know I was once sympathetic to Vicky," said Susan. "I am just now wondering what else she is up to. Sex chat lines, giving Paul the run around, well they're not nice I'll admit, but they're not that bad compared to screwing over the benefit system, that is totally out of order. Do you think we should report her?"

"Sometimes I wonder. Take Flossie, Colin said, as did that old guy in the fish and chip shop, it's what they do. They might get turned over, but they always find a way of making some cash on the side. Ducking and diving, I believe it is called."

"Do we have a plan of action for Derek?"

"I was hoping you would come up with something, don't forget he thinks I am a Russian bodyguard."

***

Pasta Postcard was quiet, with maybe only half a dozen other customers. Susan and Martin took a four-seater table next to the window, for no better reason than Martin thought it made him look like a local. They sat opposite each other, ordered some drinks and perused the menu. Martin felt relieved that at least here he knew the dishes on offer, the names were all familiar to him.

They watched Derek Primm busy himself close to the small bar where customers paid their bills, pulling up his trousers at regular intervals. He directed some of the waiters and took a phone call. He appeared to be a highly efficient restaurateur, possibly better at that than managing property. He looked across to their table, then pulled up his belt, his shoulders rising high, before he started to walk towards them.

He stood beside Susan, took her hand and bowed slightly as he kissed it. "Ah, the female private detective who is looking out for my tenants, how wonderful to see you again." He then turned towards Martin, seemed to recognize the face and was trying to associate the man with Susan, but he could not equate the two. He frowned, he could not place Martin, so Susan helped.

"Russian bodyguard, we work for the same company."

"Ah, of course." Derek took Martin's hand and thankfully for Martin, just shook it firmly. "You were with Ian's wife the last time I saw you. Are you off duty tonight or protecting this young lady from the many admirers I am sure she attracts?"

At that moment a waiter arrived at the table with their food order: Gnocchetti Sarde Luganica for Martin and Susan's order of Beef Lasagne and chips.

"I will leave you in peace to enjoy your meal, and I will return to continue our conversation later." Derek floated away from the table, tugging at his belt.

"He is so slimy; he has almost put me off my food," Martin commented.

"He is a dish, Martin; you have to admit it. Eat up, or 'syesh vsye' as you Russians would say."

Martin stopped eating and looked at Susan with a dumbfounded expression on his face. He had never thought of her as a linguist.

"Do you speak Russian?"

"Don't be stupid, I just Googled it to spook you out, you are so gullible at times." Susan laughed as they returned to eating their meals.

***

Derek, with their permission, joined them and provided a complementary bottle of wine for the three of them to share. He sat next to Susan, at first talking casually about the restaurant and the enormous collection of postcards that he had amassed since he was a teenager. He had found them fascinating. His father had a wide range of contacts across the country, who regularly sent postcards when they were on holiday. The teenage Derek became intrigued over the words people wrote on them: some bland, some funny, some personal, some sad. He felt he was a voyeur into people's lives. This feeling was enhanced when he started to collect older postcards, with their personal messages, invitations and words of excitement that Edwardian travellers reported back to their families about romantic lands across Europe. The hobby had turned into an obsession. His vast collection, Derek estimated, now comprised of more than one hundred thousand postcards, as he had just purchased a large number from the estate of a fellow collector who had recently died. Finally, he returned to the reason Susan had previously been to his restaurant.

"The last time you were here, Susan, you asked me about loan sharks. I have, as promised, made some discreet enquires, all alas, to no avail. I do not know who she might be involved with or who the people behind the scheme might be."

"Don't worry, Derek, we have learnt that there is in fact no loan shark, it was part of another scam that was being carried out," Susan admitted, before adding, "There is something else though." She looked at Martin to encourage him to carry on, which he did.

"You are giving your estate agent backhanders to obtain privileged information," Martin stated.

Derek did not seem in the least worried by the allegation, his facial expression could easily have been interpreted as a badge of honour for doing such a thing.

"To be clear, Steve Ellis has a real ability to create dishes and as such, I was really pleased when he agreed to offer his services in advising me on which dishes should be presented on our menu. In fact, the Gnocchetti, you have hopefully just enjoyed, was one of Steve's first recommendations. Now you mention privileged information; I think that is a little too far-fetched. We talk about property, prices, trends, what's happening in the market, as any professional would. To say ''privileged information' is very dramatic, even for a Russian." Derek smiled and refilled Susan's glass.

"There is also a housing benefit fraud occurring with your properties, again your close friend Steve admitted it all."

This time Derek's face did change to a look of complete surprise. Was he that good an actor? Martin could not be sure, but the allegation certainly appeared to have a dramatic impact on him.

"What properties are we talking about?"

"The six flats that are allocated to vulnerable people as part of the agreement your father made with the council. They should be rent free, but all of them are claiming housing benefit."

"The little shit!" Derek slapped the flat of his palm hard against the table, the glass and condiments jumped in surprise as did Susan. "I will see to it that is stopped and old man Duffield will hear of this. I will not have anyone abusing the system like that. Thank you both for bringing this to my attention." Then he added, "Consider your meal paid for, it is the least I can do."

Martin continued, "There is one other thing we need to talk to you about."

This was the question that he and Susan had disagreed about as they drove towards the restaurant. Susan could not see the point of telling Derek that they suspected, or rather Martin still suspected, Steve of purchasing drugs and selling them on the estate via Flossie. Susan thought that if they said that then assuming Derek was involved, he would just deny everything and stop the whole thing for a while. They needed hard proof that he was involved. Martin did not share that view. He felt that by pointing out that they knew, or at least they said they knew, about the prescription drugs being sold by Steve, it would spur Derek into action. At the same time, his reaction to the news might give them a clue.

"Steve, we believe, could be involved with supplying prescription drugs on the estate."

"God, it gets worse; I'm only glad you two are good at your job. I will see that he is sacked. I just cannot afford to have such a - how would you describe him - a criminal, working or having any connection to my business."

Susan watched his face but could not tell if he was guilty or not. She thought it might be time to ask a question of her own, one that she had not run past Martin in the car. She hoped she was not getting out of her depth.

"Your business, I've looked at the accounts and concluded that it is not that strong. Your property portfolio is undervalued."

"Ah, so you're an accountant as well as a detective?"

'Shit', Susan thought, had she gone too far. "Teetering on the edge?" Susan added, and just dug deeper.

"You do understand just how a company comes to value its portfolio for accounting purposes. I have a mix of investment and other property that falls under the provision of section 17 and not FRS102. This mix is legal and meets all tax rules, or do you disagree?"

'I have stepped right into it,' Susan thought to herself, wondering what she should say next. Before she could think of anything more, Martin butted in, saving her.

"We are not account experts, we leave that to another fine colleague we work closely with, very well qualified and astute, an expert in her field, Becky, a close friend of Susan's." The sarcastic comment was not lost on Susan. "Her general evaluation is that you need to complete the deal with the council to sell back the shops and the flats in order to get a healthy cash injection."

Derek took a moment to think before gently nodding, "Well, completion of that transaction will help me invest further, that is true, but I am not on the brink of financial disaster, if that's what you are both getting at. Plus, I am certainly not involved with any sort of drug dealing. Wait, you said prescription drugs. Ah, you think I am in collusion with Steve for the simple reason I own three chemist shops. Well, I'll have you know that I have very little to do with the day-to-day management of them, but I would guess that it is very hard to 'lose' some pills to sell on the streets. I think you will need to look elsewhere to find where Steve is getting his drugs from."

Derek stood up from the table, hitched his trousers up propelling his shoulders high in the air. "I must leave you now, I have a planning meeting to attend at the town hall. It has been an interesting conversation with you both. Please feel free to stay as long as you wish, I have told the staff you can have whatever you want, it is my treat." He looked at Susan. "I am not that badly off. I bid you both farewell."

"I think we need to brush up on our interrogation skills before we do this again," Martin observed, acknowledging that the only thing they actually had achieved tonight was a free meal.

"Detecting is a lot harder than it looks on television, it would be so much easier if everyone told the truth." Susan added, as she emptied her glass.

Martin looked at her as she quickly refilled the glass, "Maybe we should Google it, seems to work for languages?"

"No one ever tells the whole truth. Yet I do think Derek knows nothing about the drugs, why would he? He is busy with his tenants, chemists, the restaurant and his postcard collection. Don't forget," Susan pointed out, "even our so-called super accountant girl said that if he was money laundering he was doing a bad job."

"Ok, let's finish up here and I'll take you back."

"Let's not rush, Martin, free drinks remember?"

"Due to the fact that we are in the back of beyond miles from a tube station, I am driving. No alcohol, sadly."

"Best get used to fruit juice tonight then." Susan waved at a waiter and ordered a round of drinks.

They drank and chatted for most of the evening. Between them they put forward scenarios that might fit into what they knew to the facts: Flossie getting drugs, a cloned car with Martin's registration, Steve passing on information to Derek, the housing benefit fraud (that no doubt Steve instigated), Vicky shoplifting, her part-time job, her sex-chat line. Where, Martin asked his mind untainted by any alcohol, are the links to any of these?

With alcohol playing a big part in Susan's mind, she began going off on all sorts of tangents. Some made sense to Martin, others did not. The strangest one did spark something in his mind. Susan suggested that Steve was the most likely candidate to be supplying Flossie. The big question was where he was getting the pills from. Susan then pointed out, with her speech a little slurred, that they knew that Vicky had a part time job in a Tesco supermarket; what did she do there? Possibly they had a pharmacy; she might even work in it, and she was clearly not one to bother about breaking the law. Could she be the link? Martin warmed to that idea. After all, she was very keen to try and dissuade them from going after her phantom loan shark; possibly she was concerned they might stumble across something else. He also pointed out that she must have gone around her own flat breaking the light switches and plug sockets, as well as actually hitting herself, to make things fit the lies she was telling. Martin felt that even an intoxicated Susan could come up with some sensible ideas.

It was now getting late and the restaurant was almost empty. They stood up in preparation to leave. It was then that Susan noticed a waiter carrying three boxes, each about a foot square, and maybe half that size in height. He was walking from the bar saying goodbye to the other waiters and heading towards the door. He was olive-skinned, possibly Italian, about six-foot-tall and, in Susan's opinion attractive. Given he was good-looking, she was surprised that she still noticed the brand on the side of each of the boxes.

"Martin, Oxynorm, isn't that what Colin told us Flossie sells, the pills, she called them oxy's?"

As Martin put his coat on, he watched the man leave the restaurant and agreed that Susan was right.

"Derek must be behind all this after all. Come on, let's follow him."

Before Martin had a chance to protest, Susan was going out of the door. The good-looking Italian slipped into a sleek, red Alfa Romeo, after putting the boxes in the boot. Together Martin and Susan dashed back to Martin's car and set off following the waiter.

Martin drove as best he could to keep up with the red car given that he was completely lost. They followed it along the South Circular, through Woolwich, past Plumstead and finally onto Thamesmead. It had taken the best part of twenty minutes.

They watched as the tall waiter parked his car carefully on a small driveway of a terraced house, locked it, and disappeared into what they assumed to be his home. Martin put his car into gear and prepared to turn around, setting his sat nav for home. That was the only way he would ever find his way back to central London.

"What are you doing?" Susan snapped at him.

"Doing? I am going home. I'll drop you off first if that is what you are worried about?"

"We can't do that; we need to find out what's in those boxes. This could be our only chance of getting hard evidence against Derek Primm."

Martin put the car into neutral, pulled on the handbrake and groaned. "How are we going to get a look inside those boxes? Have you noticed they are inside a locked car?"

"Yes, Martin, I did notice," her mocking tone was not lost on him. "How hard can it be to break the lock?"

"Hard, Susan, that is the whole point of having a lock on the boot of a car in the first place. It makes it hard to get into unless you have a key. Anything else would be totally pointless."

"Martin, this is our chance. I'm sure we could force it somehow. Stop arguing and follow me." Without waiting for any response, Susan released her seat belt and opened the door of the car.

As she stepped out Martin made one last protest, he hoped it would be his trump card, "Breaking into cars is illegal, you know."

"We're stopping a bigger crime, come on." Susan was now out of the car and walking towards the parked Alfa Romeo. Martin turned off the engine wondering again what it might be like inside a prison.

They both crouched down beside the boot out of sight of the kitchen window, although totally visible to anyone who happened to be walking along the road. Fortunately for them, the road was deserted.

Susan pushed a large nail file into the key slot, then proceeded to push, twist, wiggle and push harder still using as much strength as she could muster. The nail file soon gave out and bent under the stress of doing something outside its comfort zone.

"Do you know what you are doing?" Martin asked with a hushed voice.

"Quiet!" Susan answered softly as she dug around in her handbag for another implement. This time it was a comb with a long, thin, straight handle – Martin learnt later that it was a rat tail comb. Susan followed the same procedure as she had for the nail file. Push, twist, wiggle, repeating the sequence but harder.

"It's not going to work," Martin pointed out.

"Don't be so negative, I think it is shifting the lock. Just move, you're casting a shadow and I can't see properly."

"I'm not in your light, just get on with it."

A voice that contained just a merest hint of an Italian origin spoke.

"I am sorry if I am blocking your light, lady," it was a male voice, "but just what are you doing exactly?"

Together Martin and Susan turned to see the threatening figure of the car's owner standing over them, a large kitchen knife in his hand. Almost in unison they answered the question, but with different answers.

Martin opted for a simple, "I've dropped my keys."

Susan went for a different excuse slightly more graphic, "Just having a pee."

Martin wanted to ask Susan just how she connected crouching down beside a car with having a pee, but sensibly he thought this was not the best time to try and elicit a reason. He then watched as she sprung up from her pseudo peeing position and drew herself up to her full height, which still did not compare to the waiter.

"We're private investigators and on the trail of a drugs gang. What's in your car?"

Martin stood up and brushed down his trousers, if he was going to get arrested then at least he would look smart.

The waiter, who technically at this moment was not a waiter, smiled, "Ah, you two are the couple from the restaurant tonight, friends of Mr Primm. What are you doing to my car?"

Susan stood her ground. "Those boxes you loaded into your car earlier, I want to see what's inside them."

"You think the boxes have drugs?"

"Open the boot," Susan asked sternly, impressing Martin with her fortitude.

The waiter took a key fob from his pocket offered the key to Susan. "Help yourself." Again, he smiled.

Martin was not sure if it might be some sort of trap, somebody might sprint from the boot as it opened, or it might reveal a boot full of drugs and guns. He took a step back as Susan used the key to release the boot lid, which sprung up revealing the three boxes. In the dull courtesy light, the logo of Oxynorm could be made out.

Susan looked back at the waiter; he clearly was waiting for her to open one of the boxes. They were not sealed, the lid flaps just folded in, so she easily pulled them apart to reveal:

"Postcards!" Susan exclaimed.

The waiter laughed, "There are Mr Primm's postcards and very cheeky ones too; your English sense of humour is well known for being saucy. Lots of seaside postcards, fat ladies and boobs plus some awkward moments, just like you are feeling now. He asked me to take them to his home in the morning."

Martin closed down the boot and took Susan's hand before looking at the waiter and saying, "I think we owe you an apology. We'll be on our way now. Good night."

As he guided Susan back across the road to his car, she put her mistake quickly behind her and focused on the hand holding that did not let up until they reached it. All in all, she thought, not a bad night.

CHAPTER SEVENTEEN

"Martin, is there any public transport that you are happy to travel on?"

"Only if it does not contain the word public," Martin retorted as he slipped his already creased ticket into the barrier at Charing Cross station. He had originally wanted to take his car to Deptford, yet for some incomprehensible reason that Martin could not fathom out, Susan insisted that they take the train.

"What's in the bag?" She pointed to a plain white plastic bag that Martin was carrying.

"Nothing," Martin replied immediately. "Let's just get this public train." He had no plans to share the contents of the bag with Susan just yet.

They had not heard back from Colin after his visit to Flossie yesterday and took it to mean he had no additional information about the drug dealer. Martin and Susan were in the same situation. Apart from waiting until next week to try and ambush the dealer, there was little they felt they could do. They decided it was time to tell Paul that his girlfriend had invented a loan shark, and that she was part of a housing benefit fraud. They guessed he would not be pleased with either circumstance. Although Susan did point out unhelpfully, that both being criminals, they would make the perfect couple.

With that in mind, Susan claimed that such news should be delivered in person. Martin had the opposite view and instead wanted to make a simple phone call to tell him the facts, then replace the receiver and let him deal with it in his own way. He could imagine Paul bursting into tears and then what? He had no plans to embrace any man, crying or not.

Susan insisted, as Susan often did, that in person was the only way to deliver bad news. Once Martin conceded, he picked up his car keys, which immediately brought the response from Susan that they had driven enough over the last couple of days and that they should do more to protect the environment. Martin tried to convince her otherwise but only succeeded in failing. As he boarded the train, he mentally told himself: Susan two, Martin nil. It was going to be one of those days.

The train rattled over Hungerford Bridge, then trundled into Waterloo East, where it stopped. Much to Martin's horror a mother talking loudly on her phone sat opposite him; alongside her there was a small girl clutching a well-worn teddy bear.

As the train pulled out of the station Martin avoided eye contact with the child, whose stare was rigidly fixed on him. Her mother was telling the person on the other end of the phone, whose name appeared to be Elaine, about her appointment to have a Brazilian on her hair next week, in time for Harriet's - whoever she might be - birthday party, who it would seem, according to all involved, looked a lot older than the thirty-seven years she was going to be celebrating.

Now Martin had heard of women having a Brazilian; he was just not sure it was something you should be discussing in front of your small daughter. The daughter that so far he had managed to avoid eye contact with.

Susan leant forward and asked the little girl, "What's your teddy called?"

Martin tried to convey silently his horror that Susan was communicating with this little girl. He had a sense of foreboding.

"Theodore Robert Rufus Long."

"That's a big name for a little teddy bear?"

'Please,' Martin thought, 'stop there, Susan, this will only end in tears'. Who might be crying in the end, he had no idea?

"Mummy called him that; I call him Teddy. Is he your boyfriend?" The little girl asked, pointing at Martin, who froze.

"No," answered Susan, "he's my boss, we work together."

"Do you sleep with him? Mummy slept with her boss and Daddy left. I see him at weekends at a place called 'Under Super Vision', but where we go is not super."

Mother, who was still firmly engrossed with her friend Elaine, did not hear her daughter's allegations.

"No, we just work together." Susan leaned back into her seat, finally realising what Martin had feared all along, talking to this little girl, or any small child, was going to be perilous.

"Do you have a baby tunnel?"

That surprised Susan, who was now starting to feel she was sinking into a mire of tricky questions, which indeed she was. Martin felt smug in that he had taken the correct course of action and ignored the child in the first place.

"All ladies do," Susan spoke with a staccato tone, "it means we can have babies."

Martin's complacency was short-lived as he saw the little girl's eyes turn to him.

"Why did God let my kitten die?" She asked him.

This seemingly simple question stumped Martin on several levels. Firstly, he did not really believe in god. There had been occasions when he had asked the deity for help, but he guessed that god, as forgiving as he might be, did not take kindly to people asking for help only when it suited them. The second thing was kittens. Martin liked cats. He had always wanted a cat of his own, which would fall asleep in his lap as he stroked its soft fur. It was just that his mother could not abide any form of animal in her home. So, to think of a little sweet kitten dying touched an emotional nerve in Martin, resulting in a pang of compassion for the little girl.

"If all kittens lived forever, there would be no room in the world for new baby kittens. Perhaps your kitten died because somewhere there is a very lonely young kitten who needs the loving home you could provide for him or her."

"Mummy says I can't have another cat 'cause they shit everywhere."

"Well, they all need to be trained," Martin added, "just as babies do."

"Kittens don't wear nappies."

"No, but they do have litter trays they can go in."

The little girl, having got bored with that question, changed tack and subject.

"How heavy is the sky?" Again, the question was directed at Martin, much to Susan's relief.

Martin was sure that some clever scientist, having grappled with the question for most of his working life, had the answer to that question. An answer, no doubt, that would be far too complex for a little girl and equally mystifying for him. Rescue came in the form of Susan pointing out that the train was now slowing down and coming into Deptford. Martin had never been so pleased to arrive at a run-down inner-city railway station.

As they walked, taking the stairs towards the street, Martin had to ask the question which he was sure Susan would know the answer to.

"The girl's mother," he started. "On the phone she talked about having a Brazilian. Now I am not an expert but is that the sort of thing you should be discussing on a train, or even need when you are going to a birthday party."

Susan stopped, they stood on different steps, with her on the higher one. She looked down into his confused eyes.

"Now I guess you are thinking about a Brazilian wax; the way ladies tidy up their lady garden. Am I right?"

Martin nodded.

"I imagine she was talking about a Brazilian hair treatment, a way of straightening your hair. A world apart from the Brazilian wax that you imagined. If you ever consider having one, make sure you get the right one."

"Neither appeal to me."

They continued down the stairs and onto the street, where they stood opposite the Deptford Centre, waiting for a break in the traffic.

"You know, Martin, you are sweet at times: offering Vicky money to pay off her debt, giving a loveable answer to that little girl and her kitten question."

"I might not have been quite so keen to give the money to Vicky if I had known at the time she was on the fiddle. As for the little girl and her kitten, I imagine the mother drowned it for shitting everywhere. Sometimes, it is best to steer clear of everyone's problems."

***

This time there was no tramp sitting outside the Deptford Centre. They walked in and felt its still crowded and warm atmosphere. The drone of multiple conversations filled the environment. Just a few faces turned to see who was coming through the door, but Martin and Susan no longer warranted a second glance.

As they walked towards the counter, they combed the room for any sign of Paul, but he appeared not to be around. Then Martin spotted a face he recognised making his way through the array of tables and chairs.

"Brendan, how you are doing?"

Brendan looked up and upon seeing Martin his face changed to one of concern as Martin approached him.

"Please sir, don't say anything about where we met last time," Brendan spoke in almost a whisper as he leant in towards Martin. There was a slight hint of unwashed clothes between them. "If others knew what I do, they'd be there, and I'd lose out."

Martin smiled, "No worries. I thought you might like this?" Martin passed the plastic bag to Brendan. Immediately the young man opened the bag and peered inside.

"Two Waitrose Carrot Cakes. Oh, thank you, thank you, thank you!" Brendan sounded as if he had just woken up on Christmas Day believing that Santa Claus was not going to stop at his house, and then found that Santa Claus had left him a pile of presents.

"I hope you enjoy them, only I am no expert on carrot cakes," Martin smiled.

"Oh no, I won't be eating them both. See Bob over there in the tartan shirt and Mohican hair he loves carrot cake as well, so I'll give him one. That is if you don't mind?"

"Of course not. By the way, have you seen my friend Paul today?"

"He's out the back, sorting sandwiches."

Susan and Martin walked towards the grey door that Brendan had pointed out.

"Who's an old softie then?"

Martin ignored her and followed her through the door.

Paul was working diligently in one of the back rooms of the club. In front of him was a large tray full of donated Pret A Manger sandwiches. The only requirement was for them to be unpacked and placed neatly onto plates to be distributed around the club. Working with Paul was another volunteer, a heavily built man with a thick neck. He was in his late forties but looked older; his face lined with a life that had been cruel to him. Together they chatted and unwrapped the sandwiches. They had a connection: the presence at the club for both of them was at the behest of the criminal justice system.

"You two back again?" Paul asked as Martin and Susan walked into the room. The heavily built man looked at them suspiciously.

Martin replied with a diplomatic request that they wanted a word with Paul about Vicky, and some things they had found out about her that he needed to know about. Martin also tried to infer that he might want to hear their news in private.

"I have few secrets from my namesake here, Big Paul," Paul nodded towards the large man. "We're here unpacking sandwiches for almost the same reason."

"You doing community service as well?" Susan asked, as she looked at the sandwiches, which reminded her that she was feeling hungry.

The other Paul known as Big Paul for obvious reasons, offered her a sandwich, which she readily accepted.

"No, I'm on licence from prison. Working here is part of my release programme."

"What are you in for?"

"Manslaughter."

Susan was about to take a bite out of her sandwich until his admission stopped her in her tracks. "Manslaughter, what like you killed someone?"

Little Paul offered some guidance to Big Paul, "Just give her the full story. She is one of those women who like to hear all the gory details."

Big Paul did explain in a concise way, which he had learnt to do during his time in prison, it was part of the introduction sequence when a new cellmate arrived. He continued unwrapping sandwiches as he told the room:

"I was a lorry driver - articulated lorries - delivering pallets around the country. What I didn't know was that I suffered from a condition called: narcolepsy. I didn't sleep well, but I just thought that was normal. I never realised that narcolepsy could cause you to suddenly drop off to sleep.

"The first time it ever happened to me, I fell asleep at the wheel of my truck, a very inappropriate time. I hit a car and killed the driver. They gave me seven years, saying I should have known about my condition. I still have trouble sleeping, as I can never forget that I killed a woman; she was a mother to three young children. Before you ask, I will never hold a driving licence again. It's just that is the only job I've ever had. At least I have the chance to start my life again, more than that poor woman."

"Such a sad story for everyone," Susan observed. His voice had sounded racked with guilt.

"Makes my punching a delivery guy seem trivial. Big Paul is here as part of his being integrated into society again. A nicer and kinder man you'll find nowhere, so whatever you want to tell me, you can tell me in front of Big Paul."

Martin did not deliver his news to Paul softly or sweetly. He just laid out the fact that Vicky had lied about the sex chat phone line and the loan shark to get money out of him each week. Martin then, unwisely, mentioned that maybe

Paul's mother was right, and he should give up the voluntary work here once he had done his time, and give up Vicky. It seemed that Martin bringing up Paul's mother in front of Big Paul annoyed Paul. It turned out there were things that Paul did not want talked about in front of Big Paul after all.

Paul picked up two plates of sandwiches in readiness to take them into the club. He stood by the door and spoke with his back to the others in the room.

"Really Martin, it is none of your business who I see or who I give my money to. My interfering old mother might see things differently, there again, you know as well as I do that is what Mothers are good at. I have no plans to stop seeing Vicky. Why should I? I am my own man." He then pushed the door open with his elbow and left them.

Martin was not finished yet. If Paul was not worried about his privacy, then Martin was as sure as not going to be either. Both Martin and Susan followed him out into the club, leaving Big Paul alone. Although Susan was tempted to say to him, 'don't fall asleep while we're gone' she thought that was in bad taste, even for her.

They caught up with Paul as he was placing the plates on the counter. This time Martin added the fact that Vicky was illegally claiming housing benefit for a flat that she did not even pay rent on. Paul did not seem the least concerned. Martin got the distinct impression that he was ignoring everything that he was telling him. In fact, he was not, inside he was seething.

He shouted at Martin's face, "Nicking a few pounds off the benefit system is not a major crime. Who is getting hurt? No one, really. Just forget it, Martin, walk away and do not worry about it. You used to be good at doing that."

"I am trying to help you Paul. I can't see why you're throwing your life away going after someone like Vicky."

"Martin, you have always been an arsehole! Even at school you thought you knew best for everyone. I like living my life in my way, and if that involves being with someone you don't approve of, tough shit! You can just fuck off and be the old woman you have always been!"

A familiar voice interrupted the heated discussion the ex-school friends were having.

"That's no way for a well brought-up young man to speak to anyone. You clearly are picking up some bad habits in this place." It was Colin who was now standing beside Paul and Martin. "Why don't we go somewhere private so I can get you two to be friends again. I do hate it when pals fall out."

CHAPTER EIGHTEEN

Within a few minutes, Colin had organized what he liked to describe as a pro-active focus group as efficiently as any executive's personal assistant might have achieved it. They all sat in a small meeting room above the club, which was provided by Harry Branston who Colin insisted, for reasons he did not share, should be in on the meeting. In addition to Colin and Harry, there were Paul, Martin, and Susan present; all of them were interested to hear what Colin had to say.

"Paul, - I don't think we have been formally introduced - but I want Martin to understand why you are so keen to stay with Vicky. I know his interfering can be a little annoying at times. Right, let's tell Martin a little more about you, shall we Paul?" Colin did not wait for Paul to answer, he simply looked at Martin and carried on with what he wanted to say.

"Up until a few weeks ago your friend, Paul, owned a white Ford Focus, his pride and joy. That was until he started getting several tickets for parking illegally; something his mother was not exactly smitten with, as she paid them all. Paul needed a plan." Colin continued to speak directly to Martin as if Paul were not in the room. "By chance he had seen you getting a ticket and watched your reaction, with the parking warden. That gave Paul an idea, recalling how at school you'd rather pay for something than have a confrontation, you'd prefer to take the easy way out. Sounds familiar, Susan?"

She nodded in agreement.

"Paul's new car emulated his hero: Martin, so he bought a blue Honda Civic."

"But," Susan interrupted, "Paul drives a red Toyota, I know, I've been in it."

"That, Suzie Baby, is his mother's car. He borrows it to come here, to Deptford. He did not want to get his nice new car damaged being parked around such a rough area."

"That explains the old lady's cardigan in the back and there I was thinking he was a transvestite."

"Suzie baby, you need style to be a 'tranny', sadly, as you can see, Paul does not have any. Anyway, I'll continue."

"What are you getting at? I have the same car as Martin; there are loads of them on the roads." Paul pointed out.

Colin glanced towards Paul, gave him a look of daggers, then turned back to Martin.

"As I was saying: Paul does use his car for work. A despatch manager I think he told you, Martin. He did, however, omit to tell you he is a despatch manager for a pharmaceutical company. There he works three days a week, well, to be more accurate, two days and a night shift on Tuesdays. Nights there are not that many people around it gives Paul the opportunity to tweak the paperwork, lose some pills and put them in the back of his blue Honda which, by now, has the same registration plate as yours.

"Sweet Paul then, once he has finished his shift, drives down to Turner Road and drops off a couple of plastic bags worth of pills for our friend, Flossie. Hence it was the same day and almost the same time each week. It was also a useful time as his girlfriend, who lives across the road, was unlikely to be up. Although to be safe he did dress in a way which would make it difficult to see through the coat, hat and scarf."

"You have no proof of this," Paul argued, "it's all conjecture and falsehoods, not a shred of evidence that would stand up in court."

Colin once more turned to Paul, "You really must be more patient."

He pulled a small notebook from his handbag, flicked a few pages over until a look of discovery washed over his face, he had found what he was looking for. At that point Harry also had a look of recognition.

"I knew I knew yer. You're old bill, seen you around a few times. You still in the filth?"

"Everyone asks me that, I then refer them to my current attire and, weirdly, they understand that I am no longer with the Metropolitan Police force, as I like to call it. Don't worry Harry, you're here to observe, an independent witness no less. You're not getting nicked

"Right Paul let's continue. A name for you: Mr Chaudhury, he runs a small supermarket about a mile from Flossie's drug shop. The supermarket has a delivery every Wednesday about midday. That was why Mr Choudhury noticed a white Ford and then lately a blue Honda regularly parked outside his shop, blocking the parking space for the large supply lorry that was due to turn up. The man in that car always went upstairs to the flat above the supermarket, a flat where all the locals, including Mr Choudhury, knew that you could obtain prescription drugs without a doctor's signature. I have found out by being a busybody, this blue Honda appeared to be doing the rounds supplying at least six locations that I know of. Are you with me so far?"

The room remained silent.

"I'll continue then. One Wednesday, Mr Chaudhury saw a suspicious young lady run out of his shop clutching a large bottle of vodka. He pursued, only to bump into the aforementioned young lady and a man who he knew to be a drug dealer; the man in the blue Honda, to be clear. Mr Chaudhury was not going to argue with a drug dealer over a bottle of spirits, he valued his life more than that bottle, so he let it go. I suspect the dealer giving him a twenty-pound note and not wanting change also helped him decide. A lucky day for Vicky, who now had a bottle of vodka and a new boyfriend."

"I am still waiting for some sort of proof: any witnesses, descriptions," Paul taunted. Even Martin chimed in,

"It does sound a little far-fetched; Paul is more of a wimp than a drug dealer I would have thought."

"I might agree," Colin said. "The only real description is a posh-talking bloke in his thirties driving a blue Honda. Even in this room we have potentially two suspects. Now the lady above the supermarket selling the drugs could only give the same banal description. The dealer was one of those nondescript people that no one really sees. Then, there is Flossie."

"Flossie who does the drugs?" Harry asked.

"The very same. A long-term trader in sex and drugs, not sure if she does rock n' roll as well," Colin smiled. "Flossie has a steady stream of women and some men arriving at her front door, none of which she takes much notice of. Her only concern is how much money she can wheedle out of them. Even when she regularly invited her dealer into her house, the best description she could give me was: posh-sounding geezer, mid-thirties or so, white guy, not heavy built, maybe a bit on the thin side, a little taller than her. Well, every little helps, I think is what they say.

"Now I've known Flossie for a few years, and I know that she does have a better memory when she comes to giving men 'their doin's' as she calls it. A man without his clothes on, does seem to help plant a comprehensive image in her mind. Fortunately for us, she mentioned that was exactly the way she had met the posh geezer in the blue Honda in the first place. Now then, what could she tell me about the man when he was naked. As it turns out, a lot."

"Look Colin, or whatever your name or sex is, just get on with it. Why be so theatrical about a load of lies. I am not your drug dealer," Paul protested, gesturing wildly with his arms. "I work for a pharmaceutical company, so what! I have the same car as Martin, so what does that prove? I should point out my car has a different number plate. Give me more than just what's in your imagination."

There was a moment's silence in the room before Colin smiled at Paul. It was a smug smile that hinted he was about to drop into the conversation something that would be incriminating.

"Not in my imagination but on CCTV as you go into the depot on nights. A blue Honda with Martin's registration plates, no doubt just tacked on with some tape. But on other days, it is a blue Honda with your own correct number plate."

"There you go, it could be another car you're looking at when I am on nights."

"Maybe, but physical evidence is hard to refute. That is why I take you back to Flossie who recalled the first time she met her drug dealer; you recollect while he was getting some relief from Flossie, without his clothes on.

"Flossie recalled that he had a strange manhood. When erect it had a very distinctive curve, imagine a very curved banana, she was convinced that if he were not careful, he might stick it in his belly button. Peyronie's disease is the correct description for the medical condition the dealer suffered from.

"You do know, Paul, that Martin shared with me your schoolboy habit of whipping your cock out in the middle of the classroom and banging it against the wooden desk, which I think is extremely dangerous, but boys will be boys!"

Susan eagerly interrupted Colin, "So, that's what it was, well, no wonder you didn't want to tell me, that is a gross habit. Mind, if you want me to conduct an identity parade, I'm happy to help."

Paul ignored Susan's quip and looked around the room nervously. All eyes were now on him, well, his crotch to be precise.

"I would also add," Colin began his conclusion, "Mummy controls your money, so the extra cash you were earning, some of which you gave to Vicky, was still cheaper and marginally better than Flossie giving you a massage.

"Well Paul, unless you want to whip out your manhood and prove to us all that you are as straight as a die in that department, can I suggest that you and I take a stroll outside and I'll introduce you to a couple of police officers who would like to have a word with you."

Colin walked out with Paul, neither of them speaking. Once they had left, the silence persisted as each person examined their thoughts about what they had just witnessed. Finally, Susan spoke,

"It just proves what I always knew; teenage boys are just plain disgusting."

CHAPTER NINETEEN

Harry was the first to recover from the revelations, pointing out from his wealth of experience with the legal system, that he did not expect Paul to be coming back for a while. With the previous form Paul had shown in landing a fist on the delivery guy, sentencing for dealing in drugs would no doubt lead him straight into prison. With his posh voice, Harry also pointed out, he was not going to be able to slip quietly into the background of prison life.

It was then time for Martin to ask Harry for a favour. First, he outlined the fact that Vicky was going to be in trouble for fiddling her housing benefit, ably assisted by his school friend, Steve. Martin intended to report the whole scheme to the authorities later in the day. Deep down he hoped they would not be too hard on Vicky, as he was convinced the driving force would have been Steve. With six young, vulnerable women in his sights, the chance to get a few extra pounds would have been a little too tempting for them all. He asked Harry if he would be able help Vicky.

Harry said he knew all too well the temptations that existed to earn a few extra pounds for those he encountered each day, all struggling to make ends meet. He promised to keep an eye on Vicky and help her where he could. He, again drawing on his experience in these matters, guessed she might get some sort of suspended sentence; he knew her to be a good girl really.

Colin walked back into the room, did a twirl, his shirt rising upwards. A large smile on his face.

"Hayden Investigations comes up trumps again! What say we go off and find a bar to celebrate? I promise no bubbly this time. The bonus is that if we find a place around here, no one will mind if Suzie Baby jumps up on the bar and sings her sweet little heart out."

Susan, never one to turn down a drinking opportunity, turned to look at Martin, but he looked glum.

"No celebrations this time, Colin, the end of Hayden Investigations has sadly arrived." Martin went on to explain about the visit from Jenny and the removal of the very advantageous terms and conditions of renting his current office. Colin, the smile having left his face, went through the same set of options that both Martin and Susan had already mulled over. Finding any sort of office for next to nothing seemed impossible.

"Sounds to me like you need a bit of Harry Branston to get things sorted," broke in Harry.

"Harry," Colin exclaimed, "don't tell me you have some offices that have 'fallen off the back of the lorry'; in my day it was just TVs."

"Nah, all legit. When the local council gave me a grant to convert this place, we ended up with the upstairs converted for all sorts of things including office space, medical space, advice space. In fact, there is this meeting room, then my office, and then there is what was meant to be the medical room, but I've never been able to get any grants to make it happen. What I'm saying is, there is a spare office here which you can have for nothing, well, maybe help us out if we need a bit of investigating done. Harry's always 'appy to help."

"That's a generous offer," Colin suggested.

"Bloody brilliant!" Susan added. "Hayden Investigations lives on. Well, shall we have a double celebration?" She now sounded extremely excited.

It took Martin to dampen their enthusiasm. "Hold on a moment," he looked around the windowless, cramped meeting room. "Thank you, Harry, that is kind of you, but this is way out of the area of where most of my clients are."

"What clients?" Colin asked.

"Exactly," Susan added, wholeheartedly supporting Colin.

"We are a growing business and you never know what will happen in the future. It is a long way for me to commute. Thank you for your offer Harry, but I really must decline."

Martin stood up, shook Harry's hand firmly, and gestured for Colin and Susan to follow him out of the door and back towards the rail station.

***

On the train back to Charing Cross, Martin did not encounter any young children asking tricky questions, but instead he was faced with two adults who were set on convincing him that a move to an office in Deptford would not be as bad as it might seem. However, Martin was of the opposite opinion.

"You need to look at this from my perspective," he began, "not only is it miles and miles from where I live, Deptford is not exactly renowned for its bars and restaurants. The whole point of having an office in town is so that I can pop in during the morning, have a coffee, arrange a lunch and then grab a tube or walk to wherever I am dining. It would be like a bloody trek to come out here first. I'm sorry, but I'm not taking Harry up on his offer."

"Even if it means me losing my job?" Susan tried not to sound as if she was pleading, which in fact she was.

"Do not try and appeal to my soft side, Susan. Of course I want to keep working with you, I have told you before I enjoy your company, but you can get another job and we can still meet up from time to time, have dinner, be friends. The fact is unless I can find a cheap, and I mean ridiculously cheap, place to occupy, this is the end of Hayden Investigations. I will just need to come up with some other sort of plan to ensure I continue to get my allowance from Mother."

"You sound just like Paul," Susan told him. It was a jibe, she hoped he would not take it too much to heart.

"At least he is not as bent as Paul," Colin's observation made all three of them laugh hysterically.

CHAPTER TWENTY

Beside Martin's desk were five brown cardboard square boxes. There was not much that he needed to take with him when he left the Duchess Street office for good. Packing up was always a poignant occasion, packing up at the end of a holiday, sorting out worn clothes at the end of a weekend away with friends. Then there was the time he collected his father's belongings following his death in hospital, each item holding a memory. Today felt a little like that; the end of a period in his life, a period he had enjoyed more than he could have imagined. He knew that was down to being with Susan who had made the last couple of months hugely enjoyable.

"Martin, do you think I could be a research assistant?" Susan asked as she scrolled through potential jobs on the internet.

Even though Martin could have delayed packing up as there were still another three weeks left on his notice period, he could see no good reason why he should just hang around. He had agreed to pay Susan until the end of the month, then a further two months wages to help her with any hiatus she might have between jobs.

It had been five days since Harry had offered the free accommodation and at times Martin had come awfully close to calling him and accepting his offer, but each time he had shied away from a life travelling between home and Deptford.

"I think you could be good at anything you put your mind to."

"That's just a polite way of saying no."

"It is a way of saying nobody should restrict their choices in life."

Martin gathered his collection of colourful business cards from his top drawer. He fanned a few out in his hand. Most had originated from the copious amounts of restaurants and bars that he had frequented. He compared his collecting to that of a beer mat collector, both were a little bit pointless, save for providing a valid excuse to go drinking or eating.

After stashing the cards in one of the boxes, he closed his laptop down, folded the screen, then coiled the charger lead before covering it all in bubble wrap. Finally, he placed it solemnly into the cardboard box. He tore off another sheet of bubble wrap, this time intended for the PC mouse, and then waved the sheet towards Susan. "Would you put this on your wall?"

She looked up from her screen, happy to be distracted. "What like wallpaper? Are you mad?"

"That is exactly what it was originally designed for, a three-dimensional plastic wallpaper. You might have already guessed from your reaction it did not take off. But as a packing material, well as they say, the rest is history."

"You know some bloody odd things, Martin. I see you're packing up the computers and stuff; do you want my laptop now? There aren't many jobs that I can see would suit me. I think I could do with Colin helping me to find one again."

"No, keep the laptop, I'll have no use for it," Martin told her.

Before she could reply the door to the office opened and Mrs Barrington-Smythe strode into the room. She lightly greeted them both, in the form of a very curt hello, before taking a seat on the leather sofa. Carefully she placed her handbag securely beside her, as if she were expecting it to be stolen by either of them.

Paul's mother looked around at the boxes and emptied drawers with a disapproving look, before dismissing the idea of asking what exactly was going on. She had no plans to concern herself with it for now.

She began to speak as if she was talking to a class of schoolchildren.

"My son, like his father before him, is a complete disappointment to me, Mr Hayden. You have only served to reinforce that notion, as well as clearly show he has extremely poor taste when it comes to choosing female friends. That Vicky girl sounds a totally horrendous person. Hopefully, prison will change him and make him grow up, understand his responsibilities.

"My visit here today, Mr Hayden, is to offer you my sincere thanks for bringing at least a temporary end to my son's immoral behaviour. How sharper than a serpent's tooth it is to have a thankless child!"

"What?" Susan thought she must have misheard the old lady.

"Shakespeare, Susan, I'll explain later," Martin helpfully offered.

"Ah, you must be Susan, the drunk who was sitting or rather lying comatose on this very sofa the last time I attended this establishment. King Lear, act 1 scene 4. I guess they did not cover Shakespeare at your secondary modern school, why am I not surprised. Paul did mention you, nothing flattering, I should point out.

"I understand, Mr Hayden, that there were some parking tickets that my son incurred whilst in pursuit of his clandestine activities, which implicated you and as a consequence were paid by you on his behalf without knowing. I will be happy to reimburse you, assuming you are able to supply the necessary paperwork to support your claim."

Martin sat, or a better description would be slumped, onto his desk. "Don't worry about it, it is not worth the trouble."

Mrs Barrington-Smythe was, if nothing else, an inquisitive type of lady, so she could not suppress the compulsion to ask, "Exactly what are you doing with all these boxes?"

Susan closed her laptop and answered, "Moving out, we just need to find other premises."

"You have nowhere to relocate? That is an odd way of doing things. My cousin has some sort of property business, I am sure he could find suitable accommodation, he has a lot of offices across London."

"Expensive, I bet." Susan pointed out.

"I am sure, young lady, that every square foot he rents is fairly priced. I will happily ask him if you wish?"

"If he offers free office space then we would be interested." Susan saw a glimmer of hope that she might be able to continue working with Martin after all. Her glimmer was soon stubbed out.

"He does not promote charity. Tell me, what is it with certain classes that they think charity is their birth right?"

Susan did not welcome the implication of that statement. Martin recognised her imminent temper and quickly stepped in.

"Please do not worry your cousin, I have a number of options available to me, it is just a matter of a final decision and completing the paperwork.

"Well, it was good of you to take the time to show your gratitude, but unless you have another wayward son who needs convicting, we would like to get on."

Mrs Barrington-Smythe, not used to being told what to do by anyone let alone someone younger than her, tutted sharply, gathered her handbag and made her way to the door.

"Nothing will come of nothing," she quoted as she closed the door behind her.

Susan looked at Martin, who was now standing and putting one of the boxes on his desk. "I do presume that 'just need to complete the paperwork' was a blind?"

"If you mean a lie, yes, it was. It was justified to stop you exploding and giving the old bag a large loud piece of your mind."

Susan smiled, "You know me so well."

***

On her knees taping up the last box Susan asked, without looking up at Martin, about the large leather sofa, which stood beside the kitchenette, "Are you leaving it behind?"

"No, I have arranged for Harry to pick it up and make use of it for the charity. I have no need of it any longer."

The office now looked bare, worse than it had the first time when Susan had tentatively arrived for her interview. Pictures were taken down, desks emptied, kitchenette stripped of every utensil, and beside the door five boxes were neatly stacked. Handwritten on each of them was the name of the person they belonged to, Martin had three and Susan two. She looked around the office that had been her workplace for the last couple of months, time that had flown by. The best job she had ever had and now it was coming to an end.

"Without a base, how are you going to convince your mother you are still working as a high-powered private detective?"

"I'm going to try my best, but Mother is a hard person to convince at the best of times. I will just have to put my thinking cap on and come up with some sort of sneaky plan. Maybe I'll set up an office at home in some quiet corner, for the short term at least."

"Well, I can always pop round from time to time, if you like?"

"That would be good; I think we should keep in contact. I mean we are..." there was a hint of hesitation in his voice as he considered the best word or words to describe their relationship beyond employer and employee, "...special friends."

Susan liked that idea. But she did not want the conversation to stop there; she had a set of follow-up questions ready to deploy.

"I guess now that Jenny is out of your life, you'll be looking for someone else, another married woman?"

Martin sat down on the sofa beside Susan, where she had been since finishing stacking her boxes.

"No, I think I have had my fill of older married women. I need to mature and find someone more my own age or at least someone with whom I could have a long-term relationship."

"Does that mean you're over Paula?"

"What, my fiancée who took my trust as well as a few thousand pounds? I often wonder if she is still with her boyfriend or if she disappointed him as much as she disappointed me. Yes, I'm over her now. I think you have helped me to regain my trust in the fairer sex. In fact, you have taught me a few things about myself. You have been good for me Susan; a little angel sent to sort me out."

"Ah," Susan took the moment to slip her arm into his and pulled him close to her. "I do try and help, and it's been fun." She felt the warmth of his body next to her; it felt good.

"Susan, if I was to ask you......" Martin stopped as the door to the office opened and a man stood in the doorway pulling up the belt of his trousers.

"I'm sorry, am I interrupting?"

"No, come in, Derek." Martin beckoned him as he and Susan stood up. Derek walked towards them giving one further pull on his leather belt before he spoke.

"In this day and age, there are so many ways to communicate: emails, phones, video conferencing. However, for all that, nothing can replace a physical presence, which gives me the opportunity to greet and appreciate such beauty." He took Susan's hand and kissed it, then shook Martin's hand as he continued to speak.

"I wanted to thank you personally, both of you, especially Susan for leading some amazing detective work and uncovering the nasty fraud that was being carried out by Steve Ellis. I had believed he was an asset to my business with his public school education and obvious good breeding; how wrong was I. Thanks to you, Susan, no doubt assisted by your in-house bodyguard, that was shown not to be the case.

"If his scam had continued and been uncovered at a later stage, say when I was in final negotiations with the council to sell them that parade of shops and flats, then it could have seriously damaged my reputation and business."

"I'm glad we could help," Susan replied, having been placed firmly as the lead investigator by Derek. "I can understand fully where you are coming from Derek. In my experience men who have been churned out by the public school system end up with some unbelievably bad habits, don't you agree Mikhail?"

"No idea, I went to a comprehensive school where the girls also have bad habits; some even go stealing at lunchtimes, which would never happen in Russia," Martin countered back at Susan.

"Exactly," Derek agreed. "Fortunately, it has shown those who matter that I am an honest businessman who does not stand for any type of skulduggery."

Susan wanted to point out that he was paying someone to give him confidential information, although she wisely decided this was not the best time to mention such a fact.

"Also, Mikhail, thank you for compensating Roberto, my waiter, for the damage his car suffered at the hands of your enthusiastic chief." He smiled at Susan, "I can understand totally; I shall in future consider what branding is on the boxes when I am transporting my postcards.

"As a thank you I would like to offer you both and your partners a complementary meal at my restaurant. Anything you want, provided it is in season, plus as much as you can drink, no limit. It is the least I can do."

Martin wondered if Derek realised just how much alcohol Susan might get through during an evening on the town, he guessed not. But Derek had done well out of the whole affair in avoiding any controversy.

"That'd be amazing! I loved that white wine you gave us last time, nice bit of vino, I would say." Susan was already planning what she might wear, eat and drink. Then it struck her, an evening out with Martin, who by the time they took up the offer, would not be her boss. He would be fair game!

"I see you have boxed up your office, moving to new, larger premises?"

Martin was getting a little fed up explaining about the decamping from the office into a vacuum, but he did so politely as he had already done to others. This time he kept to the basic facts, or to be more precise, lies. These included: end of rental agreement on the current office, too big an increase requested by the landlord, moving out until they find somewhere affordable.

Martin forgot that if he was going to lie, then it was always best to do it out of earshot of Susan who liked to add a little more information. This normally resulted in highlighting to those listening that he was either not telling the truth, or he was not fully aware of the entire situation.

"When Mikhail here, who looks after the admin side of the business, says affordable, we are really looking for something ridiculously cheap, or very, very cheap, like in free, that would be good."

Derek looked at Susan, then gave an odd look to Martin. He acknowledged they might be a good investigator and bodyguard but they did both seem to lack a bit in business acumen.

"Well Susan, good luck with finding such an office space in the capital. If you do, let me know, bound to be some profit in it for me. I'll leave you both to your packing."

Derek turned and walked towards the door, pulling his belt as he went. Together, Susan and Martin watched him.

Then he stopped in the doorway. Once again he pulled up his trouser belt and then turned back to face them; they saw a wistful look on his face.

"How big an office are you looking for exactly?"

"Small is good, tiny is fine, it's just the two of us. All our other staff are freelancers," Susan explained, never having imagined herself as an executive, but liking the feeling of being asked such questions. Martin just observed, he thought like any good bodyguard. Derek walked back into the office.

"I have recently purchased one of those business centre things, you know, a block of small boxes, each one an office space for enterprising start-up entrepreneurs. It's just off Tower Bridge Road, not that far, good connections for the tube and rail networks. There is, amongst the fifteen office spaces, one odd-shaped space, which I can find little use for. It is not big, but it does have a window and a door. As I say, it is not big, but you could get a couple of small desks in there, a phone, not much else though. Would you be interested?"

Susan looked at Martin, deciding to delegate her newfound responsibility. "What do you think?"

"What sort of rent and service charge were you thinking about?" Martin asked, expecting to hear a figure way beyond what he could sensibly afford.

"Shall we say a peppercorn rent? I have no other use for it; it'll be good to see it put to good use. I trust if I ever needed a favour from you then it would be reciprocated. Does that sound like a fair offer?"

"You have yourself a deal then, Mr Primm." Martin strode forward with his hand outstretched keen to seal the deal quickly. Then he heard Susan say,

"Is the free meal still on offer?"

Derek smiled as he firmly shook Martin's hand. "Yes indeed, I look forward to greeting you soon."

***

Martin and Susan turned to each other as Derek closed the door behind him. They looked like two thrilled children who had just learnt Santa Claus was planning on coming twice this year. Martin enthusiastically grabbed Susan's upper arms.

"Well, Miss Morris, I am pleased to inform you that Hayden Investigations is still in business and this Russian bodyguard is still in need of a personal assistant; would you consider accepting the job offer?"

Susan beamed as she looked up into his eyes. In a Russian accent she replied, "Comrade Hayden, I would be delighted to accept your kind offer."

Martin then pulled her close to him, a full embrace. He was so near, Susan could feel his breath on her face as he spoke, "This deserves some sort of celebration; what do you think?"

To be fair, Susan tried to restrain her thoughts as she went through possible ways of celebrating while in the arms of Martin. She had several pre-planned scenarios, most of which required the door to be locked and the leather sofa being put to good use. For now, she confined herself with just willing him to kiss her fully on the lips. Was he hesitating, not confident how she might react, she could not be sure? She had planted a long kiss on him while they were in the theatre, but that was technically work related. Certainly Martin had not complained, even though he had no idea at the start just why she was kissing him.

This was the time, the opportunity that she should not throw away, if he had not actually kissed her in the next three seconds, she would kiss him.

One...Two.... Th... the door opened, distracting them both as they turned to look at who the visitor might be.

"I'm sorry to trouble you, Mr Hayden." Ernie the caretaker stood in the doorway, he watched as they released their embrace.

"No trouble, Ernie, what can we do for you?"

"Oh, you have already packed up; I didn't realise you were leaving so soon. I have been meaning to ask for your help with a personal problem I have, but not to worry. I'm sure I can work it out on my own."

Martin gestured Ernie into the office. "Come in and tell us about it. I am sure we can help."

The End

Acknowledgements

As ever, any work of fiction is not the result of just one bleary-eyed person bashing away at a keyboard, drinking copious cups of coffee and enduring sleep deprivation over several months.

In the making of *The Reluctant Detective Goes South*, there were in fact six people working away at keyboards, flipping over pages and missing out on sleep. These dedicated people are my friends who ploughed their way through the chaos of my final draft!

As I have never offered them any financial gain for their sacrifice, the least I can do is to acknowledge their dedication and valued advice. This is a big thank you to: Claire, Gavan, Angela, Peter, Irene, Brian, and Anthony. Finally, Linda, my wife, who has spent countless hours reading, suggesting amendments and making sure the whole book is comprehensible.

AUTHOR NOTES

If you have read the first Martin Hayden Mystery, *The Reluctant Detective*, I do hope that you have enjoyed this second adventure for Martin and Susan. They have once again managed to get through a set of circumstances, which have shown that absurd things can happen alongside serious issues.

When we think of drug dealers, we often think of hard drugs like cocaine and heroin and the junkies they supply lying comatose in some scruffy squat. Sadly, there is another side to drug abuse, the misuse of prescription drugs. This is a problem that is not always fully acknowledged yet exists amongst some of the poorest in our society.

Flossie and Vicky are an amalgam of people I met whilst working for a charity in south London. They find employment difficult, life mundane, and often they exaggerate events in their lives to make themselves believe that they are 'having a great time'.

Whereas a man drinking himself into a stupor is not always frowned upon, a female single parent doing the same is looked at as being irresponsible. Hence the concealed use of prescription pills to help deaden the boredom and despair many feel.

As with so many problems, there is no one simple answer. Poverty, depression, health issues, poor housing and broken relationships all contribute to the problem of drug misuse. Possibly the first step to finding a solution is to fully understand the problem, and to not just stereotype and put to one side people we do not understand.

If you have enjoyed *The Reluctant Detective Goes South*, then it would be helpful if you could leave a review on Amazon or goodreads, both of which help not only to promote my books, but reviews can help other readers when choosing their next book.

I am currently writing the next adventure for Martin and Susan, ably helped by Colin and Becky. If you would like to be one of the first to hear about the publication date, then please subscribe to my mailing list.

You can contact me, join my mailing list, find more about me, the books I write, and what I am up to on my website www.adrianspalding.co.uk or find me on my Facebook page Adrian Spalding Books. I look forward to hearing from you.

Adrian.

OTHER TITLES BY ADRIAN SPALDING

Sleeping Malice

The Reluctant Detective

The Night You Murder

www.adrianspalding.co.uk

The Reluctant Detective
by Adrian Spalding

A humorous crime mystery

The Hayden Detective Agency has no need of clients. The very existence of the Agency allows Martin Hayden to claim his large monthly allowance from the family fortune - without lifting a finger.

Martin's biggest problem is his interfering mother, who understands her idle son too well. She takes steps to find him not just clients but also a personal assistant to keep an eye on him.

Under pressure from the women in his life Martin agrees to take on his first client. How hard can it be to follow a 90-year-old woman who spends her time losing money at roulette tables? As it turns out harder than Martin ever thought possible, especially with the old lady dying in strange circumstances.

Soon the Reluctant Detective is grappling with shady estate agents, an intellectual artist, missing charity money and an irritating Indian waiter. Luckily for Martin there is help in the form of Colin, a transvestite who, apart from having particularly good fashion sense is an expert at breaking into houses.

<u>Available now from Amazon</u>

Sleeping Malice
by Adrian Spalding

Your past never forgets.

When journalist Helen Taylor lands her dream job on a newspaper, she could never have imagined that her first assignment would become her worst nightmare.

Travelling to France for a simple story, Helen encounters Phillip, a puzzling Englishman who avoids contact with anyone. When she meets him, she feels there is something dark about him, which may provide her with a major scoop.

Greg, an out-of-work journalist, also arrives in the village asking questions about a missing man. With the appearance of two journalists, one English family fears they are being hunted for the secret they hold.

When Her Majesty's Government stretches its merciless talons across the English Channel, Helen and Greg have to work together to discover just what has been hidden in the village.

As they begin to uncover the facts, their own suppressed secrets start to emerge. They learn that when your past comes back to haunt you, no one around you is safe.

<u>Available now from Amazon</u>

The Reluctant Detective Goes South
Text Copyright © 2020 by Adrian Spalding. All Rights Reserved.

All rights reserved. No part of this book may be reproduced in any form or by any electronic or mechanical means including information storage and retrieval systems, without permission in writing from the author. The only exception is by a reviewer, who may quote short excerpts in a review.

This book is a work of fiction. Names, characters, places, and incidents either are products of the author's imagination or are used fictitiously. Any resemblance to actual persons, living or dead, events, or locales is entirely coincidental.

Printed in Great Britain
by Amazon